The First 48:
Money Making Meeka 2

By: Nakiala Comeaux

Thank you for purchasing, "The First 48 2: The Finale," Feel free to browse Amazon for the rest of my catalog, I hope you enjoy and thank you for the support. Below is a list of my previous work and social media contact.

- Forever my Savage: A Yungin and His Lady 1-4

- Daughter of a Trap King 1-4

- I Love you For My Soul 1-3

- She was a Savage, He was the realist 1-3

•He Was My Thuggish Valentine (A Novella)

- No Matter What, I Choose You 1 and 2 Finale

- Married to a New York Menace 1 and 2 Finale

- One Kiss For All My Troubles (A standalone novel)

- Ain't No Love In Hip Hop: Love vs Fame 1 and 2 Finale

- I Got Love For A Philly Thug (A standalone novel)

- I Want to Be Thugged By You

Social Media Information

Facebook: Author Nakiala Comeaux and Authoress Nakiala Comeaux

Instagram: @_authorravonne_

Snapchat: Authorki16

Facebook Like Page : Author Ravonne R.

Are you looking for a publishing company to express your writing? Well, look no further! Nakiala Comeaux Publications and Ravonne and Ronshon Publishing house are accepting manuscripts in the following genres: urban romance, romance, and interracial love. Submit 3,000 words, contact information, and synopsis to nakialacomeauxpresents@gmail.com

For street literature/ urban fiction, erotica, paranormal, Christian fiction, interracial, horror, mystery and suspense. submit the following information to ravonneronshonpresents@gmail.com. Please allow 48 hours to review information.

Like our Facebook page to keep up with more updates! : Ravonne and Ronshon Publishing House/Nakiala Comeaux Publications.

Chapter 1

Within three days, the rumor around town was that Philly was behind Santana's death and hearing that only made Meeka's heart ache even more. Several rumors circulated about why he killed Santana. One rumor was that Santana stole ten thousand dollars from Philly. The second rumor was that Santana attempted to set up Philly, but Meeka knew that was true. The third rumor was that Santana threaten to tell everyone about his relationship with Philly. For some reason, Meeka felt it in her heart that it was true.

"Are you okay, Meek? Do you need me to bring you anything?" Quix asked. Meeka could hear that Quix was crying and it made her sad. Meeka used her shirt to wipe her tears and her wet phone screen. Then she said, "No Q, I'm fine, but I'll call you later."

"Okay, girl, please do. I love you."

"I love you too." Meeka disconnected the call and reached for the box of tissue. She pulled four tissues out and blew her nose. Every day she cried, and it felt like the tears were never going to stop.

She sat at the round table and stared at the wall. She couldn't stop thinking about Santana. Her face was covered with smudged makeup and tears. Hustle's words replayed in her head like a broken record. Her chest ached, and her heart throbbed tremendously. It didn't matter how much medication she took, her entire body was still in pain.

Marlo slowly walked into the room with Izzy in his arms. He stood behind Meeka and grabbed her shoulder. Meeka dropped her head and sobbed louder and harder, and she dug her nails deep into Marlo's hand to mend her pain, but it didn't help. Marlo sighed and dropped his head. He wrapped his arm around his sister's neck and held her tightly.

"Marlo….this pain, THIS FUCKING PAIN! Oh, my God, this shit feels so unreal. This can't be life. This HAS to be a nightmare or a terrible joke! Santana has to be playing a joke on me. There is no way in the world that Tana is dead. My heart is broken, Marlo. It doesn't feel the same and isn't beating the same. Not Santana, not my baby Santana, Marlo. Please tell me everyone is playing a joke on me. Please tell me he's going to walk through that door within the next hour. He's going to have on some loud spandex jumpsuit and a badass blonde lace front. His Chanel bag will be in one hand, and his dog will be in the other hand. He's going to walk in here like he usually does. I won't question him, I swear I won't. I swear to Allah, I won't question him. I just want my friend back!!" Meeka shouted and pulled her hair. She banged on the table and stood to her feet. She flipped the table over, and it crashed into her glass sliding doors. Marlo quickly jumped back to protect Isabella's body. Glass shattered everywhere, but she didn't care. Meeka's loud outbursts startled Haylee and she began to cry.

"Sis it's going to be okay," Marlo rocked Haylee, but it wasn't soothing her. Meeka's chest expanded up and down. She paced back and forth and ran her fingers through her hair. She was a nervous wreck, and she didn't know what to do.

"It won't be okay, Lo, so you don't have to tell me that. I want my best friend back!! I can't eat, I can't sleep, I can't do anything. I can't function without him. It just doesn't seem real. How could they kill him because he told the truth? They lied on him, and all he did was tell the truth! He didn't break up a happy home, and he didn't expose anyone or snitch on anyone. All he fucking did was defend himself so he could clear his name. How do you beat someone to death? How Marlo, how can you hate someone much that you kill them with your bare hands? How am I supposed to process all of this? This is a hard pill to swallow, and I can't do it. I can't do it, I can't do it, and no one can make me!!"

"Sis, you have to calm down. Let shit die down for a few weeks. After that, we're going to handle it. If those niggas think they have a chance of living, they're crazy. I'm down for pull-ups, drive-bys, walk-ups, and all."

"We can't tell Hustle anything. I don't want to hear his mouth. I know he's going to try and talk me out of it."

"That's the last thing we need. We have to do this for Santana. If it was one of us, he would hang out of the window with a Choppa." They both laughed. Meeka wiped her tears, but she started to cry again. She thought about the time Santana was hanging out of the window on I-10. She wiped her tears again and smiled.

"Yes, he literally would. I'ma miss that nigga so much, Lo. It'll be years before I come to peace with his death." Meeka said.

"I know, and that's okay. I love you, sis."

"I love you too bro and thanks for being here for me."

"We have to kill Philly, Marlo, we have to do it."

"I know, but let's be real, we both know this won't be easy," Marlo said.

"I know, I know, but if we get the right team we can. I know a few people who wouldn't mind help me."

"Who, sis?" He asked. Meeka stared at the ground and smiled. She wanted to answer his question, but her thoughts had her quiet and excited. She placed her finger in the air and said, "I'll be right back!" Meeka stood to her feet and ran out of the room.

"Just give me a second Marlo, I'll be right back." Meeka ran into her bedroom and scrambled to the floor. She wiggled under the bed and searched for the medal box. She quickly flipped the box over and ripped a gold key off of it. Her hands shook as she unlocked the box. She opened the box and pulled out a small black cell phone. She pressed the power button and anxiously waited for the phone to come on.

"Hurry, hurry, hurry!" she whispered to herself. The phone powered on and Rocko rushed to her call log. She only used the phone to speak to one person. She pressed the green button and waited while the phone rang. Within three seconds the screen began to count the seconds of the conversation.

"Hello, Rocko?" Meeka whispered.

"Meeka, what did I tell you about calling me that shit?! You know it's Jupiter man, you're slipping BIG TIME!" Rocko shouted, but her voice was cluttered and raspy.

"I'm so sorry, Jup."

"It's all good, but don't let it happen again. What are you doing calling me anyway? You know we have a set time I call you. Are you trying to get us caught up Meek? Besides that, do you know what time it is here?!"

"No, Jup, but it's important. You won't believe what I'm about to tell you. I don't even know how to put my lips together to say it!!" Meeka shouted, and tears began to stream down her face. She used her sheets to wipe her tears and snotty nose.

"Tameeka….what's wrong, talk to me. Is it Izzy or Hustle? Did something happen to them?"

"No, it's Santana, he was killed."

"Noooooooo, Tameeka you're lying!"

"I swear, Jupiter, I'm not joking. I'm dead ass serious, Philly killed him!!"

"What, I know you didn't say who I THINK you said." Meeka could hear Rocko's tone of voice change. She knew hearing that name sent rage through Rocko's body.

"Yea, I said Philly," Meeka said.

"This can't be true, what happened Meeka?" Rocko asked.

"To make a long story short, Philly is gay! He killed Santana because he thought Santana was going to expose him."

"Oh my God, are you serious Meek?" Rocko's voice began to crack. She could feel a headache coming soon. She tried to get out of bed, but her legs were too weak.

"I wish I wasn't, but I'm not. This shit is crazy Jupiter, and I don't know what to do!"

"Meek, you need to calm down first. Let me talk to Kane, I'm going to call you back." Rocko said.

"Okay, but please call me back," Meeka begged.

"I will, bye." Meeka disconnected the call and turned to Kane. He was sound asleep with his mouth wide open.

"Kane!"

"What, baby?" He mumbled and rolled over. Rocko was hit with a little bit of Kane's morning breath, but she didn't care.

"Get up, I can't believe I'm about to say this, but we're going back to the States."

"What?" Kane's mumbling quickly annoyed Rocko. Right now, he needed to clear his raspy voice and wake up. She squeezed her fist tightly and deeply. Rocko pushed Kane a little and smacked his lips. He sighed and then opened his eyes. He stared at Rocko and said, "Diana, what's wrong?"

"You won't believe this, but Philly killed Santana."

"Santana, what, are you sure?" Kane rose in the bed rubbing his eyes. Rocko turned away and nodded her head.

"Damn, what the fuck?" Kane whispered and dropped his head. He rolled out of bed and stood to his feet. He leaned against the wall and placed his heads on top of his head.

"I was on the phone with Meeka a few minutes ago. Philly's name is behind it, that muthafucka has struck again. Oh and you won't believe this, Philly is gay!"

"Gay, are you serious?"

"Yea, Meeka said Santana was going to expose Philly. That could be the motive to why he killed him."

"Mmmmmaaannnnnn, this shit is crazy. If Philly was messing around with Santana that means he's gay, gay."

"He's bend over and let me put my finger in your butt gay!" Rocko laughed, and so did Kane."

"He's put a strap on and fuck a bitch gay." Kane laughed.

"Hell yea, he definitely went with his move. I can't believe this shit."

"I was his friend, and I didn't see this shit." Kane shook his head.

"Forget him being gay. This nigga has killed someone again, Kenneth. Because of Philly, an innocent person has died."

"I know baby, and that's fucked up. I hope he doesn't get away with another murder."

"I wouldn't be surprised if he gets away with it. We have to go back, Kane! I don't want him to sit in jail. I want to feel his warm blood splatter on me. I'm going to laugh when droplets of it hit my lips." Rocko slowly touched her lips and softly laughed. Kane didn't understand why she was laughing or why she had an evil look across her face.

"Bae, what are you saying?" Kane asked.

"I'm saying we are going to Opelousas to kill him," Rocko said.

"WHAT, DIANA ARE YOU CRAZY??" Kane shouted.

"No, I'm not crazy. I know Meeka called me for a reason. She needs our help, and we HAVE to help her Kenneth! Once again, Diana is you crazy?? We haven't been to Louisiana since 2012 or in the United States in a year. Maybe you should go back to sleep and clear your mind."

"I don't need to go to sleep. What I need to do is start packing my clothes so we can catch the earliest flight." Rocko tried to get out of bed, but Kane stopped her. Rocko leaned to the left and Kane sized her up. She knew that meant to lie down and that's what she did.

"I'm not dealing with this right now. I would love to help Meek, but I'm not putting my freedom on the line again for Philly. He won, and let's leave it at that. We got away, and he's still hiding here and there. Let it go, Rocko, just let it go."

"Kane, every day I think about how I held your sisters as they took their last breaths. I think about the way your grandma screamed as she was shot. Some days I thought about it nonstop when you weren't here. I had to deal with that alone, and it killed me. What hurt me most is that their killer was still out there. For a while, I thought he was in jail, but now I know he isn't. Look at us Kane we don't look like Rocko and Kane anymore. It's going to be easy for us to maneuver through the city. We have the chance to kill the person who brought so much pain to our lives. Tell me you never thought about standing over him and sending him to his maker?"

"Yea, I thought about it. I thought about it plenty of times. When we separated in Chicago and didn't reunite like we intended, I was literally sick. I never felt a pain like that before. Now that we are together, I never want to separate again. Going back home could separate us Diana, and I'm not going through that again. I'm not feeling that pain again." Kane said.

"Baby I understand all of that. I honestly do, but Meeka needs our help. We can't leave her hanging like that. The way I look, Philly wouldn't even recognize me. Shit, half the time I look in the mirror, I don't recognize myself." She chuckled.

"I have to think about this, Diana. I can't just give you an answer and start packing. This shit can go wrong and ruin everything. I went through so much to be with you, and I'll be damn if I lose you because of Philly."

"Kane I promise you won't lose me, ever again. I love you, and you know that." Rocko smiled and moved across the bed. She pointed at Kane and signaled for him to come closer. He smirked a little and walked to Rocko. He kissed her forehead and climbed back into bed.

"I love you too baby. Now let's go back to sleep."

***

Sydney sat on her black leather couch waiting for her kids to walk through the door. By the way, things were going downhill she needed to sit down and have a talk with them. It was also time for her to tell them the truth about Santana. They were asking questions about him, and she knew she couldn't hide the truth any longer.

Her oldest son, Pacson, is eight years old, and she figured he would understand death. Issac and Karlous were only four and six years old, and she wasn't sure if they would fully understand. Mostly, Issac was the one she knew wouldn't fully grasp it. His attention span was very short.

Sydney's phone began to ring, and by the ringtone, she already knew that it was Meeka. She cleared her throat and answered the call.

"Hello," Meeka said.

"Hey Meek," Sydney spoke in a flat tone.

"How are you?" Meeka asked.

"I'm doing, but what about you?"

"Same thing, I can't even lie," Meeka said and exhaled.

"I swear it's like my head is about to pop off of my head."

"I thought I was the only person feeling that way. Did you talk to the boys yet?" Meeka asked.

"No, not yet, they aren't back from the barbershop yet. I've been trying to figure out what to say, but I'm still not sure."

"You need to start by telling them the truth," Meeka said.

"I know, but they are so young. I shouldn't have to have this conversation with some kids."

"True, but they need to know the truth. Our men are being killed for pointless reasons. I hate to say it, but one of your boys could be the next Santana. We're living in a world where only a straight white man is safe. This shit is crazy, and it disgusts me! God needs to wrap his arms around this world. We need a serious hug as soon as possible."

"Girl I second that, this still doesn't seem real, Santana is -"

"Please don't say it, Syd. I finally got my appetite back. I would love to actually eat something good today." Meeka rubbed her stomach and walked into the kitchen.

She opened the icebox and grabbed the box of pizza. She tossed two slices on a plate and placed it in the microwave.

"I'm sorry Meek." Sydney reached for her remote and flipped through the channels. Nothing caught her attention, so she continued flipping through the channels.

"It's okay Sydney," Meeka said.

"Did you talk to Mrs. Asha again?" Sydney asked.

"Yea, I told her I was coming to visit her soon. I need to bring some of Santana's things to her. The rest of the things I'll donate to charity."

"Save me a wig and a jumpsuit," Sydney said, and they both laughed.

"I sure will. I told her I'll go and identify the body once it's transported back from Arizona. I don't want her to see him like that."

"That's a good idea Meeka. If I had the heart to I would tag along with you." Sydney sighed.

"I know, but Brink is coming with me," Meeka said.

"Is this real Tameeka? This can't be real man! They found his body in a ditch. Like someone just tossed him to the side and they never looked back. Santana was such a good person. How could he do that to him?"

"I don't know Syd. This shit is messing with my head. We're going to get to the bottom of this, even if we have to rock out on a couple of people."

"You know I'm down for whatever Meek. We can't let Philly get away with this."

"I promise we won't. I have a trick up my sleeve, but I can't discuss it over the phone. We need to meet up later so I can tell you."

Sydney could hear a car pulling into the driveway, and she knew it was Xavier.

"Okay, that's cool. Xavier and the boys are back. I'll call you later." Sydney disconnected the call and rose to her feet. Pacson rushed into the house and dropped his book bag on the floor.

"Pacson, pick up your book bag. I tell you this every day." Pacson tossed his head back and turned around. He grabbed his book bag and placed it on the countertop. Then he ran to Sydney and gave her a huge hug. She rocked side to side and kissed the top of his forehead.

"Hey, mom!"

"Hey, baby." She said.

"Do you like my haircut?" Pacson spun around to show his mom his haircut. She gave him a high five and laughed.

"I sure do, it's perfect. How was school?" She asked.

"School was okay, but we're having a jean day this week. It's only a dollar, please mom!" He begged.

"Sure baby, but I need to talk to you and your brothers." Xavier walked into the house with Karlous and Issac. He gave Sydney a disappointed look and pointed at Karlous. Lately, he was getting into trouble at school, and Sydney knew it was the same thing today.

"Sit down you two," Sydney said. Karlous and Issac flopped on the couch and stared at their mom. She dropped to the floor and rubbed their hands. She was trying to gather her words, but nothing came out of her mouth. Sydney turned away and bit her bottom lip. For a moment, the clouds look like Santana, and she smiled.

"Mom, are you okay?" Pacson asked.

"Uuhh, yea baby, I'm okay. I have to talk to you three about something important."

"About what mommy?" Issac asked.

"What if we had to move? Would you guys like that?" Sydney asked.

"We don't want to move mommy," Issac said.

"Why would we have to move?" Pacson asked.

"Because of daddy, he isn't happy with himself, and he's being really mean to mommy and her friends."

"Is he being mean because you don't love him anymore?" Issac asked.

"Despite the way he is acting I still love your father and I always will. He may not know that, but I really do." Sydney said.

"Why don't you tell him that?" Pacson asked.

"I have baby, plenty of times. Your father doesn't want to hear that. He's bitter and upset, but I can't change that. We'll get into details later about that. I have to talk to you three about something else."

"About what money?" Issac asked.

"It's about uncle Santana.

"Where is he mommy? He was supposed to come over and watch TV with me like he always does." Issac said.

"Yea and he told me he was going to help me bake a cake for you," Pacson said. Sydney sighed and rubbed her thighs. Her boy's questions had her feeling uneasy already.

"Something happened to Uncle Santana, someone…killed him, I'm sorry."

"What?" Pacson asked.

"Mommy who killed him?" Issac asked.

"I'm not sure baby. We're still trying to find out."

"Why would someone want to kill him?" Karlous asked.

"Baby he was killed because of what he is."

"What's that?"

"Gay," Sydney said.

"Mommy, what's gay?" Issac asked.

"Uuummm, gay is when you like the same sex. Like a man liking a man. Santana liked men, and that's why he was killed."

"That's not fair mom. Uncle Santana should be able to like whoever he wants too right mom?"

"Of course he does, well did. Baby, we're living in a world where the safest person is white. Your religion, sexuality, and skin color can get you killed or hurt." Sydney said.

"Why do people feel like they can hurt you because of that? Why would they want to hurt you because you aren't white? That's stupid mom." Pacson said.

"It is stupid, and I wish I could answer those questions. Those are some questions that every African American, Jewish, Muslim, and Mexican would love to know the answers too. What I can say is that you never judge a person because of what they look like or their sexuality. If the person sitting next to you is gay or Mexican, ole well, your life is still going on. You wouldn't want someone judging you because of your dark skin tone. Do you guys understand what I'm saying?"

"Yes, mam." They said.

"It doesn't matter what you hear, Santana was a great person. I'm sorry the rest of the world couldn't witness that."

"We saw it though. That's all that mattered." Karlous said and smiled.

"You're right, and you guys have some great memories with him. Just because he isn't here physically, he's here spiritually. Santana is now our guardian angel and is watching over us." Sydney said.

"Mommy is it okay to be sad because I'm sad."

"Awww baby, it's okay to be sad. We lost someone that was very important to us." Sydney hugged Issac and held back her tears. Xavier cleared his throat and said, "Okay boys, it's time to go to your rooms. I need to talk to your mother.

"Okay." They said and ran off.

"Mr. Karlous, you, and I will have a talk later. I don't why you're acting a fool at school, but I'm going to fix that issue today."

"Yes, mam," Karlous said and closed his door.

"Sydney rolled her eyes and fell backward. She lied on the soft carpet and stared at the ceiling. Her mind was racing, and she could feel a headache coming. Her emotions were everywhere, but she needed to pull herself together fast.

"Everything is going to be okay baby. Please don't stress yourself over this." Xavier laid next to Sydney and pulled her closer to him. Sydney buried her face into his chest and whimpered.

"That's easier said than done. I never thought I would have this kind of conversation with the boys."

"I know, but how the world is going, I'm glad you did," Xavier said.

"Today was horrible at school, but I really didn't want to tell you," Sydney said.

"What happened?"

"Two parents are pulling their kids out of my classes."

"You can't be serious Sydney. Why are they doing that?" Xavier asked.

"Because of the lies, Austin is spreading about me in the streets. He's slowly ruining my reputation. Before you know it he's going to damage my career."

"No he won't, don't say that."

"It's true, and you know it. You can't go anywhere without someone whispering or pointing at you. I'm so sorry that I dragged you into my mess!" Sydney said.

"Stop saying that Syd. You didn't drag me into anything. I wouldn't let this push me away or leave you. That's what Austin wants. He's going have to come a little harder than that." He laughed. He stroked his beard and stared at Sydney. She cracked a smile, but it faded away.

"How can you laugh at this Xavier. I see how your family is even changing on you. They treat you different when I'm around. It doesn't matter how many times I explain the situation to them. They still will believe what they hear in the streets."

"Fuck them I don't care what they think. I damn sure don't care about what they have to say. You're my woman, and I love you. Before you know it, it'll all over with. Austin will find someone new to pick on."

"I hope so baby. The only reason why Meeka hasn't killed him is because all eyes are on her."

"I know, but she has to do something soon," Xavier said.

"I know, I know. This is spinning out of control. I could lose my job because of this. I'll never be able to get a decent job again."

"It's not like you need a job. They should be calling you *Money Making Sydney*." He laughed.

"Ha, ha, very funny, but I'm serious. "Meeka said she has some tricks up her sleeve. We're meeting later to discuss it." Sydney said.

"We all know what that means. Shoot'em up bang, bang!" he laughed.

"You got that right. Santana was everything to Meeka. I know she's taking this hard even though she isn't showing it much."

"Tameeka is a tough girl. She just mourns differently."

"I know, but some of your toughest people break down. I'm this close to packing our shit and leaving. I swear I will never turn back for anything or anyone." Sydney held onto the table and climbed to her feet. She walked down the hall and entered her bedroom. She stood in front of her wide mirror and stared at herself. Her makeup was ruined, and her freckles were fully exposed. As a child, she was insecure about her freckles. Once she became confident with her flaws, she flaunted them every chance she got.

Xavier stood behind Sydney and held her hips. He gently kissed her neck and ran his fingers under her shirt.

"Why don't we?" He asked.

"Why don't we what?" Xavier asked.

"Why don't we pack up and leave? Let's leave before things get too crazy and out of hand."

"I can't do that baby. I can't leave Meeka alone to clean up my mess. I'm the reason why all of this is happening."

"I understand that baby. If I was in your shoes, I would probably do the same thing. You're a true friend, and I love that about you."

***

Meeka sat near the dining room window and watched the raindrops fall. The streets were basically empty, and cars barely drove by. The only person she spotted walking was Pippy. He didn't care what the weather looked like. That didn't stop him from making a dollar.

The sound of rain was soothing and felt like music to her ears. Since Santana's death, her phone rang non-stop. Her mom always said when someone died the rain poured. It was God's way of crying out, and Meeka heard him loud and clear.

"Please come back Tana, just for a few seconds." She mumbled.

Meeka thought about all of the good times she shared with Santana. He knew some of her deepest and darkest secrets. Without Santana, she felt alone and empty. Neither Isabella nor Brink could fill that emptiness she was experiencing.

"I wish I was there with you Santana. Things would have gone totally different." Meeka whispered to herself and closed her eyes. Tears started to fall and wet her chest. As much as she cried last night, she thought she was all cried out. Today she had to identify Santana's body. Seeing him lifeless on that table scarred her for life.

"Hey, Tameeka." Meeka opened her eyes and found Jamie standing in front of her. Jamie's eyes were swollen and red. Her clothes were wrinkled, and her hair was covered with a loose bonnet. She looked a mess, but her appearance was the least of her worries.

"Uuummm, hey Jamie, how did you get in here?" Meeka rubbed her eyes and yawned. Her eyes were so heavy that she could hardly keep them open.

"Hustle let me in. I just wanted to stop by and see how you were doing." Jamie squatted to the floor and sat next to Meeka.

"I can't lie, I'm not good. This shit is crazy and feels so unreal."

"It does and saying that Santana is dead feels weird. I know you don't care what the police say; you're going to take matters into your own hands." Jamie said.

"I'm glad you know me so good Jamie." Meeka chuckled.

"I've been around you long enough to know how you get down. Anywho how did it go today? Was it really him?"

"I'm not sure how I'm supposed to answer that question. It was him, Jamie, he's dead. What fucked me up is how he looked." Meeka said.

"What do you mean?" Jamie asked.

"The funeral home said he was shot multiple times in the back and chest area. I think he said it was twelve times. The gun did damage to the chest area. From the neck on down, he was covered with a sheet. I took a peek of the rest of this body. He was rolled over also. They gave me his belongings. It's crazy how he was still wearing his purse through all of it." Meeka laughed.

"Wow, that's crazy." Jamie shook her head.

"He looked like….he looked like he was sleeping. I started saying, wake up Tana wake up! If I didn't know any better, you would have thought he was sleeping. His face was still beat of course. The only thing that was ruin was his makeup, it was a little smudged. He honestly looked like himself. My Santana is dead, and I can't do anything about it. I can't fix this problem, and I hate it, Jamie!! I hate it so fucking much its killing me! Any problem Santana brought to me I fixed it. I fixed everything, but whatever was going on I couldn't fix it."

"Meeka don't beat yourself up, we honestly don't know what happened. Do you think Philly has something to do with it?" Jamie asked.

"I wouldn't be surprised. Philly has a track record out of this world, and I haven't seen him in a while."

"Once he killed Kane's sisters and grandparents he vanished into thin air," Jamie said.

"I'm surprised that he was involved with Santana. I didn't even know Philly was gay."

"Girl I almost passed out when you told me that. Now we finally know who this little boo is." Jamie laughed, but it was a fake laugh.

"That's crazy, right? You never know who's gay now and days."

"It really doesn't surprise me who is gay. I'm going to hate myself forever. He died, and I was holding a grudge against him. I'm so fucking stupid Tameeka! How could I be that damn stupid to let a no good nigga abuse and mistreat me. Everything that Santana said was right, but I'll never get the chance to tell him that."

"Hey, don't beat yourself up because of this," Meeka said.

"How can I not Meeka? When Santana was in the hospital, I didn't visit him one time! He would call and text me, but I wouldn't respond. Some days he would come by the house, but I wouldn't answer. I would literally watch him call non-stop from the doorstep. The girls would ask about him so much, and I lied."

"You know Santana wasn't holding a grudge against you. He worried about you so much. Santana was hurt when you never visited him in the hospital. I tried my best to cheer him up, but it didn't work. He just wanted his cousin by his side." Meeka said.

"Thanks, Meek, this made me feel a lot worse," Jamie said as she wiped her tears and rolled her eyes.

"I'm sorry Jamie I wasn't trying to make you feel bad. I'm only telling you the truth. I don't hate you because of your actions. So don't think that. All I want you to do is learn from this. Next time you won't put a poo ass nigga before your family. All he was trying to do was save you from a lot of pain and heartache."

"I'm serious this time Meek, I'm done with him. I changed the locks and my number. I don't need that kind of person in my life or around my kids."

"That's good for you Jamie. I'm glad you finally saw what we were telling you. Sometimes you have to go through the pain yourself." Meeka said.

"I sure did go through the pain. I'll never take that kind of bullshit from someone again." Jamie said.

"Good for you Jamie. Know your worth. I have something to tell you," Meeka said.

"What's up Meek?"

"I have some friends coming into town to help me handle Philly. They always referred to that nigga as a cat."

"Why?" Jamie asked.

"Because he almost misses death, kind of like he has nine lives. I promise Jamie, I won't let Philly get away. It's going to be hard to capture him, but I won't stop until I do." Meeka said.

"Who are these friends?"

"It doesn't matter, but they are the truth. They hate Philly as much as I do. They probably hate him even more than I do." Meeka smirked.

"Damn, thanks a lot of hate." Jamie laughed.

"Yea, but that's life. I need to clear my head. Let's go and get a drink and some food." Meeka wiped her snotty nose and jumped to her feet. Jamie stood to her feet and gave me a big hug. She began to cry, but Meeka wasn't sure why. She patted Jamie on the back and said, "It's going to be okay Jamie, I promise."

"Meeka please don't get yourself hurt."

"Hey, look who you're talking to. I live for this shit, and I'm built for it." Meeka laughed, but Jamie didn't. Since she didn't laugh, Meeka's ignorant comment made her feel stupid.

"I'm serious Tameeka. I don't want to have to bury you too. I can't have that on my heart. I just can't."

"You won't Jamie, you have to trust me."

***

Meeka, Hustle, and Isabella sat in Waffle House waiting for the waitress to return to their table. She said she would bring the bill shortly, but Meeka spotted her outside smoking a cigarette. Meeka didn't care though. She was enjoying the little time away from home. Meeka had mix feelings about leaving her house. One minute she was trying to run away from it because it felt like the walls were talking. Then the next minute she was too depressed to leave the house.

"Pedro talked all of that shit and was at Juju's house last night." Meeka scooped the hash brown onto her large spoon and shoved it into her mouth. Hustle used his long pinky nail to dig between his teeth and laughed.

"I know, but you know how that goes. Just imagine all of the times I said I was done with you." Hustle chuckled.

"Ha, ha, ha Brink, you're very funny."

"You know I can't stay away for too long." He smiled.

"Do you remember our first date?" Meeka asked.

"Yea, after chasing you for two years I finally got a yes. I took you to Kyoto Japanese Steakhouse in Lake Charles."

"Yep, I can't believe you remember that." Meeka played it cool, but she was a little surprised. Their first date was years ago, and she barely remembered it.

"How could I not? You're my baby Tameeka. I never told you this, but I fell in love with you a week after we met. Everything about you had me in a daze. You're smile, the way you laugh, and even the way you walk on your tip toes. I just hope Isabella stops walking like you." He laughed.

"I hope so too, but can you honestly see yourself with me only me, forever?" Meeka asked.

"Hell yea, I'm with you now, and I'm happy. Yea, we've had our ups and downs, but they don't outweigh our good times. I feel like you and Izzy are the best things that have happened to me. I don't know what I would do without you two." Hustle reached into his back pocket and pulled out a black wave brush. He brushed his hair a little, and then placed the brush back into his pocket. Meeka shook her head laughed. Hustle was obsessed with his waves, and so was Meeka. His hair was wavy and perfect. That was the first thing she noticed about him. He took pride in his appearance and Meeka liked that. She was a bad bitch and stayed in designer. She needed the man next to her to be the same way.

"I really do love you Brink I mean that shit from the bottom of my heart. Every day I battle with should I be a cold-hearted bitch to the world or should I let my guard down and love. I want to give my all to you and feel free. I don't want to worry if you're out there cheating on me or if you're going to leave me." She said.

"Are you worrying or concerned with that now?" Hustle asked.

"Not, not at all," Meeka said.

"Okay, and why is that?"

"Because I know you're not doing anything. If you were, I wouldn't care." Meeka said.

"Why wouldn't you care? When you stepped out on me, I cared." Hustle said.

"Because you're going to do what you want regardless so I rather not care, so I don't get hurt. I'm kind of tired of getting hurt."

"I understand that, but when have I hurt you, well at least not purposely?" Hustle exhaled and locked his fingers together. He stared Meeka in her eyes, but she turned away.

She couldn't stare him in his eyes because she knew everything he was saying was true.

"My point exactly you know I love you with everything in me. I would die behind you Tameeka. You should know that and trust that. All I need you to do is get out the game. We can't continue to live like this. First, it was Santana so who's next?" Hustle asked.

"Austin doesn't have anything to do with that," Meeka said.

"How do we know that?"

"We really don't know that, but I highly doubt it. As for me getting out of the game, change doesn't happen overnight. I told you to give me time!" She grunted loudly.

"I am giving you time, but know your time is whining down." Hustle said.

"Yea okay." Meeka rolled her eyes.

"Yea, whatever." Hustle smacked his teeth and looked around the restaurant. It was crowded and dirty. The floor needed a good mop and sweep. Tables were left with dirty dishes and trash and needed to be clean.

"Before Izzy came along our date nights use to be lit." Hustle laughed and took a sip of his orange juice.

"Hell yea trips for weeks at a time. We were never home or even in the country."

"New Zealand was my favorite place," Meeka said.

"I wish we could pack up and leave tonight." Hustle said.

"I know, but this is life as we know it, eating waffles on a Thursday night," Meeka said.

"I wouldn't have it any other way." Hustle leaned forward and gave Meeka a kiss on the lips. She smiled and rubbed his hand.

"Thank you, baby," she said.

"Thank me for what Tameeka?" Hustle asked.

"Thank you for everything you do and especially now. I know it's a lot, but it seems like you're handling it all."

"You don't have to thank me for anything. I'm your man, and this is what I'm supposed to do. When you're down, I pick you up. It's simple as that and no questions asked."

"More and more I see why these girls are crazy over you." She laughed.

"Shid, I thought you been knew that." They both laughed.

"Isabella, are your waffles yummy for the tummy?" Meeka asked in a high pitch voice.

"More syrup mommy," she giggled.

"More syrup what mommy?" Hustle asked with the bottle of syrup in his hand.

"More syrup mommy PLEASEEE!" she shouted, but she quickly covered her mouth and laughed. She knew her squeaky laughter would make Hustle forget about her loud outburst.

"Tameeka where does she get this little attitude from?"

"That's funny Brink, you know she gets it from her daddy." Meeka teased.

"Oh really, I thought she got it from you." Hustle laughed and poured a large amount of syrup onto Isabella's waffle. Meeka grabbed her utensils and cut the waffle into six pieces. Isabella grabbed a piece of the soaked waffle and stuffed it into her mouth. Syrup was all over her hands, so she licked it.

"Eww," Meeka said, but Isabella laughed.

"No mommy, not ewww. It's yummy."

"Isabella, where are your manners?" Meeka asked.

"At home mommy." She giggled.

"She definitely gets her start mouth from you." Hustle said.

"I can't deny that. She definitely gets that from me."

"How are you feeling today?" Hustle asked.

"I'm feeling I guess. I can't answer that with an honest answer."

"I understand that. You know I'm here every step of the way." Hustle said.

"I know and thank you."

"Hi, are you Tameeka?" A girl who stood about six feet tall stop next to the table, her heart-shaped face, and gorgeous green eyes were breathtaking. Her sandy blonde hair was trimmed perfectly at her shoulders.

"Why?" Meeka asked. The girl was a little disturbed by Meeka's rudeness. She simply cleared her throat and smiled.

"I'm sorry, I should have introduced myself first. I heard him say your name and it caught my attention. I've always heard good things about Tameeka. You're beautiful just how he bragged, and in the pictures, I've seen." The girl stared at Isabella and smiled. She attempted to grab Isabella's arm, but Meeka grabbed it. Joseline rubbed her arm and stared at the dirty floor. Hustle and Meeka locked eyes.

"You must be Isabella. Oh my God, she is your twin Meeka."

"How do you know all of this? Let me guess, Austin sent you in here?" Meeka asked.

"NO, I'm not sure who Austin is. I'm Santana's cousin Joseline."

"Oh, can I help you with something?" Meeka asked.

"Yea, I'm looking for Santana. I've been calling his phone, but I'm not getting an answer. I called Jamie's phone several times, but she isn't answering either. Jamie is so wishy-washy! I can't stand my own cousin sometime."

"Shit." Hustle whispered and turned to the window.

"Damn, you don't know," Meeka said.

"I don't know what? Is something wrong? Did Tana move or something?"

"Uumm, you should sit down for this. Move, no, the something, yea." Meeka pointed to the chair, and Joseline turned around.

"Okay, what's wrong?" Joseline pulled a chair to the table and sat next to Meeka. Meeka stared at her plate trying to gather what words to use.

"A few days ago I got a phone call from a detective in Scottsdale, Arizona. He was...killed Joseline."

"WHAT, ARE YOU SERIOUS?"

"Yes, I'm serious. I'm so, so, sorry you had to find out this way."

"Oh God, this is a lot to take in. I'm in shock, are you serious?" Joseline asked.

"I wish I wasn't, but I am. I identified his body yesterday. It was him, unfortunately." Meeka didn't want to cry in front of Isabella, but she couldn't stop her tears from coming out.

Joseline seemed lost and suddenly pale. She wasn't sure what to do or what to say.

"Joseline, are you okay? You look a little flushed." Meeka said.

"I'm good, I'm just shocked. Are the cops working on the case? Is there a suspect in custody?"

"Yes, the cops are working on the case. If I have to go back and forth to Arizona, I will. Santana will get the justice he deserves." Meeka said.

"Did you talk to Asha?" Joseline asked.

"Yea, but she isn't doing well. I'm going to visit her tomorrow and check on her. If you still in town you're more than welcome to ride with me. It's going be my boyfriend and I."

"Yea, that's fine. I -I -I -I still can't believe this HAPPENED! To him, why man!" Joseline dropped her head and held her stomach. The tears dropped on her watch, but she didn't care. Meeka sat closer to her and rubbed her back.

"Trust me, I ask myself those questions all day. Santana was my right-hand man, and now he's gone."

"This is a lot to process. Excuse me for a second. I need to visit the room."

"Okay, take your time. I know I hit you with a lot." Joseline rubbed her forehead and stood to her feet. She took one step and collapsed to the floor. The loud thump scared Isabella, and she started to cry. Meeka and Hustle jumped to their feet.

"Oh my God Joseline!" Meeka shouted and dropped to the floor. Meeka waited for her to respond, but she didn't. Hustle check her pulse, and it was still beating.

"She isn't dead." Hustle said.

"Oh thank God, call 9-1-1!" Meeka shouted to Hustle. A few of the workers and customers ran to assist Meeka and Hustle. Everyone was in a frantic and wasn't sure what to do. Joseline's white skin turned pale and became sweaty. Hustle pulled his phone out and instantly dialed 9-1-1.

***

Meeka, Isabella, and Hustle sat silently in the hospital waiting room. Meeka leaned her head against Hustle's shoulder and watched television. Isabella was sound asleep with her head buried in Hustle's lap. Meeka rubbed her fingers through Isabella's tangled hair. Meeka was surprised that Isabella didn't wake up.

It was 10:23 pm and the emergency room was surprisingly empty. Hustle was sleeping, he was tired as hell. Meeka was sleepy as well, but she couldn't sleep. She had too much on her mind and plate, but her eyes were heavy. Her head fell backward and forward, and her eyes were closing on their own.

Meeka's phone began to vibrate, and it was Sydney calling. She yawned a little and answered the called.

"What up Syd?"

"I'm walking in the ER," Sydney said.

"Okay, you'll see us. We're the only people in here." Meeka laughed and disconnected the call. She kissed Isabella's head and walked to Sydney. They embraced each other with a hug, and then sighed.

"I need a drink man. Every day it's something new."

"I know, but too bad Don's isn't opened." Meeka laughed.

"I'll be there tomorrow early. Can I get a large Swamp Water plleeaassseee," Sydney threw her head backward and chuckled.

"I'm starting to understand why people do crack. I can't catch a break Syd, like what the fuck!" Meeka shouted in a whisper. Sydney rubbed Meeka's neck to comfort her, but it didn't help. Meeka's neck was tight and tense.

"I'll be damn if I let you turn to drugs." She laughed.

"Seriously Sydney, everything is happening back to back. I don't even know this girl, and I'm spending my night in the hospital with her!"

"That's because you're a good person Meeka. Besides, that's Tana's people. How is she anyway?" Sydney asked.

"I'm not sure, as of now, they didn't find anything wrong. They are running test and stuff right now."

"Okay, that's good. Is that the cousin Joseline who lives in Dallas?" Sydney asked.

"Yea that's her, well I would hope that's here. I couldn't ask her many questions. She did say she hadn't spoken to Jamie yet."

"Did you call Jamie? I'm sure she would want to see her cousin."

"I called her, I'm waiting for her," Meeka said.

"That's good, that's good, Jamie needs to take care of her cousin. We have other things to worry about." Sydney folded her arms across her chest and rolled her eyes.

"You're right about that," Meeka said.

"Have you spoken with Juju?"

"No, did you?" Sydney asked.

"No, I tried calling her, but she didn't answer. I saw her ugly ass brother today, but he didn't see me. Thank God, I was not in the mood to argue with him. I can't wait until all of this is over."

"Have you thought about getting a restraining order on him? I know a piece a paper won't keep him away, but it's a nice paper trail for when you pop him upside his head." Meeka laughed.

"I thought about it, but I changed my mind. That might make him madder. It's like I can't win with him. I can only imagine how he's going to tear me down in court."

"Hopefully he's dead by then. Fuck all that shit. It's only so much I'm going to take from him. I'm really letting him play me like I'm a pussy."

Jamie rushed through the sliding doors and searched the room for anyone who could help her. Meeka and Sydney spotted Jamie standing by the door. Meeka waved her over, and Jamie ran over to them.

"Where is she Meek? Is – is she okay?" Jamie asked. She was so nervous, she couldn't stand still. Sydney held Jamie by the shoulders and said, "Baby you need to calm down.

"I can't calm down. Where is my cousin?"

"Jamie you really need to calm down. We had to step out of the room for a few minutes. They're getting blood, urine, and running test. Most likely she got overwhelmed with everything. The better question is why weren't you answering when she was calling you?" Meeka asked.

"I dropped my phone in my mop bucket today, and my screen went black," Meeka said.

"Oh, well you need to get that fix," Meeka said.

"Yea, like ASAP Rocky." Sydney chimed in. Jamie sized her up and down. Jamie and Sydney didn't get along too well. They were friends before, but now they were sort of enemies. Years ago, Sydney swore she saw text messages from Jamie to Roman. Jamie was begging Roman to get in bed with him, but he declined her and threated to tell Meeka. Sydney decided to tell Meeka, and the shit hit the fan.

Sydney and Jamie got into a huge fistfight, and since then they could barely be in the same room. Jamie said hurtful things to Sydney like Sydney was a broke down version of Meeka and him how Sydney was secretly jealous of Meeka. Sydney wasn't bothered by anything Jamie said about her. She only wanted Jamie to be a woman and Meeka to know the truth. Even when Roman told Meeka what happened, she still didn't believe it.

"Anyways, I have it from here Meek, I can see that you're tired and you have Isabella with you," Jamie said.

"Are you sure? You know I don't have a problem staying with you."

"No, I'm good, but thank you."

"Okay, have a good night. Call me when you guys leave." Meeka gave Jamie a hug a Jamie walked away. Behind her back, Meeka was giving Sydney all kinds of ugly faces. Meeka didn't see it, but Jamie was no good. She'll never admit it, but Jamie wanted Roman badly. Maybe Meeka did see it, but she didn't care.

"You need to chill out Syd. We have enough shit going on right now. The last thing I need is for you two tearin' it down like savages."

"Yea, like the savage I am." She joked. Meeka pitched Sydney's shoulder and laughed.

"Girl you are crazy. I'll see you tomorrow girl, I love you." Meeka said as she reentered the building.

I love you too Meek. Let's do breakfast before I go to work."

"Okay, cool."

Chapter 2

It was a cool, but sunny day, so Xavier decided to take the boys to the park. He knew they would enjoy the summer breeze and fresh air. Sydney recently started a tutoring program after school and wouldn't be home until 6:00 pm.

"What are the boys doing?" Sydney slowly walked through the classroom to make sure the students were doing their homework. Once she noticed everyone was busy, she walked out of the classroom.

"Running around the court like crazy people," Xavier laughed.

"That's about right. I can hear Karlous screaming at the top of his lungs," she laughed.

"Pacson, give your brother the ball, please," Xavier said.

"Okay!" Pacson shouted and ran off.

"How is the new principal?" Xavier asked.

"That bitch is annoying me already. She's watching my every move like someone is making her do it." Sydney sighed and leaned against the wall. Then she removed her glasses from her face. She rubbed her neck a little and closed her eyes. Lately, she wasn't getting much sleep. When she did, she tossed and turned throughout the night.

"I wouldn't be surprised if she's working for him."

"Ugh, another muthafucka I have to watch." Sydney rolled her eyes and bit her lip. She wanted to bit her nails, but that was an awful habit she was trying to stop.

"I love you Sydney, I mean that."

"I love you too baby. Thank you for everything you do for us. I wish the world had more men like you. Shit, I wish I would have met you first. Then I wouldn't be in this mess." She giggled, but she was serious. She often thought about why God didn't guide her to Xavier first and kept Austin completely out of her life.

"Don't think of it like that. Good things come to those who wait." Xavier said.

"Yea, you're right about that." Sydney opened the door and quickly peeked in, and the students were still quiet, so she gave them thumbs up.

"DADDY!!" Karlous shouted, and they ran towards the fence. Xavier stood to his feet and stretched his eyes wide. Austin glanced at him and laughed.

"Daddy, did Karlous call you daddy?" Sydney asked. Pacson and Issac followed behind Pacson and stood by the water fountain.

"No, he's talking to his bitch ass father."

"WHAT?? Xavier, do NOT let him around my children!! I mean that shit."

"Trust me I won't, but let me call you back." Xavier disconnected the call and dropped his phone into his pocket. He walked to the fence and stood in front of the boys.

"It's time to go home boys." Xavier didn't bother making eye contact with Austin. In his eyes, Austin wasn't close to being a man.

"Boys, you talk like you're their father," Austin said.

"I may not be their father, but I'm the closest thing to a man that they know." Xavier laughed.

"What the fuck does that mean?" Austin closed his fists tightly and walked around the fence. Xavier pushed the boys to the side a little and walked towards Austin.

"Why are you so hostile?" Xavier smirked.

"Like I said, what the fuck does that mean?" He asked.

"It means what I said. There was no hidden or subliminal message." Austin sucked on his teeth and walked around Xavier. Xavier wasn't bothered at all. He looked over his shoulders and laughed.

"You think you're hot shit because you have my wife? I can make all that change within seconds. You wouldn't want to try me, you're still that lil' nigga from the projects in my eyes." Austin chuckled.

"Yea and you are still the rookies in the police uniform to me. The same rookie who was scared to patrol at night because the boys from the Dead End had you shook. I remember nigga, I remember. Without that badge, you're a what? You're a bitch and a half. You know the song." Xavier clapped his hands and laughed. Austin's blood began to boil. Xavier's word's hit hard, and he hated the truth.

Xavier's deep laughter, struck a nerve and Austin snapped. He pulled his gun from his hip and pointed it at Xavier. Xavier's body frozen and it also felt like time froze. A group of people nearby screamed and ran in different directions. Xavier didn't panic he knew Austin wasn't going to pull the trigger.

"DADDY NO!" Pacson cried out. With the gun pointed directly at Xavier's chest Austin laughed. He didn't care that he his kids were standing a few feet away from him. He had a point to prove, he wasn't that coward rookie anymore. Just a coward detective, but that he would never admit.

"Daddy please don't kill Mr. Xavier." Issac weeping was loud and heartbreaking. Xavier could see in his eyes that Issac was terrified. Karlous's weeping made Xavier's ears ring.

"Daddy stop you're making my brother cry!" Pacson screamed while crying. Right now, he hated his dad and wished he could pull the trigger on him.

"Do what you want to do ROOKIE!" He laughed, but Austin lowered his gun and slowly backed away.

"You wasn't going to use it anyways." Xavier laughed. Austin ran to his car and got in. Within seconds he sped out of the parking lot. Xavier watched as Austin sped down Martin Luther King Boulevard. His heart was racing, but he tried his best to stay calm. He gathered the boys into the car and started the car. Issac and Karlous were screaming at the down of their lungs with major tears.

"It's okay boys." Xavier drove off, but he was in a rage. He wanted to follow Austin and shoot up his entire car, but he knew that wasn't possible. Unlike Austin, he would never pull a gun out in front of Sydney's kids.

The boys were asking question after question, but Xavier couldn't think straight. This was something he didn't want to tell Sydney, but he had to. He would hate for her to find out another way.

"Where is my mom?" Pacson asked.

"She's at work. I'll call her as soon as we get home." Xavier tried to dial Sydney's number, but his hands were shaking out of control.

As Xavier pulled into the driveway, he noticed the front door was wide open. Since he was the one who locked the door, he knew something was up. He didn't want to panic in front of the kids, but he was getting nervous by the second. He reached under the seat and grabbed his Glock 17.

"Boys, stay in the car. I'll be right back."

"Why is the door open Xav?" Issac asked.

"Uhh, your mom left it open, remember what I said do not get out of the car okay."

"Okay." Xavier took his gun off safety and got out of the car. The closer he approached the house he noticed a big shoe print on the white door. He ran into the house and saw that the alarm was smashed. The house was a total wreck. Furniture was tossed over and damaged. Dirt from his plants was all over the floor, and broken glass was shattered everywhere.

He carefully walked through the house with his gun in midair. Sweat began to form on his forehead. He prayed that no one was still in the house. He would hate to have to shoot some in his home, but he was going to do what he had to do. He searched every room of the house, but he didn't find anyone. He walked to the front door but stopped. Sydney stood in the doorframe of the house with tears. The way the house looked had Austin's name all over it.

"What…….the hell happened?" Her voice and hands were trembling. Xavier wrapped his arms around

Sydney and gave her a hug. She tried to fight him off. But he was too strong.

"I'm not sure baby, I just got home. I need to talk to you about something."

"We need to talk about this first. What the fuck happened? This looks like some shit Austin would do. I know he made some lil' young niggas do this shit. Was anything stolen?" Sydney asked.

"I'm not sure if anything was stolen. I haven't checked yet. We left the park early because Austin and I got into an argument. It got heated, and he pulled a gun out on me."

"WHAT??!!!" Sydney shouted.

"Syd calm down please."

"How do you expect me to call down?? Where were the boys when all of this happened?"

"They were right there baby, I'm sorry."

"I'M GOING TO KILL HIM XAVIER!!! I SWEAR I'M GOING TO KILL HIM! HOW COULD HE DO THAT IN FRONT OF OUR KIDS, MY KIDS! This time he is wwaayyyy out of line and needs to be held accountable for his actions."

"Baby calm down, don't get yourself all worked up because of this. I knew he wasn't going to pull that trigger. We both know he isn't built like that."

"Calm down, how can I calm down? How could YOU be calm right now?? First, he pulls a gun out on you. Then he gets someone to rob or crash your house!"

Sydney this is material things. I can replace this in a few hours. If this is supposed to get a reaction out of me, it isn't going to work. I told you before he has to work harder."

"That's not the point Xavier. Money can't replace a life. I can't continue to do this to you!" Sydney punched the wall and ran into their bedroom and reached under her bed and grabbed a duffle bag.

"Sydney what the hell is you doing?" Xavier tried to snatch the duffle bag out of her hand, but he was too slow. Sydney reached into the dresser drawer and grabbed a few pieces of clothing.

"BOYYYYSSSSSSS, GET IN HERE NOW!" She shouted. Karlous, Issac, and Pacson ran into the house. Sydney pointed to their rooms and said, "GO and PACK your things."

"Mommy why?" Pacson asked

"BECAUSE I SAID SO!!"

"Sydney why are you shouting at him? Better yet, why are you making them pack their things?"

"Because I am their mother and I can do what I want!" Sydney opened the closet door and ripped a few dresses and shirts off the hangers. She stuffed as many clothes as she could into the duffle bag, then she zipped it. She tossed the heavy bag out of the room and grabbed the big tote bag that was hanging on the door. Xavier grabbed the bag and stuffed it in his pants. Sydney was upset and out of breath.

"Xavier give me my bag back!!!"

"Sydney no please tell me what's wrong!! What did I do to cause you to act this way!! Please tell me so I can fix it, I'm sorry." Xavier dropped to his feet and started to silently cry. He held Sydney by the hips and kissed her stomach. Sydney felt like a piece of shit. She rubbed the top of his head and cried.

"We just, we just need some time apart. The boys and I need to go away for a few days Xavier." Sydney's tears were full of emotions. She didn't want to leave, but she felt like it was the best thing to do right now.

"Okay, then what?" Xavier asked.

"I don't know Xavier, but I can't continue to drag you into my mess. That would be selfish of me, and I love you way too much for that. All of this is my mess, but no one wants to admit that to me. Everyone thinks it's going to hurt my feels, but it won't. It's the truth, and maybe I need to hear the truth."

"Sydney this is not your fault. I told you time and time you are not dragging me into anything. I chose to stay, and that's that, why can't you see that Sydney!"

"How long are you going to stay until you get fed up with this nonsense? Six months, a year, shit maybe even two more months. Then you're going to get tired of it and leave. I need to clear my head and figure all this shit out, Xavier. You don't see it, but I do. I'm basically dragging you to hell with me. Austin isn't in his right mind anymore. This is for the best, just a few days apart."

Xavier didn't make eye contact with Sydney, but he nodded his head. He rose to his feet and walked to the closet. He grabbed a few more pieces of clothing and dropped it into the bag. He wiped his face and walked out of the room.

"I'm going to make sure the boys have their things packed. Then I'll put them in the car as well."

"Thank you." She whispered. A headache started to rush to the front of her head. She held onto the dresser and massaged her brain. When she noticed her boys were walking out of she rushed to grab her bags and walked out of the room.

"Mom where are we going?" Pacson asked.

"Somewhere Pacson, don't start with the questions. Now let's go."

Xavier followed behind Sydney with her bags in his hands. After her irrational behavior, he remained the same sweet man. He opened her trunk and dropped the bags inside. As he closed the trunk, he wiped his tears away. He turned to Sydney and said, "I don't want you to leave, but I'm going to give you your space. I love you Sydney."

"I love you too Xavier. Are you going to call the cops and report a break in?"

"Yea, I will." He said.

"Alright, once I calm down and settle in I'll call you."

"Okay, be careful. I'll see you later boys." All the boys waved at Xavier and smiled. Xavier kissed Sydney on the lips and walked away.

"Mom, why are you crying?" Issac asked. Sydney quickly raised her head and wiped her tears.

"Put your seatbelts on and be quiet." Sydney didn't like how she was taking her anger out on her son, but she couldn't control her emotions. Within hours, things spiraled out of control. More and more Austin was raddling her life. Sydney sped through the streets and rushed to Meeka's house. She noticed Hustle's car wasn't there and she was glad.

Sydney ran to the door and banged on it three times. Meeka peeped out of the window with a hammer in her hand. When she noticed it was Sydney, she swung the door open and said, "Syd what the hell? Why are banging on the door like that? Isabella is sleeping!!"

"Meeka, I'm sorry." Sydney dropped to the ground and began to cry. Meeka didn't know what was going on, but she dropped the hammer and asked, "Sydney what the hell is wrong with you?"

"Austin, I can't take him anymore!!!! I'm going to kill him, Meek, I swear to God!! If you don't, I will, and I don't care if I get caught. I wouldn't mind spending time behind bars for him!"

"You need to tell me exactly what happened. Where are Xavier and the boys?" Meeka walked closer to the car, and the boys waved at her.

"Hey boys, get out the car and let's go in the house." Meeka smiled and opened the door.

"Okay, but do we need to take our bags down?" Pacson asked.

"I'm not sure baby. Why do you have bags?" Meeka asked.

"I don't know, but our mom told us to pack our bags. We were at the park, and my daddy pulled a gun out on Mr. Xavier. Then when we got home, someone broke into the house. Why would someone want to do that Mrs. Tameeka?"

"Wow baby, you guys had a busy day. I'm not sure why someone would do something like that. Maybe they were looking for those yummy cookies we baked the other day." Everyone laughed.

"Maybe so, but can we make some cookies again?" Pacson asked.

"Of course we can. Grab your bags and let's go in the house."

"Okay." They all said. Meeka ran to Sydney, but she was still on the concrete crying. Meeka grabbed her by the arm and stood Sydney to her feet. She wiped her tears and said, "Pacson told me what happened. I understand you're overwhelmed, but you have to pull yourself together."

***

It's been two weeks since Meeka was out of the house. Her first stop had to be the strip club. While she was home grieving, Sydney was at the club collecting Meeka's money and making sure everything was running smoothly.

"Hey Meek Milly, it's good to see you're out of the house." Cindy smiled at Meeka as she prepared her usual drink. She handed it to Meeka, and they toast.

"It feels good to be out of the house. If I would have stayed in the house another minute, I would have lost my mind. I think about Santana all day man. This shit is fucked up."

"I totally understand Meek. I still can't believe he's gone. It's going to be weird not seeing him walk in the club dancing. I swear he was the life of the club." Cindy laughed. Her eyes were filling with water, and she was ready to change the subject.

"I know, swinging those wigs like he grew the hair himself." Meeka chuckled and took a sip of her drink.

"Guess who is here?"

"Who boo?" Meeka asked. Cindy smiled.

"You know who, don't play dumb Tameeka."

"Girl who, I'm not playing dumb?" Meeka asked. Cindy pointed at the roundtable that was near the slot machine. Meeka squinted her eyes to get a better view then chuckled. Roman and two of his friends were sitting at a table full of stacks of money and drinks. Two but naked dancers sat on Roman's lap and it kind of made her jealous.

"Oh okay, Ro is here as usual."

"He came here six times looking for you," Cindy said.

"I'll holla at him when those tricks get off his lap."

Tia and Mia, but Meeka liked to call them The Double Mint Twins, were all over Roman. While Meeka and Roman were dating the twins tried to get with him numerous times. The only reason why she hadn't killed them was because she had a soft spot for their mom. She was the bank teller at MidSouth Bank. She never questioned Meeka about the large amounts of money she deposited.

It's didn't matter how many times they threw themselves at him, he never gave in. It didn't matter that he was no longer with Meeka. He was still loyal to her, and she respected him for that.

"I swear, I can't stand those two. I don't understand how they are still working here. They start so much drama, it's ridiculous." Cindy said.

"Because they both are fucking the owner," Meeka said.

Roman looked over his shoulder and spotted Meeka at the bar. He slightly pushed the twins off his lap and stood to his feet. When they noticed where he was headed, they rolled their eyes. Meeka laughed and nodded her head towards them.

"Come on Tameeka, stop being messy, you're way too pretty for that." Roman laughed and gave Meeka a hug. Meeka wanted to hug him tighter and pull him closer to her being in his strong arms made her feel secure. A feeling she hadn't felt lately.

"Whatever Ro, you already know how I feel about the double mint twins." Meeka flipped her hair and adjusted her collar. Roman stared at her with glossy eyes, but he didn't say anything.

"What why are you looking at me like that?" She asked.

"I'm just admiring your beauty. Sometimes I forget how beautiful you are. I swear it feels like I'm looking at an angel."

"How could you forget that?" She giggled.

"Maybe because I don't wake up to that beautiful face anymore and on top of that I haven't seen you in two weeks." He said.

"Yea, that could be why."

"How have you been since everything?" He asked.

"I'm not sure. I'm trying to learn how to block everything out. My head is all over the place. I'm not sure how to feel."

"I understand that boo. I know you're a tough woman, but it's okay to cry. Let it all out and heal yourself."

"I know, but I have so much going on right now." She said.

"You need to make time to take care of yourself Tameeka. Did you get the flowers I sent you? I sent sunflowers because I know that's your favorite."

"Yes, I did and thank you by the way. I also got your little note as well." Meeka smirked, and Roman laughed.

"You know there was nothing little about my note. It was all love, and you know it."

"I love it when you talk that sweet shit, Roman. It gets me every time. Luckily Brink didn't see your little note. He probably would have cried right then and there."

"I'm glad he didn't. I wasn't trying to start any confusion between the two of you. I just wanted to make you smile from a distance. I hope I did that." Roman gently grabbed Meeka's hand and gave it a kiss. Meeka cracked a smile and batted her eyes. Roman knew all the right things to say and do.

"You did and thank you. I received your messages as well, but I didn't have the energy to reply. This shit with Santana sucked all the life out of me."

"I understand boo, you don't have to explain anything to me. I know it's hard, but you'll get through this."

"I hope so. They do say time heals all wounds." Meeka smiled, but she didn't reveal any of her teeth. Her teeth were white, but Roman's pearly whites would put her teeth to shame. Roman's words were true. On the contrary, it would be a while before Meeka could believe them.

"Well, I'm going back to my table. After you make your rounds come and join me."

"Oh, I'll come alright." She licked her lips and laughed.

"Damn, like that?" He joked.

"Just kidding Ro," Meeka said.

"Seriously though Meek, if you need anything call me. You know I'm only one call away."

"I know baby and thank you. I mean that." Meeka gave Roman a kiss on the lips and a hug. As he walked away, she watched him. Roman and Meeka shared some amazing times together. She often regretted leaving him, but she knew who her heart belonged to.

"Damn girl, you still have that man wrapped around those coffin nails." Cindy laughed.

"Hey, what can I say? It's a skill that I have mastered." Meeka laughed and took another sip of her drink.

Tia walked in Meeka's direction with her hips swinging aggressively. Her long fiery red hair covered her pale white breast. Mia was truly the definition of trailer park trash. Just because she danced didn't mean she had a lot of money. Majority of it went on prescription drugs, court fees, and weave.

"Look who's coming," Cindy whispered.

"Trust me, I see those horse teeth from a mile away," Meeka said. Tia stared Meeka up and down with her hands across her chest. Meeka leaned against the bar top so she could be comfortable while taking a shit.

"Well, well, well, look who finally showed up. It's Ms. Money Making Meeka. I wonder if Hustle would still be with you if he saw you kissing your ex."

"Girl bye, Hustle could see me kissing ten bitches and fucking eight niggas. He STILL wouldn't leave me. When will yall learn that?" Meeka chuckled and slapped her thigh.

"When will they learn that Brink is pussy whipped?" Cindy asked and laughed. Meeka dapped her down and said, "I swear Syd, I've been screaming his for years. They don't want to hear the truth. Just the lies they tell themselves."

"Cindy you need to stop dick riding Tameeka and worry about making those drinks!"

"I'll make your drink, and I'll put something special in it." Cindy flipped Tia the middle finger and stormed off.

"Have a good day love." Meeka grabbed another drink and walked away from the bar. She noticed Quix was on stage and she gave Quix her full attention. Quix was an amazing pole dancer and entertainer. She always pleased the crowd with her pole tricks and twerking. Meeka waved at Quix, and her eyes grew big. She gave Meeka a quick wave and continued making her ass clap.

A few minutes later she was done dancing and ran off stage to meet Meeka. She gave Meeka a big hug. Her sweaty body had Meeka's clothes damp, but she didn't care. She was just glad to see Quix.

"Tameeka, I can't believe you came tonight." She said.

"It's only been two weeks Q. You need to calm down." Meeka laughed.

"I missed you so much, girl. You were avoiding my calls. I thought you were still upset with me."

"I'm sorry, but I was avoiding everyone. I needed some time to myself, that's all."

"I understand that. Once again, Meek, I'm sorry I had you guys worrying. Sydney and Juju still aren't speaking to me." Quix said sadly.

"Damn, I'll talk to them for you. You had us worried Q. I didn't know what to do think."

"I can tell you what to do. Keep your damn phone charger when you run off to take care of something." Meeka laughed. Quix shrugged her shoulders and laughed as well.

"Trust me I will." While everyone thought Quix was in danger, she wasn't. A family member in Virginia was in a bad car accident and needed to rush back to her hometown. She didn't have time to grab many of her things, including her phone charger. Sydney walked out of the Champagne room and locked eyes with Quix. She flared her top lip and turned away.

"See what I'm saying. She's been doing that all night." Quix rolled her eyes and leaned against the bar top.

"That's going to stop tonight. Let's go to my office." Meeka grabbed Quix by the arm and walked through the club. Sydney was standing near the stage talking to Justice. Meeka tapped Sydney on the shoulder, and she turned around.

"Meek, I didn't know you were coming tonight!" Justice gave Meeka a hug and rubbed her back.

"I didn't plan on it, but I needed to clear my mind," Meeka said.

"Did you see Roman? He asked about you." Justice said.

"Yea, I spoke to him. I need to talk to y'all. Let's go to my office."

"Okay." Everyone walked down the small hall, then entered Meeka's office. The cold air slapped everyone in the face. Meeka rushed to turn the air conditioner off and sat at her desk. She stared at the family picture of her, Hustle, and Isabella. She hadn't been away from them a full hour, but she was missing them like crazy.

"What's up Meek? I was about to do a lap dance." Justice said.

"I was about to get a Champagne room. You know Marcus leaves early on Tuesdays."

"I know, but I won't take long. Y'all need to squash whatever feelings y'all have towards Quix. Everyone knows what Quix's situation was so drop it!"

"Quix you had us terrified!" Justice said.

"I know, and I said that I was sorry a million times. Damn Ju, you ain't like I fucked your man or something. I called yall as soon as I could."

"You're right Quix, just don't let it happen again. We were worried sick about you." Sydney said.

"Okay, she's sorry and y'all forgive her. Sydney where is my money?" Meeka asked.

"It's in the top drawer, Meek." Meeka shook her head and grabbed the silver handle on the dresser. Large amounts of money were wrapped with rubber bands. She knew it was too much money to count by hand. She reached under her desk and grabbed her money counter.

"Are y'all ready for the funeral?" Quix asked, but no one replied. Everyone looked around the room and played dumb.

"Of course not," Justice whispered.

"Fuck no," Sydney mumbled.

"Hell to the no," Meeka said.

"No matter what y'all, we have to all stick together through this, even if Justice chooses the other side."

"Choose the other side? What other side?" Justice walked in front of Quix and stood toe to toe with her. Justice was a foot taller than Quix and twenty pounds bigger than Sydney, but she wasn't intimidated.

"The other side is your brother. I just find it strange how you would choose Meeka over your brother and freedom. Maybe you're pretending to do that." Quix smirked.

"Something must have been in the water in Virginia. You're talking out of your ass."

"Maybe I am, but maybe I'm not." She said.

"You had too much to drink. I'll let it slide because the Vodka is talking for you." Justice patted Quix on her stomach and walked out of the office.

"What the hell was that?" Sydney pointed at the open door and stared at Justice. Justice shrugged her shoulders and tossed her hands in the air.

"Your guess is as good as mines. I'll be in the dressing room taking a shower if anyone needs me." Justice chucked the deuces in the air and walked out of the office. Sydney followed behind her and closed the door. Meeka locked her fingers together and waited for Sydney to say something.

"Uummm, does Q know something we don't know?" Sydney walked to Meeka's desk and sat on the edge of it.

"I'm not sure. I think she would have told us something. Maybe Juju is right. Quix could be talking out the side of her neck for real."

"Yea, but I didn't see her put a drink to her lips, only water, and pineapple juice. You can ask Cindy to make sure."

"Naw, I believe you. Let's not look too deep into it. If something is wrong, I'm pretty sure Quix would tell us." Meeka pressed the power button on the money counter and neatly placed a stack of money in the holder. The machine said $1,000, but she wanted to recount it to make sure.

"Okay." Sydney reached into the drawer and handed Meeka another stack of money.

"Girl you had Roman in here looking for you with a flashlight. I could have sworn I saw him using the flashlight on his phone." Sydney laughed.

"That sounds about right." Meeka laughed.

"Do you regret breaking up with him?"

"No, not at all, if I didn't I wouldn't have my sweet baby girl." She said.

"True, but you could have had a baby by Roman," Sydney said.

"I know Isabella is my perfect little girl. She is literally Hustle and me in a diaper."

"I understand that. People don't like to admit it, but a man can make you feel a certain way about your kids. When I had Pacson, I was drunk in love with Austin. Being in love with him, made me love him a hundred times more."

"I feel you on that. Isabella is Hustle all day. She yawns like him and even crosses her ankles just the way he does. It's crazy how they pick up on the things you do." Meeka laughed.

"I know Karlous exaggerates his word JUST like Austin does. I hate that shit, but it's cute."

"Roman and I would have had a beautiful little baby." Meeka smiled. She imagined a caramel skin tone baby with big brown eyes. She had wavy chocolate brown hair and big ears exactly like Roman.

"I would be lying if I said I don't miss him or think about him often. Roman is a damn good man, but he isn't Brink. I don't know what it is about him. I really think he's my soul mate."

"Aaaww, do you tell him that?" Sydney asked.

"Hell no, I don't know how to fix my mouth and tell him those things."

"Do you ever tell him nice things?" She joked.

"Uhhh, yea bitch I'm working on being a softer person." Meeka laughed.

"I hope so. You're rough like an orange."

"Whatever trick. On some reals shit though, I don't think Roman has moved on." Meeka said.

"I don't think so either. I never see him with a woman."

"Mayyybbbbbeeee, he's gay?" She burst into laughter.

"Ha, ha, very funny Syd coming from the person who husbands is obsessed with me!" She laughed.

"Damn Meek, that was deep!"

"Too soon?" Meeka squinted her eyes and hid her laughter.

"Hell yea, way too soon." She chuckled.

"Meek, do you remember when Tana was dating that guy from Baton Rouge?" Sydney asked. Meeka dropped the stack of money and rubbed her eyes. She raised her head a little and started to laugh.

"Oh my God I can't believe you remembered that. We were like eighteen years old. Wasn't he from the south side, uptown to be exact, right?" Meeka said.

"Yea and he also had that hidden girlfriend and family." They both laughed.

"Right her name was Peppa, Piggy, or something with a P. Shit I can't remember. Tana had so many 'boos' and 'baes' in Baton Rouge." Meeka chuckled.

"Exactly, that's why I never got with anyone from B.R. Not even Baker, Denham Springs, or Zachary. I don't know who Tana was meeting on Florida."

"That damn Tana."

"I'm going to miss him Meeka-" Sydney tried to complete her sentence, but her voice started to crack. Meeka exhaled and drop the money. She thought she was all cried out, but she realized she wasn't. Her tears pushed out, but she cried silently. She stood to her feet and walked around the desk. Meeka wrapped her arms around Sydney, and they both cried.

"I know Syd, I miss him already. I don't know how we're going to get through life feeling this pain." Meeka sobbed.

"Tameeka, I want him back." Sydney's crying heart tore Meeka's heart apart. She didn't know what to say or do. She couldn't do much to mend her friend's pain.

"I know baby, I want him back also. One day we're going to get through this, and it's going to get better."

"I hope so Meeka, I really hope so what if though Meeka," Sydney said.

What Sydney?"

"What if she's working for her brother?" Sydney asked.

"I really don't know Syd, I really don't know. If something does happen, I want you to leave and never come back here. One of us has to make it out of here."

"What about you Meeka?"

"What about me?" Meeka asked.

"What are you going to do?" She asked.

"I'm going to stand ten toes down and clean this mess I made."

***

Meeka sat in front of the church in her car crying. Today was Santana's funeral, the day she was dreading.

She tried to visit his body, but her heart wouldn't let her. She ran out of the church and locked herself in Hustle's car for an hour.

"Baby, it's almost time for you to speak." Hustle stood by the car's door and held his hand out for Meeka. She looked in the mirror and wiped her snotty nose. Hustle helped her out of the car and closed the door. Her bladder felt weak as she walked inside of the church. Everyone pointed and stared at her and Hustle.

"Someone asked Justice who was her friend? They were talking about Santana's mom." Hustle whispered into Meeka's ear and laughed. She shook her head and laughed as well.

"I hate people, I swear." Meeka walked to the pulpit, and her heart was pounding loudly. She was surprised that Hustle couldn't hear it. She stood at the pulpit and stared into the crowd. The church was packed with a variety of people; gays, straights, transgender, bisexuals, and people of color. They all had two things in common, to mourn and celebrate Santana's going home. She could see Santana's mom was uncomfortable being around all the people and Meeka hated it. His mom still fully didn't accept that her son was gay.

Meeka wiped her wet eyes, but the tears didn't stop falling down her face. She wiped her face again and pulled a folded piece of paper out of her pocket. She took a deep breath and began to read it.

"Santana, but as I like to call him Tana, my best friend, my favorite shoulder to cry on, and my brother, I never saw this day coming, and I don't think he did. For hours, we would talk about all kinds of things. His death was never the topic of discussion. I know we're not supposed to question God's plan, but this is hard to not question. No one deserves to die because of their sexuality. It just isn't fair, and we all know that. I wish people wouldn't judge him because of how he appeared. If you would have gotten to know him like I did, I swear you would have fallen in love with him.

"Tameeka Giulbeaux!" Meeka stared down the aisle of the church and realized it was Detective Pipes. Everyone stared at Meeka and then stared at him. As the detective walked the aisle, Meeka held onto the pulpit tighter and tighter. She knew this wasn't going to turn out well.

"I need to take you downtown for questioning."

"What, you can't be serious. I'm in the middle of speaking at my friend's funeral." Meeka laughed, but Detective Pipes pulled his silver handcuffs out and slapped them around Meeka's wrist. The entire church gasped. He walked Meeka down the aisle and laughed.

"You can't be serious!" Sydney shouted.

"Meek, what did you do?" Justice asked as she stood up.

"What the hell!" Hustle's eyes grew big, and he handed Isabella to Quix. Hustle, Sydney, and Justice followed behind Meeka, but Pipes stopped them. Hustle sized him up and down, but Meeka said, "Brink, no! We both do not need to be in cuffs. Follow me to the police station."

"Let's go!" Pipes pulled Meeka out of the churched and pushed her into the police car.

Meeka couldn't believe this was happening especially at Santana's funeral. Everyone pointed and stared at her in the police car. She has never been this embarrassed before. She dropped her head and closed her eyes. She hadn't been in the back of a police car since 2006. She cried the entire time to the police station. Not because she was arrested. She cried because she couldn't tell Santana goodbye.

She was relieved that Austin's car wasn't in the parking lot. Pipes held Meeka's wrist tight and lead her into the interrogation room. The room was cold and dim. He placed Meeka's body into the metal chair, and then he sat down.

"Why am I here?" Meeka asked.

"Do you want any water, coffee, or a cigarette?" He asked.

"No, but I do want to know why I'm here. I'm supposed to be at my friend's funeral."

"Calm down, gay people die every day," he laughed.

"Cops die every day too B. y'all be alright." Meeka laughed. Pipes gave Meeka a foul look and reached for his briefcase.

"A few months ago a gentleman by the name of Glenn was killed." Detective Pipes opened the blue folder and pulled out a photo of Glenn. He was dead with one gunshot to the head and next to him was the fake suicide letter that Meeka had handwritten.

She grabbed the photo and stared at it for a few seconds. She didn't show any emotions because she wasn't bothered by his dead body.

"Suicide, he wasn't killed, right? That's what all the news stations reported. No foul play or signs of forced entry into his home, right?" Meeka asked.

"That is correct, but we believe that you have something to do with his murder."

"Suicide, not murder I don't want to offend you, but do you know what the definition of suicide is?" Meeka asked.

"What?" He felt insulted.

"I guess not, but let me break it down for you big fella. Suicide is the intentional taking of one's own life. That's what happened. That's what YOUR team said happened. The case is closed so why are you opening it again? I think that family suffered enough."

"We received a tip that Glenn was a target. He knew information about you that you didn't want us to know."

"Clearly you don't know me, Detective. I don't hide anything, and I let it all hang out. Ask my boyfriend, he'll tell you." She laughed.

"No thank you, I prefer to ask you instead." He said.

"Whatever floats your boat and I'm pretty sure your tip was Detective Austin. It's no secret that he hates my guts and the ground I walk on."

"The night of the killing where were you Ms. Tameeka?" He pulled out a small notepad and black ink pen. Meeka cleared her throat and said, "Just like I told your tipper Austin, I was home with my family. You can contact my boyfriend to verify that. You can check my cell phone records to also prove my location. I made calls to Pizza-Hut and China Wok. My daughter, Isabella, looovveesss their shrimp fried rice with her pepperoni pizza, disgusting combination, right?" Meeka raised her eyebrows and crossed her legs. Detective Pipes wrote down every single word that came out of Meeka's mouth.

"While you're being a puppet and following Austin's orders, y'all need to worry about who killed my friend. I had to bury my fucking friend today!!! I couldn't even attend the entire funeral because I was escorted out of it. Either you're going to let me go or charge me with a crime that I didn't commit. Go ahead and try it. I have the best damn lawyer in the state of Louisiana. Taneisha Riggs aced the bar exam with no problem. She graduated from Southern University at the top of her class. I keep her on speed dial because of cops like you. Nothing ties me to this suicide, and you know it, but just a bitter detective and his sidekick. You have to come a little harder than that Pipes!"

"Uumm, you're free to go."

"Yea, I thought so. Enjoy the rest of your day sir." Meeka stood to her feet and kicked the chair over. Even though she was furious, she walked down the hall calm. Everyone stared at her, but she didn't make eye contact with anyone. Her face was covered with smudged eyeliner and lipstick.

Meeka rushed out of the police station and saw Hustle standing next to his car. The phone was attached to his ear, and he held a large amount of money in his hand.

"Baby!" she shouted and waved at him. She disconnected the call and jogged her way.

"What happened?" Hustle asked. He grabbed Meeka by the cheeks and planted kisses all over her face. She looked over her shoulders began to walk.

"Let's get the hell away from here first." Meeka and Hustle walked to his car, and they got in. Hustle sped out of the parking lot.

"Austin is trying to connect me to Glenn's murder! That muthafucka will not stop Brink, he doesn't fucking stop!!!!!" Meeka shouted and banged on the window.

"How is that possible? What evidence does he have?"

"He literally has no evidence. Just Austin's ass talking shit, oh but best believe I'm calling Taneisha. She's going to handle this shit because it's getting out of hand."

"Just calm down baby," he said.

"How Hustle, how? He escorted me out of a damn funeral, my friend's funeral to be exact. Do you know how shame that was? My daughter had to see me in handcuffs. I swear I could kill Austin and Pipes. I never liked him from day one, but Sydney begged me to be nice to him. I should kill her for even introducing me to him. What the hell was I thinking ever talking to those Pigs."

"Tameeka calm down, you're getting all pissed off for nothing."

"I have every right to be pissed off. You weren't the one in handcuffs. I swear Taneisha is going to have a field day with this shit. I can't wait until she gets back from Italy! Where is Isabella by the way?" Meeka asked.

"She's with Sydney and Xavier. Do you want to stop and get here?" Hustle asked.

"No, let's go home."

Ten minutes later Meeka and Hustle arrived home. She ran into the house and screamed. For a second she thought she was losing her mind. She dropped to the floor and began to cry. Hustle held Meeka tight in his arms. He tried to soothe her, but it didn't help. Her cry became louder, and it turned into a whimper.

"Tameeka, just say the world, and we can leave. I swear we can leave right now and never come back."

"I can't leave Tana like this baby. No, I can't, I can't do it." She shouted.

"Baby you're not leaving him, he has already left you. It's time for him to rest. Let him rest baby."

"But he killed him Brink and left him for dead. He didn't care about what would happen to his body. Why Brink, why Santana? He could have taken anyone, but him. I – I -I need some kind of answers."

"Tameeka we need to leave. Just for a few days, that's it. You need to clear your mind from all of this. I hate to see you like this."

"We can't Bae, not now." She said.

"Yes we can and we will." Hustle scooped Meeka into his arms and carried her into the bedroom. He pulled her heels off and raised her black dress to her stomach. Hustle softly kissed Meeka's stomach and rubbed his hand against her vagina. Her legs began to spread apart as if they had a mind of their own.

***

It was midnight and Meeka, and Sydney were wide away in her dining room. For hours, they talked about how she was escorted out of the church and how they needed to put a plan in motion. Sydney was full of Patron and was ready to kill Austin tonight. Meeka, on the other hand, was sober and in her right mind. She knew that killing Austin tonight would be a crash dummy move.

"I'm telling you Meeka, I know he's sleeping right now. He's going to wake up in a few minutes to use the bathroom. Then he's going to flush the toilet and walk out of the bathroom. That nasty bitch never would wash his hands. He's going to walk down the hall and scratch his balls. Then he's going to open the fridge and open a bottle of water. He'll take two sips, and then go back to bed. It's clockwork Meek, I'm telling you! He won't wake up until 6:00 am, and he'll be out the door by 7:30 am. By 8:00 am he'll be at work getting a cold ass donut and drinking a cup of coffee. I promise you, I know my husband well."

"You know when he dies you're going to be a black widow?" Meeka laughed.

"Girl that's the least of my worries he's going to get whatever comes to him. Xavier is a damn good man, and I refuse to let him go. I just needed to clear my mind for a few days. Austin will not ruin my relationship."

"That's good I would have killed you if you would have left him."

"Meeka he was so sad when I left, but he also understood what I was saying. I still can't believe Austin pulled a gun out on Xavier. He didn't care that our kids were right there. What if he would have pulled the trigger Meeka? My kids would have witnessed some messed up shit because of him. I swear I can't stand the ground this man walks on."

"That shit is crazy. I don't care how you feel towards a person. Pulling a gun out in front of some kids are not called for."

"I swear I want to kill him with my bare hands, soft pink coffin nails and all." Sydney pretended to strangle someone and laughed.

"As long as you don't leave any fingerprints behind," Meeka said.

"Of course not you know I keep the latex with me."

"Just like I keep that 45 with me." Meeka laughed and grabbed another slice of pizza. She tried to hand Sydney another, but she declined. Instead, she grabbed the box of hot wings and took a few out of the box.

"Fuckin right, the way things are going I may need to get a 220. I still can't believe Philly though. He didn't have to do Santana that way bruh."

"I know and to leave him in the middle of the road was fucked up. How could a car not see a big ass, dead ass, human in the middle of the road?" Meeka shook her head.

"The fact that he still had his purse around his waist was funny though." They both laughed.

"I know right. I don't care what anyone says, that was Philly on that tape. You could clearly see his cross tattoo on the back of his neck."

"That's true, but I don't understand how he NEVER gets convicted or even picked up for a crime. That nigga killed four people and got away. How many times can someone go on the run?"

"Clearly plenty of times, someone in the police department is working with Philly. He has an uncle, cousin, or a friend on the force. That's the only way."

"Do you think?" Sydney raised her eyebrows and tilted her head. She didn't have to say anything. Meeka knew exactly what Sydney was thinking.

"Could he?" Meeka asked.

"Tameeka I honestly wouldn't be surprised, Austin been no good. This didn't start a few days ago. That would make a lot of sense. I wonder if they are related." Sydney rubbed her chin and went into deep thought. Meeka smacked her lips and slapped Sydney on the shoulder.

"Shit, you're his wife. Is he related to him in any way, a distant cousin, a close cousin, or related by marriage?" Meeka asked.

"No, I've never seen Philly at any family gatherings. I never even heard Austin mention his name before. Wait a minute, what is Philly's real name?" Sydney asked.

"Your guess is as good as mines. I always thought his real name was Philly." Meeka shrugged her shoulders.

"Maybe Philly is short for Philadelphia. I'm going to ask Justice tomorrow if they are related."

"No, I'll ask her. She may be salty about how you blasted her brother on Facebook." Meeka snickered and covered her mouth. Sydney raised her glass in the air and said, "Fuck him, he better be lucky that's all I did."

"What if they are related, but you don't know?"

"I doubt it, Meek, I never saw Philly around the family. Majority of the time I do see him is on the news."

"Forget it, maybe the liquor has us looking too deep into it," Meeka said.

"Yea you're right. Austin isn't the only crooked cop in the department."

"You're right about that. Matter of fact, I'll drink to that." Meeka grinned.

"You were going to drink anyways." Sydney giggled and twirled her hair.

"It was nice having you guys here, and I'm going to miss you." Meeka took a sip of her red wine and took a bit of her cheesy pizza.

"You know y'all could have stayed here instead of a hotel," Meeka said.

"I know, but it was nice to be away from everyone for a few days. After a while that fast food shit got weak." Sydney laughed. Sydney was gone from home long enough and was ready to go back home. Xavier gave her all-time she needed to clear her head. He didn't call and text her phone nonstop or bothered her. He knew Sydney's head was in another place and he didn't want to push her over the edge.

"You are drunk girl, and I'm not letting you leave my house." Meeka grabbed Sydney's keys, but she took them back. She stumbled a little, but she regained her balance. Meeka gave her a stale look and shook her head.

"Meeky, I'm fine. I miss my boyfriend, and I want to talk to him."

"Call him, that's why they made cell phones."

"I want to see him in person. That's why they made cars. I'll be right back."

"Alright, but don't take too long and call me when you're on your way back."

"Okay mother, I will." Sydney laughed and walked out of the house. Like a kid, she skipped to her car and got in. For some reason, she was missing Xavier a lot and wanted to love all over him. She pulled out of Meeka's driveway and drove off. Xavier only stayed three minutes away, so she made it there in no time.

Sydney pulled in front of the house, but a deep purple 2014 Dodge Charger was parked in the driveway. An LSU sticker was on the back glass, and the license plate read ForBen. Sydney wasn't sure who the car belonged to or who was Ben. She figured it was one of his co-workers, but she was a little annoyed. She wasn't in the mood to meet any of Xavier's friends or co-workers.

"Ugghhhh." Sydney reached into her purse for a stick of gum and a tube of lip gloss. She tossed the gum in her mouth and began to chew it. She could feel her mouth getting refreshed already. She pulled the top off the lip gloss and squeezed a small amount on her lips. She bobbed her head and rubbed her lips together.

Before she stepped out of the car, she sent Meeka a quick text. Meeka replied okay, and Sydney dropped her phone into her purse. The light was a little dim outside, so she struggled to find her house key.

"Got it." She said and slid the key into the keyhole. She quietly walked into the house and closed the door. The cold house was spotless and perfect. It made her smile. She was glad to see the place was still in place.

"Babe, I'm home." Sydney walked into her bedroom, but Xavier wasn't in there. She turned around and walked to the bathroom, but something caught her attention.

"I know not," Sydney stood in the middle of the hall and stared into Pacson's room. What she was seeing made her feel every emotion except for love and happiness. Xavier was making love to some woman as if he already knew her. Sydney was offended at how Xavier gripped the woman's waist and pulled her hair. It all seemed too familiar and normal. She screamed and shouted how much she loved Xavier. She begged for more of his long stroke, and he gave her exactly what she begged for.

Sydney used her shoulder to wipe her tears and took a step forward. She shook her head and took two steps backward. She wanted to stop watching and run away, but she couldn't. Xavier said and did the same things he did to her, and it was heartbreaking.

"Wow, now it all makes sense. The whole good guy act and giving me my space was an act." Xavier turned around, and the girl screamed. She covered her naked body with the colorful bed sheet.

"Syd, what are you doing here?" Xavier grabbed the pillow to cover his penis area and climbed out of bed. Sydney chuckled and tied her hair into a ponytail.

"This is my home, and I can come here as I please. There is no need for you to cover your dick. I see, suck, and feel the muthafucka every night!" Sydney shouted.

"Your home, you fuck her every night, what the hell is going on Xavier? You told me you were single and she was your sister."

"Aha, your sister? That's funny Xavier, very funny. I was his girlfriend, but now I'm his ex-girlfriend. I would have more respect for you if you would have had sex in our bed. Having sex on my son's Thomas and Train sheets is sooo disrespectful. I'll be back to get our things tomorrow when you're at work. Have a good day Xavier, and it's nice to meet you, whoever you are hunn." Sydney turned around and jogged out of the house. She didn't want anyone to see her crying. Not only was she hurt, but she was also embarrassed. Xavier chased behind her with a blanket wrapped around his lower half. He grabbed her arm, but she pushed him away and slapped his face.

"Xavier, how? How could you do this to me?" Sydney's legs began to feel like jello, she was so nervous. If Xavier took one more step, she was going to explode on him.

"I'm so-"

"Don't EVEN WASTE YOUR BREATH OR ENGERY TO SAY YOU'RE SORRY. It's crazy how it all makes sense now. That's why you weren't bothered by my absence. You were occupied with some bitch in my son's bed. I should kill you right now, but I don't want to get blood on this shirt."

"Sydney, please don't go. Let's talk about this!"

"Let go of my arm and if you grab it again, I swear I will leave you stankin' right here. We have NOTHING to talk about. You're just like my husband, no good!"

"I'm nothing like him! Don't ever compare me to him!" He shouted, but Sydney laughed. She only laughed because she didn't want him to see her crying.

"You say that, but you sound exactly like him. Good day, Xavier."

"Stop telling me to have a good day! Let's talk baby. Please, I'm begging you! From the bottom of my heart, I'm sorry." Xavier fell to his knees, and he started to cry. He grabbed Sydney by her legs, but she kicked him. He stumbled to the grass.

"NO, don't try it, Xavier. You are not sorry because you hurt me. You're sorry because you got caught!! How disrespectful can you get Xavier? I thought you were better than this, but I guess you're not. I'm so done with your ass."

Chapter 3

Kane and Rocko, well, Jupiter and Spencer arrived right on time in Louisiana. It took them a month to get everything situated, but they finally made it despite a minor delay at the McCarran International Airport in Las Vegas, Nevada. The weather was perfect today, and Rocko was taking in the warm sun. She loved how the heat tickled her arms, and the breeze made her glossy hair shine even more.

Rocko looked like an entirely new person with her breast and butt implants. Her cheekbones were higher, and her nose was a little slimmer. She was still rocking her pixie haircut, but her hair was bright red with a hint honey blonde highlights. Kane gained a little weight, but mostly muscle. His arms were covered with tattoos, and his eye color was now green instead of brown. He was rocking a bald head and a new nose job.

Rocko and Kane drove down Jefferson Street feeling good and looking good. They drove pass plenty of people they knew, but no one recognized them. They both were glad. That meant Doctor Paco did a good job and their money was well spent.

"It doesn't look like much has changed. I'm seeing the same clowns on the block." Rocko chuckled and shook her head.

"I'm seeing the same thing too." Kane laughed. Rocko wasn't tempted to speak to anyone she knew. While living in Opelousas, she didn't make friends with many people. Majority of the people she met was through Kane. By the way, he was staring at some people she knew he was tempted to stop and make conversation.

"I know you won't admit it, but I can tell you missed home," Rocko said.

"It's kind of hard not to, I was born and raised here," Kane said. By comforting Kane, she held his hand and gave it a soft kiss. He looked over his shoulder and smiled.

"I totally understand. That's how I felt when we were in Chicago." Rocko said.

"I never thought we would be back here especially for something like this. Slow rolling down Jefferson Street and Rail Road Avenue were the good old days." Kane said.

"Hell yea, only this time there is no drugs or guns in the car. I kind of feel bad about leaving the girls back home." She frowned.

"I know baby, but you know they are in good hands. We're going to settle this shit once and for all. I'm still trying to figure how he is still in these streets doing the same thing."

"You know they let rats run free. That nigga never stuck to the G-code, but that's not what I'm worried about. I'm trying to figure out how were you friends with Philly and never knew he was gay. He isn't just gay he's gay gay, like full-blown gay!"

"I'm still trying to figure that out myself that really threw me for a loop." Kane shook his head. He made a complete stop at the stop sign then looked both ways. He made sure no one was crossing his path before he drove off.

Are you sure he never played with your booty hole, just the tip of the thumb or the whole index finger in our butt?" She laughed.

"Don't play Diana. The only person who gets a finger in their butthole is yours." Kane laughed.

"Whatever, at least I can admit it." She joked.

"This shit is crazy. Santana was a good dude. A real shit nigga if you ask me. It didn't matter that he wore a wig and a purse. He was still a man in my eyes."

"I swear, I'm going to make Philly pay for everything he has done. For every person he has killed I'm going to make him pay. I'm going to be in his face, and he won't even know it's me."

Kane turned on turned on Sonny Street and squinted his eyes to read the addresses on the houses. Rocko strolled to her text messages and read the address Meeka gave her.

"It's the blue house on the left. Meeka said to pull park behind the house." Rocko said.

"Okay." Kane increased his speed a little and turned into the driveway. Rocko didn't realize it, but she was happy to be back home. Sonny Street was a quiet street, but it made her and Kane a lot of money. Kane turned the car off and sat low in the seat. He looked around and shook his head. Rocko gathered her things and turned to Kane.

"Baby, what's wrong with you?" She asked.

"Are you sure you want to do this? I swear we can turn around and catch the first flight back home. I'm serious Diana."

"In the United States it's Jupiter, and you know that. Okay Jupiter, Mars, Pluto, or whatever. Once we get out of this car, you know the g-shit is going to pop."

"Duh, I love that g-shit, and you know that. Now give me a kiss." Rocko grabbed Kane by the back on the head and shoved her tongue into his mouth. He grabbed her breast and twirled his tongue all through her mouth. Within seconds, Kane turned her on. She was ready to pull his pants down and pull her shirt over her head.

"Damn Kenneth, you've been turning me on since 2006." She wiped her wet lips and laughed.

"Of course, look at me." Kenneth wiped himself down and grinned. Rocko rolled her eyes and got out of the car. Kane walked around the car and held Rocko's hand. Rocko was a little nervous to see everyone because it's been a while. She wasn't sure how everyone would react to her presence and a new look. They were a little upset that her and Kane left without telling anyone.

Rocko and Kane stood at the front door, and her heart was racing. She raised her fist to knock on the door, but she stopped.

"What's wrong?" Kane asked.

"Uuhh, nothing." Rocko knocked on the door and clutched Kane's hand a little tighter. A few seconds later Quix opened the door. A red cup was in her hand, and a cigarette was hanging off the bottom of her lip. Rocko coughed and blew the smoke away. Quix bypassed Rocko and stared at Kane. She sized him up and down with a flirty look written on her face. She couldn't take her eyes off him, but Quix's sexy figure didn't interest him at all. He held Rocko by the waist and asked, "Where is Meeka and Hustle?"

"They're in here, but who are you?"

"Spencer," Kane said.

"And I'm his girlfriend, Jupiter." Rocko tilted her head to the side and gave Quix a fake smile. Quix frowned and turned around. As she walked, she made her hips swing from left to the right. Rocko and Kane both laughed and brushed her off.

"She's going to faint when she finds out it's us," Rocko whispered.

"I hope no one thinks I'm going to pick her big ass up. Q looked like she gained about twenty pounds." Kane said.

"Hell yea and it all went to her thighs, ass, and hips," Kane said.

Rocko and Kane sat on the couch and waited. Five minutes later Meeka and Hustle walked into the living room, Meeka had a huge smile on her face. She ran to Rocko and gave her a huge hug. She wasn't sure if she missed Rocko, but she began to cry.

"Oh my God, look at you!!!!! I swear I'm looking at a different person. Bitch you were bad before, but now you're bad on a whole new level." Meeka laughed and spun Rocko around. She was impressed with Rocko's surgery and was kind of jealous.

"Thank you, baby, but you're looking great as usual."

"Not like you and Kane you're looking good as well."

"Thanks, Meek." Kane gave Meeka a hug then he dapped Hustle.

"Kane, as in Rocko's boyfriend, Kane?" Rocko nodded her head up and down and laughed.

"So who are you?" Quix pointed at Rocko and asked.

"I'm Rocko, as in Rocko, Kane's girlfriend."

"WHAT?" Quix dropped her cigarette and cup. Everyone laughed.

"Yea bitch, it's me."

"Oh my God, Rock!! What did you do? You like an entirely different person." Quix tiptoed around the wet floor and gave Rocko a huge.

"I know, that was the plan, where is Marlo and Sydney?" Rocko asked.

"They should be on their way back. You know Marlo needed something to smoke."

"I see some things don't change." Kane laughed.

"Rocko you look great, I still can't believe it's you and Kane. Meeka I can't believe you didn't tell me they were coming!" Quix said.

"That's because it was a secret. This is my secret weapon." Meeka rubbed her hands together and smiled. Quix looked around the room. She was a little confused.

"A secret weapon for what?" Quix asked.

"To kill Philly, it's time for him to meet his maker," Meeka said.

"Who, the devil?" Quix asked.

"Yep, I'm pretty sure Satan misses his son."

"Even if he doesn't miss him, they're going to reunite," Rocko said.

"So Rocko how is Bora, Bora? Tell me everything and don't leave anything out!" Quix sat at the end of the couch with her hands on her chin. She was ready for Rocko to give her full details about Bora, Bora.

"It's beautiful, it's perfect, and it's perfect! It's like everyone is always happy there. I swear Picasso couldn't paint how pretty the beach and sky is."

"Aww man, I'm jealous. You're living in paradise while I'm living in the slop." Quix laughed.

"You can anywhere you want. What's holding you back?" Rocko asked.

"Nothing really and you're right. I would love to move to Paris and never come back."

"The way things are going you may be there sooner than you think." Hustle said.

"Are things that bad?" She asked.

"Bad is an understatement. Austin is doing the absolute most, like for real." Meeka said.

"Hustle, you must have Meeka turning pussy," Rocko said.

"Why do you say that?" Hustle asked.

"Because she hasn't killed Austin yet, yea, you have to be the reason why." Rocko laughed.

"Shut up Rock, that's not the reason why." Meeka walked into the kitchen and leaned against the countertop. She searched the kitchen for something to eat, but nothing caught her eyes.

"So what's the reason?" Kane asked.

"If I kill him now all eyes will be on me, and I'm trying to spare Justice's feelings."

"Fuck Justice and her feelings. For all, you know she could be working for and with her brother." Rocko said.

"THANK YOU DIANA, someone else has said it. Syd and I have been saying this from day one." Quix tossed her hands in the air and threw her head back.

"Speaking of Justice, where is she?" Kane asked.

"I'm not sure. Since Santana's death, she's been distant. She took his death hard you know." Meeka said.

"I understand that, but how are you holding up?"

"I'm holding Kane, that's all I can say."

"I feel you, but things are going to get better."

"I hope so, I really do," Meeka said.

"Does Justice know we're here?" Rocko asked.

"No, and I want to keep it that way. She only needs to know that my friends Jupiter and Spencer are here."

"Hhhmmm, I wonder why you don't want to tell her the truth." Quix flared her nose and weirdly stared at Meeka. Meeka rolled her eyes and turned to the icebox. She grabbed a bottle of water and reentered the kitchen.

"That's because I can't take any chances."

"Because you don't trust her, case closed," Quix smiled and walked out of the room.

"That girl knows she can hit a nerve yea," Meeka said.

Marlo and Sydney walked into the house laughing. With the Xavier drama and Santana's death, Sydney was on edge with everything. Since she didn't recognize Rocko, she sized her up and down. Rocko laughed and said, "Don't come in here mugging me, it's Rocko."

"Rocko!!" Sydney dropped her bags.

"Yea, I'm in the flesh!"

"What the fuck?!" Just like Meeka and Quix, Sydney ran to give Rocko a hug.

"What did you do?" Sydney walked around Rocko to check her out.

"Found a bomb as a surgeon." She chuckled.

"I see that, but you need to give me his number. I need a little surgery to boost my spirits."

"Why, what's wrong?" Rocko asked.

"I caught my boyfriend cheating on me." Sydney could feel she was getting emotional, but she fought back her tears.

"Aww damn, it's okay Syd. You'll shake that shit off."

"Yea, I will. I just need a little time to cry and eat ice cream." She laughed.

"Hey, do what you have to do to shake back. While I'm here, I'll eat all the ice cream with you."

"Bet, thanks girl," Rocko gave Sydney a warm hug. She could tell Sydney was hurt and needed some type of loving.

"No problem baby."

"What up Marlo," Rocko said.

"What up y'all, it's good to have y'all back. How long are y'all staying?" Marlo asked.

"Until Philly is in the dirt and if we have to travel back to get our girls so be it," Rocko said.

"Who did you leave them with?" Sydney asked.

"We left them with our neighbor. She's hella nice and helpful,"

"Okay, now that everyone is here, let's get down to business." Rocko signaled everyone to follow her to the back room. She walked down the hall and entered the back room. Meeka turned the light switch on, and everyone filled the room. It was a small room with only a table and chairs in it. Everyone sat at the table and waited. Meeka pulled out a lighter and a cigarette. She lit the tip of the cigarette then took two hits. Hustle shook his head at her, but he didn't say anything. She promised she would stop smoking cigarettes, but she couldn't. She took one more hit and blew the smoke out. She tapped the cigarette on the bottom of her tennis shoe and sat at the table.

"Marlo has some news for us. Tell them, Marlo," She folded her arms and nodded at Marlo.

"I overheard someone talking in the gas station yesterday. He's hiding in Greensburg, Louisiana. He is hiding at some guy's house that he met on Blackpeoplemeet.com." Marlo said. Everyone looked at each other and burst into laughter.

"Where the hell is Greensburg?" Sydney asked.

"Greensburg is near Kentwood, Louisiana. It's in St. Helen Parish. It's a very small town. It may be smaller than Opelousas, but I'm not sure." Hustle said.

"I swear I've been living in Louisiana all of my life and I have never heard of this place," Sydney said.

"Maybe you should get out of Opelousas more often." Hustle said.

"When I do I damn sure won't go to Greensburg." Sydney laughed."

"Forget where he's hiding. Let's talk about how he's on Blackpeoplemeet.com!! What's really going on with him?" Rocko asked and laughed.

"I'm still shocked that this clown ass is gay." Kane shook his head.

"The fact that he is on an online dating site looking for love, Philly used to be my nigga, but I don't know what the hell happened to him," Kane said.

"I never really liked the lil' cat, he always looked like he was up to no good. I keep cats like him out of my circle and as far away as possible." Hustle said.

"That's why his only friend is Pedro, and he's a Mexican. Mexicans are loyal as fuck."

"Fucking right Meek Milly," Hustle bit his lip and blew a kiss at Meeka. She blushed and turned away.

"I always liked when you call me Meek Milly."

"I bet you do." Hustle said.

"We need to send this story to the Shade Room. This storyline is wwwaaayyyy better than the rehearsed storylines on Love and Hip Hop. I'm talking Hollywood, New York, and Atlanta." Meeka laughed.

"Don't forget about Baller Alert! They are going to eat that shit up with hashtags. Hashtag dick in the booty as nigga, hashtag undercover ass nigga, hashtag bending niggas over ass nigga," Sydney said.

"Okay Syd, we get it," Rocko said.

"Forget all of that. What's the plan to kill him?" Quix asked.

"Blackpeoplemeet.com," Meeka and Rocko said, but everyone was confused.

"What?" Sydney asked.

"I know it sounds crazy, but Rocko is going to become his friend on Blackpeoplemeet.com and get him to meet up with her," Meeka said.

"What, that's crazy, and that won't work." Hustle said.

"Uh, yea it will. Think about it, how many times you have let your guard down around a fine ass female. This is the perfect way to bait him in, trust me." Meeka said.

"I don't know Meek this can go left in so many ways," Sydney said.

"If we do it right we won't have to worry about a thing. Y'all have to trust me on this one. If we wouldn't have said that it was Rocko and Kane, y'all would have thought it was some new friends I made." No one said anything. They knew their only option was to trust Meeka.

"Let me put the bullet in his heart. I promise he won't stand a chance against my new baby."

Marlo grabbed his 38 Super Automatic gun and waved it in the automatic gun. The two-tone colors made the reflection of the light bounce through the room. Meeka stood to her feet and snatched the gun out of Marlo's hand.

She handed the gun to Hustle, and he tucked it between his jeans and boxers.

"Marlo sit your ass down. You must be high on coke if you're waving a gun around in my house."

"Damn Meek, I'm sorry. I got a little happy, but it won't happen again." Marlo said.

"You won't be killing him. Rocko and I will handle this. Rocko looks like a whole new person. No one in town recognizes her, and that's a good thing." Meeka said.

"That also means my plastic surgeon is a fool with the knife. I'm looking Janet Jackson and Serena Williams wrapped into one." Rocko laughed.

"My baby does look good," Kane said.

"So how is everything going to play out?" Quix asked.

"First we need to connect with him online. Then from there, they will go back and forth in conversation, and once he agrees to meet up, that's when the plan will go into motion." Meeka said.

"Okay and after that?" Marlo said.

"I'm going make him take me on a nice little date, and once I catch him slipping, I'm going to slip a little something into his drink. Meeka will be waiting outside for us. From there, his time will be ticking." Rocko said.

"That's not a bad plan after all. It's simple when you think about it. I wonder how many niggas died like that?" Marlo asked and laughed.

"I don't know, but he's going on that list, believe me," Meeka said.

"That's what I like to hear. Are we done, I need to go and holla at Pedro?" Hustle yawned and gave Meeka a kiss. Then he reached for his keys and stood to his feet.

"Yea."

"Okay Marlo and Kane, are yall rolling with me?" Hustle asked.

"Yea." They said.

"I'll be back baby." Kane kissed Rocko on the cheek, and they walked out.

"Did y'all see that new dude that works at Wal-Mart? That nigga is fine. He's so yea." Quix giggled and repeatedly flipped her hair.

"Yea?" Sydney asked.

"Like yea, yea!" Quix said.

"Wal-Mart, ewww, you can do waayyy better than that Q." Meeka pretended to have chills and quivered. Quix flipped her the middle finger.

"Hey, nothing is wrong with that. I'm trying to leave these street niggas alone. If I get another collect call, I'm going to scream!"

"I can't relate." Meeka laughed.

"I'm sure you can't Tameeka. We all can't have a man like Brink." Quix said.

"No, they really can't. My baby is one of a kind, and I love him."

"Baby and love in the same sentence?? Damn, someone is in a good mood." Sydney rubbed her finger on

Meeka's arm and smirked. Meeka gently moved Sydney's finger, and they laughed.

"Wait, I'm confused. Are we using yea as a noun or an adjective? I can't keep up with the Louisiana slang." Rocko rubbed her temples and laughed.

"Both." Sydney, Meeka, and Quix said. Everyone laughed.

"Never in my life have I heard a word being used as a noun and an adjective. That shit is crazy."

"Welcome to Louisiana baby. That's all I can say. I'm going outside to smoke a cigarette. Is anyone coming with me?" Rocko grabbed her purse and walked to the door. Quix followed behind her, and they walked out of the house.

"I see someone is still smoking those cancer sticks," Sydney shouted at Rocko.

"Yep, I have to die one day. At least let me choose how I go out." Rocko shouted and closed the door.

"I swear, that girl reminds me soooo much of you. I said that the day Kane introduced me to her."

"Yea, she kind of does."

Meeka reached for her phone to make sure that she didn't have any missed calls from anyone, mainly Justice. She hadn't spoken to her in two days, and she was a little worried about her. She figured Justice was still grieving and needed time to herself. When Meeka noticed she didn't have any missed calls. She sighed and dropped her phone into her purse.

"What's wrong Meek?" Sydney asked.

"Nothing, I haven't heard from Justice in the last two days. I know she's taking Santana's death hard, but damn. She could at least return a phone call or reply to a text."

"She can't be taking it that hard with the pictures she's posting on Instagram." Sydney unlocked her phone and handed Meeka her phone. Meeka slowly scrolled through the pictures and read the captions. Little did Meeka know, Sydney was in Florida with some mysterious guy.

"Who is this?" Meeka was a little surprised.

"I'm not sure, but he kind of looks familiar. I swear years ago I seen him with Austin. He was riding with him doing a stakeout, but maybe I'm tripping."

"Have you heard from him lately?" Meeka asked.

"No, and I'm glad. Once word gets out about Xavier cheating on me, he's going to rub it all in my face."

"Fuck it don't beat yourself up for that Xavier lost something good."

"I know, but it hurts Meek. I thought Xavier and I had something good, but I guess not. How he could do me like that?"

"I can't give you an answer to that. Some people are so stupid it's disgusting. I don't want to bad mouth him because I know the feelings are still there. It doesn't matter what you need Syd, I'm here."

"I know Meek and thank you. It's so hard Tameeka. I thought this was my happily ever after. Now I'm alone again, and I have to start over."

"Nothing is wrong with starting over baby. Good is always new, remember that. Maybe you guys may get back together. Don't forget me Roman was in the picture for a while." Meeka said.

"True, but you and Roman knew where you wanted to be."

"I know, and now I'm where I want to be. I was the one fooling around, not Hustle. If you want to be with him Sydney, then be with him. Fuck what anyone has to say. If you can't take a cheater back, then don't."

"I love him, I honestly do, but I'm not sure if I can take him back. He disrespected me on sssoooo many levels. I still can't believe he had sex in my son's bed. That shit hurt Meek, HIS BED! He was fucking her how he would fuck me, and she was saying how she loves him and shit. This has been going on for a while Meeka, but I didn't see it. How stupid could I be, damn man!"

"You aren't stupid Sydney. You loved a man, that's all."

"Loving a man got me heartbroken. I don't think I can take him back. He hurt me to the core, seriously."

"If you feel like that, don't take him back. Don't be miserable just so you can be in a relationship. Enjoy being alone. Focus on our career and the boys right now. With all the drama their father is causing, they need a strong mother right now." Meeka's words made Sydney emotional, and she began to cry.

"Syd, you have a visitor. It's the guy who got caught with his pants down." Rocko sized Xavier up and down and flipped her hair. Meeka silently laughed and stood to her feet.

"Even though I want to knock your head off your shoulders, I'll let you two talk in peace. I thought you were one of the good men, but I guess not. Let's go Jupiter; I'm sure Quix smoked the entire pack of cigarette."

"Hello to you too Tameeka," As Meeka walked out of the room she gave Xavier a dirty look. It made him uncomfortable, but she didn't care.

"I guess you told her what happened." Xavier awkwardly laughed to lighten the mood. Sydney wiped her tears and rolled her eyes.

"What do you want Xavier and how did you know I was here?" Xavier approached Sydney, but she stopped him by pressing her hand against his chest.

"I saw Brink at the gas station, and he told me you were here."

"Wow, thanks, Brink."

"Please hear me out Sydney, we need to talk." She said.

"We have nothing to talk about Xavier. I said what I had to say and that's it.

"Look, Syd, I'm sorry for everything. I'm not sorry because you caught me, I'm honestly sorry. Miranda was a girl I dealt with right before we got together. Once things got serious between us, I cut her off. She didn't like how I cut her off. The night you caught us in bed was my first time seeing her in months."

"Where did you see her?" Sydney asked.

"I saw her at Chips, and she brought me a drink. I was in my feelings because of you not being home. Miranda knew about you, that was a front. She heard you were crazy, so she played the victim role. I guess she didn't want an ass whipping."

"Why Xavier, why did you hurt me like that? How could you sleep with another woman in our home? You don't understand how much you hurt me. Watching you have sex with another woman crumbled my heart. I thought you were my happy ending, I swear to God!"

"I am your happy ending baby. I know I fucked up bad, but don't end it like this. I swear I will never hurt you again. Not even once and if I do, you can leave me. I'll respect your decision. Just give me one more chance."

"It's not that easy Xavier, it's not that damn easy. YOU DON'T UNDERSTAND HOW MUCH YOU HURT ME!!" Sydney began to shout and cry. She started to hit Xavier in the face, and he stumbled to the couch. She climbed on top of him and continued to beat him. He blocked a few of her punches and held her hands together.

"Sydney stop!"

"No, you deserve every punch I'm giving!" Xavier held Sydney tighter, and she cried harder. She collapsed into his arms and sobbed. Xavier felt worse, he hated seeing Sydney cry. He promised himself that he would never make her shed a tear unless it was tears of joy.

"You're right, but I want you to listen to what I'm saying,"

"Nothing you're saying matters to me."

"Please baby, just listen to what I'm saying," Sydney tried to break free from Xavier, but she couldn't. She knew he wouldn't let her go until she heard what he had to say.

"You have two minutes, and I'm counting in my head," She grunted.

"I'm not an easy man to get with, and I don't cheat."

"You sound so fucking stupid. That doesn't make sense. I caught you cheating dummy!"

"Besides this, I've been nothing but faithful to you," Xavier said.

"Is she prettier than me? Did she fuck you better or loved you more? What is it Xavier, I need to know."

"I cheated because of me, not because of you. You're perfect in every way. Miranda can't hold a candle to you. I can admit I fucked up and I'm going to say it again baby, I'm sorry, I'm sorry, I'm sorry, I'm sorry. I miss you, and I want you to come home, please Sydney."

"I don't know what to think anymore. One minute you're saying she can't hold a candle next to me, but you still cheated on me! That is crazy, and you know it."

"Just come home so we can work things out. I'm going crazy without you." Sydney turned away. She couldn't look Xavier in the eyes. He wiped away her falling tears and kissed her on the lips.

"I can't tell you I'm coming back home and I can't tell you I won't come home."

"I understand that Syd. If time is what you need I understand that. I love you, have a good day." Xavier gave Sydney one more kissed then he climbed to his feet. Sydney didn't want him to leave, but she had to show him she meant business.

"Okay." Xavier walked out of the room, and Meeka walked in. She was still sizing him up and down, but he ignored her and walked out of the house.

"Syd, are you okay?" Meeka ran to the couch and gave Sydney a hug. Sydney placed her head on Meeka's shoulder and silently cried.

"No Meeka, I'm not okay. I'm confused, and I don't know what to do."

"Do what's best for you. It doesn't matter what anyone says. Sydney must make Sydney happy. I told you the same thing when you were ready to separate from Austin."

"You're right Meeka, but I hope I don't make the wrong decision."

"You won't Sydney, but you have to take this next piece of advice to heart," Meeka said.

"Okay, what is it?" Sydney asked.

"You won't make the wrong decision if you let your heart make the decision for you."

"What if my heart tells me to leave the relationship alone? I love him Meeka." Sydney said.

"You don't have to explain yourself to me, Syd. I know you love him."

"So tell me what I'm supposed to do. I really don't know, help me!" She cried out.

"If your heart tells you to go back then go back. If your heart doesn't, that's okay. That's your sign to see that it failed and it was never love."

***

Meeka lay in her bed watching TV while Isabella was sleeping and Hustle was on his way home from Pedro's house. The conversation between her and Sydney was stuck in her thoughts. She hated seeing her friend so heartbroken, especially over a guy.

"Damn Tana, I wish you were here for this shit. I miss you so much." Meeka began to fall asleep, but her phone began to ring. She rolled her eyes and reached for her phone. It was Jamie, but Meeka wasn't in the mood to talk to anyone. She was trying to be uplifted, but Santana's death was taking a toll on her. Her weight was slowly dropping, and she hadn't eaten anything in two days. Hustle tried his best to keep Meeka happy, but he couldn't. Nothing could fix her broken heart, but time.

Jamie called again, but this time Meeka answered it. She wanted to have an attitude, but she changed her mind. She didn't want to disturb Isabella, so she quietly climbed out of bed and walked down the hall.

"Hey," Meeka said.

"Hey Meeka, are you home?" Jamie asked.

"Yea, what's wrong?"

"Nothing is wrong, Joseline wanted to talk to you," Jamie said.

"Oh okay, well y'all come over."

"Okay, we'll be there in five minutes," Jamie said.

"Bet." Meeka disconnected the call and walked downstairs. She grabbed her can of air fresher and sprayed it throughout the living room. A few minutes later she heard a knock at the door.

"Who is it?" Meeka asked.

"It's Jamie."

"Okay, give me a second." Meeka fluffed her pillows a little then ran to the door.

"Hey y'all," she said as she opened the door. Jamie and Joseline walked into the house. Joseline gave Meeka a big smile and a huge hug. After Santana's funeral, Joseline was admitted to the hospital again. Meeka didn't know her well, but she still took time out to visit her. Since Santana was no longer supporting Jamie, she had to work double shifts every other day. She didn't have much time to visit Joseline in the hospital, so Meeka did it for her.

"You look better," Meeka said and closed the door. Joseline shook her head and sat on the couch.

"I feel a lot better, well as in my health. It's going to be a while before I heal from Santana's death."

"Yea, me too, he was a big part of my life," Meeka said.

"Me three, I'm going to always regret how things were between us when he died. This shows me to never hold grudges or take life for granted.

"That's right life is too short for the dumb shit. So, what are you two doing out?" Meeka asked.

"Before I go back to Florida I wanted to tell you thank you for everything. Everything has been crazy, and I haven't had the time to tell you thank you."

"Oh, it's was no problem at all. Santana was like family, so you're family too. I'm glad you're feeling better. If you're ever in town again, I have another home you can stay at. You'll never stay in a hotel again." Meeka laughed.

"I like that, and if you're ever in Florida, I got you. My house isn't nice like this, but I keep it clean." Joseline laughed.

"Hey, if the pots, bath, toilet, and sheets are clean, I'm good. When are you leaving?"

"My flight is for tomorrow morning in New Orleans, but I'm leaving tonight," Joseline said.

"Oh okay, be careful Joseline. It's supposed to storm tonight. Thanks to Tropical Storm Matthew, he's bringing in hella rain." Meeka said.

"Let's pray that he doesn't turn into a hurricane. That is the last thing we need in our lives." Jamie said.

"Girl I know, we haven't had a bad hurricane since Hurricane Rita," Meeka said.

"Right, but it's about that time we leave. I can hear the thunder approaching." Everyone stood to their feet and walked to the door.

"Aaww okay, I'm glad you stopped by before you left. Don't be a stranger Joseline. You have my number and use it often."

"I will and thanks again Tameeka. Santana had a great friend."

As Joseline and Jamie were walking out, Hustle was walking in.

"Hey Brink," Jamie said.

"What up Jamie, how are you?" Hustle asked.

"I'm okay, I can't complain. I'll see y'all later, Meek call me tomorrow. We can go get lunch or something."

"Okay girl and kiss the girls for me." Meeka waved and closed the door. Then she removed her glasses from her face and placed them on the table. Her eyes were heavy and red, she needed some major sleep.

"Hey, baby." Meeka wrapped her arms around Hustle's neck and stood on her tip toes. She passionately kissed him as if she hadn't seen him in months. He gripped her ass cheeks and grabbed the back of her head. Then he pulled away from her and sat on the couch. He removed his fitted cap from his head and kicked his shoes off. Meeka could tell he was tired as hell.

"Remind me to never volunteer to help someone move again. Pedro had shit from 2004 in that back room.

"What?" Meeka asked and laughed.

"I'm serious, I'm so tired baby. I couldn't wait to get home to you." Hustle pulled Meeka closer to him and placed his head on her lap. She stared at the wall and stroked the side of his face. She grabbed her hand and gave it a soft kiss.

"I love you, Brink."

"I love you more Tameeka." Hustle said.

"If you love me more than I love you, then that's a lot of love."

"It is a lot of love. You know my heart beats for you." Hustle said.

"I like the way that sounds. Was Kane with you?" Meeka asked.

"Yea, but he left early. He wanted to visit his grandparents and sisters house. No one is staying in either house."

"Oh okay, but I don't blame them. The way Philly killed them no one SHOULD want to live there." Meeka yawned and stretched her legs out.

"I know I wouldn't want to live there. I don't care how much they remodel the house. That tragedy will forever stay there like a stain." Hustle shook his head and sighed.

"When Philly did that shit, he had the entire city shook. The streets were extra hot, and the money was slow. That was crazy I thought things like that only happened in movies." Meeka said.

"I know, I never thought something like that would happen in Opelousas."

"I bet it was hard to leave the way they did. Kane couldn't bury his family or even grieve like he wanted to. The police labeled them as Jane and John Doe's and cremated their bodies. Just thinking about it gives me the chills. You know what's crazy?"

"What?" Hustle asked.

"Technically Anne Frank died because they cremated her," Meeka said.

"What?" Hustled chuckled, but he was confused.

"I'm telling you, baby. She was in a concentration camp. I think it was the Bergen-Belsen concentration camp. Anne was so tired and drained from lack of food that they thought she was dead. When they were putting her on the burner, she tried to scream, but she was weak. They didn't hear her until she was burning. I'm not sure if that's true. I've read other articles that she and Margot died of Typhus."

"How and why do you know so much about this?"

"I find all of it interesting, it's really amazes me. I hope Isabella loves history just as much as I do."

"I'm pretty sure she will." Hustle said.

"You know there is no official death date for Anne and her sister Margot. The Dutch authorities gave the date March 31, 1945."

"Wow, that's crazy they just gave them a death date. No one will ever know when they exactly died. I wonder how they can do that?"

"I'm not sure, but I'm going to research that. That should be illegal, but then again Hitler was doing what he wanted to."

"That is true baby. I will never understand how one man could create an army and march around the world to kill people. How do you have the guts to do that?"

"I guess when people don't look like you, you hate them. Poor Anne, her and her diary became famous. She'll never know how famous she is."

"You said Anne like you personally knew her." Hustle laughed.

"Shit, I read her book like fifty times. I feel like I shot marbles with her." Meeka laughed and kissed Hustle again.

"I bet you do. Where were Jamie and Joseline going? Her name is Joseline right, like the Puerto Rican Princess?" Hustle laughed.

"Yea like the Puerto Rican Princess she's going back to Florida. Her flight leaves tomorrow, but she's going to New Orleans tonight. That's where her flight is taking off from." Meeka said.

"Oh, okay, that's what's up. I still feel bad for her. The way she had to find out how her cousin died was messed up."

"I know something like that can damage you for a lifetime," Meeka said.

"Have you spoken to Rocko since earlier?" Hustle asked.

"Yea, about an hour ago actually and her new look is giving me all kinds of life. I think I want a little surgery now." Meeka dropped her face and stared Hustle dead in the eyes. He shook his head and laughed.

"In your dreams, you can get all of the surgery you want."

"Excuse me, did you tell me no in a different way?" Meeka asked.

"I sure did, it's a first time for everything."

"Don't you want me to look like those girls on Instagram? Don't think I didn't see you liking those pictures." Meeka pinched Hustle's arm and rolled her eyes.

"Pipe down baby, it's only pictures. I don't want you to look like those plastic bitches. I love you exactly how you are, flaws and all. Besides, these niggas bitches are already chasing after you."

"As long as my baby is happy with my body, speaking of baby, Izzy is sleeping in our bed," Meeka said.

"That's fine with me a nice and calm night with my girls. I couldn't ask for anything better."

"Oh, yea and thanks for telling Xavier where she was."

"I'm sorry, I thought he knew that." Hustle said.

"I still can't believe he cheated on her. Would you ever cheat on me like that?"

"I should be asking you that question."

"Ha, ha, very funny Brink I may have done some things to you, but I would never cheat on you like that. I would never cheat on you again. I realize what I have, and I don't want to lose it." Meeka said.

"So that means you'll be making an exit out of the game soon."

"Aw baby not tonight with that. I can't deal." Meeka tossed her head back and rolled her eyes.

"No worries, but don't forget your time is whining down. Now let's go to bed."

Chapter 4

Sydney sat in the break room eating a tuna fish sandwich and potato chips. Her lunch was only thirty minutes long, but she wished it was an hour. She could use the other thirty minutes to cry in the staff's bathroom. Being away from home was odd, and she hated it. Xavier was trying his best to get her back home, but it wasn't working. Sydney was holding onto Meeka's words tightly.

"Excuse me Sydney, you have a visitor." Jason, the 4th grade English teacher, peeked into the break room.

"Huh?" Sydney reached for a napkin and wiped the corners of her eyes. She stood to her feet and walked to the door. Jason opened the door, and Xavier was standing behind him. He held a bouquet of red roses and a box of chocolates in his hands. Sydney wanted to curse Xavier out for coming to her job, but she didn't want to make a scene at work. She hated seeing him since she saw him at Meeka's house, even though she was upset with him. It was still good to see his handsome face. He purposely wore the blue cashmere sweater that Sydney liked. She always said it complimented his skin tone and eyes.

"Thank you, Jason, and I'll come by your classroom shortly. She needs to discuss the field trip those kids are still bugging me about that." She smiled.

"You're welcome and okay." Jason smiled back and walked away. Sydney rolled her eyes and returned to the table. She ignored Xavier as she wasn't standing by the door. She grabbed the remote and turned it to *The Price is Right*.

"Hey baby," Xavier slowly walked to the table and sat next to Sydney.

"Sup." She said and continued to watch TV.

"These are for you," Xavier handed Sydney the gifts, but she laughed.

"Are these I'm sorry I got caught fucking someone in your son's bed gifts?" Sydney smelled the roses and tossed them on the table.

"No Syd, it isn't. I know these are your favorite things, and that's why I got them. I did things like this from day one. I have no reason to stop now." Xavier said.

"I guess Xavier, but why are you here? Shouldn't you be at work or fucking someone?" Sydney smirked.

"Come on Syd, stop with that. I called into work today, that's why I'm not there."

"Well, you should instead of being here."

"Sydney, please stop, you know this isn't for you and me." Xavier grabbed Sydney's hand, but she pulled it away. He hated how Sydney was treating him, but he knew he deserved it.

"You made your bed now sleep in it."

"I am, and I'm sleeping in my real bed alone. I miss you, baby, will you come back home?" Xavier asked.

"No."

"Just for one night, I'm going crazy without you."

"That sounds like a personal problem Xavier. You should have thought about that before you cheated on me. How would you react if I cheated on you?" Sydney asked.

"I would be upset, hurt, and probably angry. I love you, and I can't imagine another man touch and rubbing on your body. Call me crazy, but I wouldn't leave you. I would rather fix our problem instead of starting over with someone new."

"It's easy for you to say that. I'm the one who is hurting, not you. You can easily say what you would have done. It hurts that YOU of all people did this to me. I have to deal with Austin and all of his bullshit he is bringing in my life. Not in a million years did I ever think you would bring so much pain to my life too." Sydney wanted to cry, but she was tired of crying. Crying wasn't fixing any of her problems or mending the pain.

"That's not the reason why Sydney and you know that. You always say you're dragging me in your drama, but I never look at it like that. The average man would have left a long time ago, but I didn't. Yes, I cheated, and once again I'm saying I'm sorry. I'm admitting my wrong like a man. I swear, I never meant to hurt you. You have to believe me when I say this."

"Yea, I hear you, Xavier." Sydney rolled her eyes.

"Are you going to think about coming back home? Even if it's just for one day, I want to hold and kiss you." He said. Xavier pushed closer to Sydney, but she pushed her chair further away.

"I'll think about it Xavier, that's all I can say."

"I'm fine with that baby. Can we have lunch on Friday? I really want to take you somewhere and spend some time with you."

"I can't, maybe some other time. Friday Austin and I are meeting with our lawyers." Sydney said.

"For what?" Xavier asked.

"We need to discuss this divorce. He's trying to get joint custody, but I'm going to fight it. I do not want him around my kids. I need you to come with me. They have to know about the gun situation."

"Sure baby, whatever you need. You know I'm here for you. I love you Sydney, I mean it."

"I love you too." Xavier kissed Sydney's forehead and held her hand. Just because she was being nice didn't mean she was over what he did to her. She was still hurt from his actions. It would take more than a few sweet words to make her forgive him.

"I have to go. My mom has an eye appointment in an hour. Can I call you later?"

"Yea, you can."

"Okay, see you later." Xavier gave Sydney one more kissed and walked out of the room.

Part of her felt good, but the other half of her felt stupid but she wasn't over what Xavier did to her, and she wasn't feeling going home even if it was for just a day. She did miss him, but she felt like she was being weak by giving in.

Lately, Sydney's days were stressful and long. She didn't want this to take over another minute of her thoughts. She shook her thoughts off and put her attention back on the television. She wasn't interested in watching *The Price is Right*, but she needed to get her attention off Xavier. She was wearing her emotions on her shoulders, and she hated it.

A few minutes later Jason walked into the break room, and his strong cologne hit her nose hard. It was a familiar scent, and she hated it. It was the exact cologne

Austin would wear. She closed her fist tight and exhaled. Jason walked to the table and tapped Sydney on the shoulder. Then he smiled and tilted his bag of grapes to Sydney. She smiled back and took a few of the green grapes.

"Did you boyfriend leave?" Jason asked.

"Yea, he did," Sydney said.

"Oh, okay, I didn't want him to walk in here and see me sitting next to his woman." Jason laughed.

"Ha, ha, whatever."

Jason Webster is originally from Blanchard, Louisiana, but he lived in Abbeville. He recently moved to Opelousas three months ago to be closer to his mom. About a year ago she was diagnosed with stage three kidney failure. Jason is a handsome brown skin brother and all the female teacher's lust after him. It didn't matter if they were old, divorced, or married he made all their panties wet.

He was twenty-six years old and graduated from McNeese State University a year ago. With his long dreadlocks and tattooed covered arms, everyone was quick to judge him. He was a sweet, but quiet guy. Sydney only held a few conversations, and he always had positive things to say. She was glad she didn't judge him by his appearance.

"I'm just saying. I know how some guys can be when they are dating a beautiful woman."

"Nowadays I'm not caring about his feelings. He'll be okay and if not, ole well."

"Why would you not care about your boyfriend's feelings, if you don't mind me asking?"

"No, I don't mind. Things aren't going well with us right now. By the way, things are going I may not be his girlfriend for much longer."

"Damn, I'm sorry to hear that." Sydney tried to pay attention to Jason, but she couldn't. His handsome face was distracting and making her think a naughty thought.

"Uuhh, it is what it is. He shouldn't have done what he did." Sydney shrugged her shoulders.

"Oh, so it's his fault?" Jason asked.

"Yea, I damn sure didn't do anything. Has anyone told you that you look like Jacquees the singer?" Jason shook his head and laughed.

"Yea, I hear that all the time. I'm not sure if that's a compliment or an insult. What do you think?" Jason rubbed his teeth and smiled. His perfect white teeth were fully exposed and seeing him smile made Sydney smile. She tried not to blush, but she couldn't help it. She didn't realize he was this handsome or charming.

"That's a good thing, Jacquees is a handsome fella. If he wasn't so young, I would be at his concerts throwing my panties at him." She laughed.

"You shouldn't be that much older than him. You don't look a day over twenty-six."

"Ha, ha, that's funny. I haven't been in my twenties in a while." Sydney said.

"My mama always said you never ask a woman her age so I won't even do that." He laughed.

"Your mom raised you right. Just know I'm in my 40's youngin." She smiled and stood to her feet. She slowly walked to the door so he could get a better view of her figure. Her hips and ass were poking out in her black skirt. Sydney was glad she put this skirt on and not the loose fitting dress she wanted to wear. Jason followed behind her and rushed to open the door. They exited the room and walked down the hall. Everything was quiet and calm. For some reason, she was tempted to hold his hand. She felt like they were kids who were skipping class and up to no good.

"Handsome and you have manners? I bet those little bitches are going crazy over you." She laughed, and so did he.

"Something like that, but none of them have caught my attention. I guess I'm focused on my career and getting used to this new city. It's been a lot of drama out here."

"It isn't much to know about this city. Park Avenue, Rail Road Avenue, and Jefferson Street can take you through the city." She chuckled.

"I'm not familiar with all of that. I was hoping you could take me for a ride through the city."

"Hhmmm, are you sure your mom will be okay with that? You know you're a baby." She laughed.

"You're funny, you should be a comedian." He laughed." I'm pretty grown if you ask me. I'm serious though, I could use a good friend. I'm not trying to push up on and get in your pants. I know you're going through something with your boyfriend and I understand that."

"I'll think about it youngin. I need to get back to my class. I can't teach for summer school, and they still fail." She laughed.

"Me too, I'll see you later." Jason and Sydney walked away in different directions. She slightly looked over her shoulder to see if he was looking. He was, and she quickly turned. Jason had her feeling some type away, and she liked it.

Sydney walked into her class and sat at her desk. She pulled her phone out and saw she had a text message from Meeka and it asked, "Did you talk to Juju?"

"No, have you?" Sydney asked.

"No, I checked her Instagram, and she's back in Louisiana. I'm going to the club tonight. Maybe I can catch her there. I need to figure out what's wrong with her. Are you working tonight?"

"Yea, we need to figure this out soon. I'm not sure, but I'll let you know." Sydney said.

"Okay cool and cheer up baby. Everything is going to work out in your favor." Meeka said.

"Yea, I hope so," Sydney said.

Sydney dropped her phone and began to think. She knew something had to be going on with Justice. Her actions were becoming scary and not funny anymore. She tried calling Sydney, but the call went to voicemail. She tried calling again, but this time she called private, and Justice answered the phone. Sydney rushed to disconnect the call. She was shocked and confused. If Sydney didn't answer her calls but could answer a private call, that meant that she had her blocked from calling her.

Sydney thought about telling Meeka, but she changed her mind. Maybe she was overreacting, but she needed to get to the bottom of it.

***

Meeka sat low in the unmarked car and patiently waited for Wendell to arrive. Wendell was a twenty-two-year-old rookie on the police force. He also worked for Meeka as well, but no one knew. Not even his girlfriend, family, or friends. This job didn't pay him nearly what Meeka paid him, but he still loved his job. When Meeka approached him about working with her, he didn't hesitate jumping on the payroll. Meeka knew he wouldn't say no for the simple fact he was a starving rookie.

"Where are you Wen?" Meeka stared and tapped on the window. It was a little foggy, but she still managed to see. Between the low temperature and raining, Meeka was slightly annoyed with Wendell's tardiness. She told him to arrive 4:45 am, but it 5:30 am. The temperature was in the high 30's, and the rain was slowly increasing. Meeka was ready to get back into her bed and catch up on some sleep. In the past week, she could count on one hand how many hours of sleep she had. She was glad they slept at the house on Sonny Street and didn't have to drive far to get home.

Ten minutes later Meeka spotted a bright red pickup truck approaching her car. She waited until Wendell was closer to her car and got out. She used her hands to cover her hair and got into his truck. She dapped him and said, "What up fool?"

"Shit Meek, just chilling. I'm sorry I took longer, but I have some crazy information for you."

"Oh Lord, is it that bad? Lord knows I can't handle any more bad news or bullshit." Meeka roughly rubbed her bare face and leaned her head against the window. Wendell reached under his reached and pulled out a small voice recorder.

"I'll let you be the judge of that." Wendell pressed the red play button and placed the recorder on the seat. As the voices grew louder, Meeka's hurt dropped. It was Justice and Austin, and she could feel that the conversation between them was going to get crazy.

"Look Juju, all you have to do is testify against Tameeka and Sydney it's not that big of a deal like you're making it sis."

"I don't know Austin. I can give you some people out of the Oil Mil that works for Meeka. I can give you Marlo or Hustle. They hold just as much weight in the game." Justice said.

"NO, I DON'T WANT ANY OF THEM! I WANT THOSE BITCHES ON A SILVER PLATTER!"

"Austin it isn't that easy, and you know that. You know how Meeka moves. I swear she has eyes and ears everywhere. She probably has ears in this interrogation room. Don't sleep on Sydney because she's the same way. You would think Meeka carried her for nine months and birth her!" Justice said.

"Come on now Juju. You're being a little pass dramatic." Austin said and slammed his hands on the table.

"No, I'm not! If I testify against them, Meeka will kill me or get me killed. I've seen Meeka in action and I know for a fact death would be my only way out."

"What kind of things have you seen her do?" Austin asked.

"Right now that doesn't matter."

"You're right we'll get back to that later. You need to stop overthinking this situation and listen to me. If you testify, we will put you in The Witness Protection Program. Your identity and everything will change, and you have to lose contact with everyone you know."

"Not no, but hell to the no! I'm not going through all of that just to help you get revenge to Meek and Sydney."

"It's not revenge it's getting two people off the streets. This is my job, and I'm also trying to save your ass because you are family, my sister to be exact. If you don't switch sides, you'll be going down with that. I have no choice Juju."

"You really don't have anything on us, but rumors you have heard through the streets." Justice rolled her eyes and turned away. Austin grabbed her by the shoulders and made her face him. She was a little scared, but she didn't show any emotion.

"Oh is that so?" Austin smirked and asked.

"Yea, that's 'so' my nigga."

"Right before Glenn mysteriously committed suicide he told me a few things," Austin said.

"Like what?"

"I know all about him working as a male escort in White Castle, Baton Rouge, Opelousas, and Franklin. My WIFE is a high paid hoe that I knew nothing about. Oh, yea, thank you for telling me that. I thought it was family over everything, but I guess I was wrong." Austin said.

"Hey, don't blame me. I thought you knew she was a hoe." Justice laughed.

"No, I sure didn't. I thought she just did a little stripping on the side."

"You were stupid for even thinking that. She does wwayyyyy more on the side." Justice turned away and mumbled.

"How could she be so low down and dirty?! That is my wife and the mother of my kids! I'm married to a paid hoe Justice. Do you know how that shit feels? No, you don't!"

"Watch your mouth. The correct term is escort."

"An escort and hoe is the same thing if you ask me." Austin laughed.

"See that's the reason why she is leaving your ass. You are so close-minded."

"She's leaving me because of that bitch Tameeka."

"Okay Austin, whatever you say. I honestly can't get on a stand Austin, I'm sorry. If you love me like you say you do you wouldn't let me get tied into all of this mess."

"If YOU love yourself you wouldn't get tied into this mess. Do you know what kind of charges Meeka can get hit with? Distributing cocaine, conspiracy, prostituting, running an organized crime and the list goes on. Just imagine how embarrassed the entire family would be. You are so innocent in grandpa's eyes. Picture his reaction when your face is all over the news." Justice stood to her feet and paced through the room. She had a clear view of her family in her head, and it wasn't good.

"Okay, I'll do it." She mumbled.

"What?" He smiled and laughed.

"I said I'll do it, but what exactly am I doing?" She asked.

"Instead of testifying I have a better idea, an idea that won't get you killed," Austin said.

"Okay, let me hear it."

"All you have to do is plant a few microphones in her house and wear a mic at all times. With that evidence, you won't have to take the stand."

"Is that it?" Justice asked.

"Yea that's it. I told you I would save you, but you must help me a little. I got you, sis, don't I always?"

"Yea you do, but my name can't come up at all!!" Justice said.

"I promise it won't, so are you down?" Austin asked. Justice exhaled and said, "Yea I'm down."

Good, I'm going to get the microphones today and hit you up. We're going to meet outside of Opelousas. I don't want anyone to see us together anymore. I want everyone to think that we aren't on speaking terms."

"Okay." Wendell stopped the tape, but he didn't say anything. Meeka could feel she was getting sick, so she opened the door wide. She held her stomach and began to gag. Shortly after that, vomit began to rush out of her mouth. She tried to collect herself, but the vomit continued to come out.

"Oh shit, let me get you a bottle of water." Wendell reached to the back seat and grabbed a bottle of Fiji water. He handed it to Meeka, but she stopped him. The vomit didn't stop; it ran like a faucet. She started to cry, and her tears were at the same pace with her vomit.

"Tameeka are you okay? Do I need to call you an ambulance?"

"No Wen, I'm good, but thanks. Where is that bottle of water and do you have a napkin or something that I can wipe my face with?" Wendell shook his head and handed Meeka the bottle. Then he reached into his pocket for his handkerchief and gave it to Meeka. She popped the cap off the water and took a big gulp. Then she patted her face and took another sip of the water.

"Are you sure? I haven't seen anyone vomit like that ever."

"I'm good, that recording caught me off guard. When did you get this?" Meeka asked.

"A few minutes ago that's why I was late. What I originally had was some information about Philly." Wendell said.

"Oh yea, what kind of information?" Meeka took a sip of water and swished it around her mouth. A few seconds later she spit the water out and closed the door. The bottle of water was nearly empty, but she still held onto it.

"In a week Philly is planning to flee the country. We're not sure where he's going or where he's currently hiding, but if this reliable source comes through, we'll know all of that." Meeka smiled to herself, but she wanted to laugh. Rocko was the reliable source that called into Crime Stoppers and gave the fake tip. She thought Wendell had some valuable information, but it was only her own information.

"Wow, that's crazy. I hope they catch him before he flees because if they don't, he's going to get away forever." Meeka said. She was ready to end this conversation and go home.

"Trust me Tameeka the authorities are working on this case."

"I believe you, but can I have the recorder?" She asked.

"Of course." Wendell handed Meeka the recorder. She dapped him down and said, "Thank you Wen, but I have to go. I'll fuck with you later."

"Okay." Meeka rushed out of the car and got into her car. She was so destroyed. She wasn't sure if she could drive home without wrecking. Sydney and Meeka always suspected Justice to be a snake, but they never had any proof. To hear everything Justice said was mind-blowing.

Meeka slowly drove home, and she made it there within seconds. She grabbed the recorder and turned her car off. She didn't care that the rain was coming down heavily. As she walked to the house, her entire body became soaked with rain. She walked into the house in tears and searching for Hustle. She peeled the wet clothes off her and covered her arms. The house was cold, and she started to shiver.

"Brink, where are you?" Meeka walked through the house and found Hustle in the laundry room. He was holding Isabella on his hip while she was sleeping. He turned are and pressed his finger against his lips.

"We need to talk NOW!"

"What's wrong baby?" Hustle opened the icebox and placed the jug of milk back into it.

"You have to hear it to believe it. Can you go and put Izzy in her room?" Meeka asked.

"Yea."

"Okay, I'll be in the room." Meeka walked into the bathroom and grabbed a towel. She dried her hair and wrapped her bottle with the towel. Meeka walked out of the bathroom and Hustle was sitting on the couch waiting for her. She walked to the pile of clothes and grabbed the recorder. She ran into the living room and dropped the recorder on the table. Meeka pressed the play button and sat down. Meeka's legs were shaking. Listening to the recorder again made her feel sick again. Her lips trembled, and her head started to throb. Once the recording was over, Hustle grabbed it and placed it on the couch.

"Wh-Who is this talking?" Hustle asked.

"Who does it sound like Brink?" Meeka dropped her head and rubbed neck. She wanted to replay the tape again, but it would only make her feel sicker.

"It sounds like Austin and Justice. Tameeka, is that Austin and Justice talking?"

"Yes Brink, it is!!!! I can't believe this bitch, and I can't believe him. He wants Syd and I to seek revenge on us, not to make this world a better place. He's not going to stop Brink!" Meeka buried her face in her hands and cried. She wanted to play tough, but she couldn't. She felt hurt, angry, and betrayed. Justice was her best friend, but that didn't matter to Justice. Hustle walked to Meeka and gave her a hug. She pulled away, but he held her tighter.

"You need to calm down baby."

"How Brink, how? Did you hear everything they said?"

"I never thought I would have to say this and be serious, but I have to kill her. I have to kill Justice. If I don't, we're all going to go to prison, and I can't leave you and Izzy, no!"

"What, you can't kill Justice. What about Pedro? He's going to lose his mind." Hustle said.

"Fuck how Pedro would feel and his feelings. If this shit goes down like Austin wants it to then this investigation will be big, and the feds will get involved, and shit will spiral out of control from there. We ALL will go down and including Pedro."

"Tameeka you can't just make a move without all the information. Maybe was lying to him. Wait and see if she's going to tell you."

"I have all the evidence I need. Justice is going to save herself. She's dying, and that's that."

"Are you going to tell Sydney?" Hustle asked.

"No, I won't. Sydney has enough going on. She'll know once they're zipping her sister-in-law up in a body bag. You're the only person who can know. I'm not even telling Marlo or Forty."

"How did you find this out?" Hustle asked.

"Wendell."

***

I'm glad you're back home baby even though it's only for the night."

"Yea," Sydney wasn't sure what to say to Xavier.

"I'm going to go back in the house and finish cooking. If you need anything, let me know." Xavier kissed Sydney on the forehead and walked into the house. She made sure he was in the kitchen before she pulled her phone out.

It was 6:45 pm and Sydney was sitting on her patio. The wind was slightly blowing, and the sun was shining perfectly. The scenery looked like something on a postcard or in a magazine. Her wine glass was full of Barefoot Moscato, and she was feeling the buzz. She wanted another bottle, but she knew she would be passed out.

It was her first day sleeping at home, but she felt uncomfortable. All day she replayed Xavier having sex in her son's bed. Since she couldn't get the image out of her, she made Xavier purchase him a brand-new bed and bedspread. She also had him purchase her a few pairs of heels and handbags. She didn't care that she maxed his card out. She deserved every penny that was spent.

"Just because I'm here doesn't mean anything. I only came because he asked me like a million times." Sydney whispered and looked over her shoulder. Even though she was outside and Xavier was in the house cooking, she was still cautious. After a week of charming Sydney, she finally gave in and gave Jason her number. She regretted not giving him her number sooner. His conversation was great, and he kept her laughing. She still couldn't believe she was entertaining a twenty-six-year-old, but she slowly wasn't caring anymore. She hadn't told Meeka about him, but today she was telling her.

"Okay, Sydney, whatever you say. You looked nice today. Blue is definitely your color." He laughed.

"Thank you, but every color is my color." She laughed.

"You are right about that. Where are you now?" He asked.

"I'm outside sitting on the patio. It's a nice day today. It's been so hot lately. I'm enjoying this cool weather."

"It is nice out here. Once I got off work, I worked out outside." Jason said.

"Oh really? I think I should join you next time. I packed on a few pounds." Sydney raised her shirt and realized another jelly roll mysteriously appeared.

"Where your body is perfect, but I wouldn't mind watching you do squats," he laughed.

"I wouldn't mind you watching me do squats," Sydney covered her mouth and looked around as if someone was watching her. She didn't want to admit it, but Jason had her wide open. Sydney couldn't control the things that were coming out of her mouth.

"Oh, really?"

"Your lil' young ass will get me in trouble." She giggled.

"No baby, I'm not trying to do that at all. Where is he at by the way?" Jason asked.

"He's in the house cooking. Are we still linking up later?" Sydney asked.

"Hell yea, I wouldn't mind seeing you twice in one day." He said. Her phone started to vibrate, and it was a text message from Meeka. She replied and continued her conversation with Jason.

"Hhhmm, I bet. We can meet up at the south park. My friend is here I'll call you when she leaves."

"Okay, I'll be waiting."

"Okay, bye." Sydney disconnected the call. She stared at the phone and smile. Meeka walked outside and sat next to Sydney. Meeka grabbed the wine glass and took a sip.

"Why were you smiling at your phone?"

"What?" Sydney asked. She didn't think Meeka saw her blushing.

"What were you smiling at?"

"Meek, it's a loonngg story. Are you ready for this?" Sydney asked.

"Bitch, what happened, spill the tea!"

"The tea is hot, get your cup out. There is this new teacher who I've been conversing with, his name is Jason."

"What, really?"

"Yea and he is sexy as hell; pretty brown skin fella with some long dreads. Perfect face, perfect smile, perfect EVERYTHING. He reminds me of Jacquees."

"Damn, he really must fine. When did meet him?" Meeka asked.

"He's a new teacher at the school, but I really didn't pay him any mind. Last week Xavier came to school to give me some flowers and candy. He was the person who walked Xavier to the break room. We started talking, one thing lead to number. It took me a week to give him my number, but I finally did."

"What, YOU gave someone your number? I can't believe it." Meeka laughed.

"I know right, but he's a nice guy. There's a catch to it, and I'm embarrassed to admit it," Sydney shook her head and covered her face.

"Oh Lord, what is it Sydney? Is a gay, married, or related to Austin?" Meeka asked. She was a little nervous to hear what the catch was.

"He's twenty-six," Sydney mumbled and turned away. She stared at her miniature garden and waited for Meeka to say something crazy. She knew the Cougar jokes were coming shortly after that.

"Girl, he's what?" Meeka jumped to her feet and stared at Sydney. Sydney squinted her eyes and shook her head up and down. Meeka burst into laughter and held her stomach. Sydney flared her nose at Meeka and laughed.

"I swear Meek, I hate your guts. I knew you were going to clown me."

"I'm sorry Syd, I didn't want to laugh like that. Age isn't nothing but a number. That's what Pretty Ricky and Aaliyah said." Meeka tried not to laugh, but she couldn't help it.

"It's not that funny Meek, he's a nice guy. He's easy to talk to."

"I'm sorry, for real this time. So, you said he's a new teacher, right?" She asked.

"Yea, it's his first year at Grolee," Sydney said.

"Suddenly he's interested in you?"

"Yea, but what are you getting at Meek?" Sydney crossed her legs and asked.

"What if he's working with Austin? Think about it Sydney," Sydney's smile disappeared, and she grabbed her glass. She took a sip of her wine then handed the glass to Meek. Meeka stirred the wine then took a sip.

"I don't think so Meek he has never mentioned anything about Austin and I sure won't mention anything. The less he knows, the better. I don't need his young ass getting tied into any of this."

"That is true, but stay aware don't let his good looks knock you off your game. You never know who Austin has working for him. I wouldn't be surprised if the janitor or lunch lady was watching you." They both laughed.

"Hey, I wouldn't be surprised either. I honestly don't think he's working for or with Austin. He seems like a nice guy, but I need to get adjusted to his age. I can't believe myself, but that nigga looks so good. Girl, I can only imagine the things I would do to him," Sydney closed her eyes and started to touch herself. Meeka grabbed her hand and said, "Eeww, you freaky little bitch. Let me find out your crushing on him."

"I think I am girl. I honestly enjoy his conversation and company at work. I'm not saying I'm going to marry him or have his baby. I wouldn't mind having him in my life as a good friend." Sydney said.

"I don't think anything is wrong with that. It's nice to have a friend to talk to. Does he know about what's going on with between you and Xavier?" Meeka asked.

"He knows enough, but he doesn't know why I originally left home," Sydney said.

"Oh okay, but what's going on between you and him anyway?" Meeka asked.

"I guess you can say we're taking baby steps. Just because I'm here, it doesn't mean I want to be with him. It also doesn't mean I'm back here for good. He's been begging to spend the night, so I gave in."

"Keith Sweat begging ass nigga." Meeka laughed.

"Hell yea he was. I'm not sure how to feel about him right now. I'll take it one day at a time, that's the best thing."

"Yea, but remember what I told you. Let your heart guide you along the way." Meeka said.

"I am, but this heart of mines better lead me to the right place. Have you spoken to Rocko since they left?" Sydney asked.

"Yea, she texted me this morning they landed in Bora, Bora about 8:00 am. Philly hasn't been on the website, so he hasn't seen her message yet. I pray this plan goes through."

"Me too, I will never be at peace knowing Santana's killer is loose on the streets," Sydney said.

"I often think about if Tana suffered or not? Did he see his death coming or was he blindsided? My thoughts run so wild, it's crazy."

"Me too Meek and it still doesn't seem real. I wish he was here now laughing with us. I know he would have had jokes for days about Jason and I." Sydney laughed.

"Girl you know it. Santana always kept me laughing. It was never a dull moment with him." Meeka said.

"I know right. When I was having Pacson, he was on the floor doing the worm. I was laughing so hard, that's how he came out." Sydney chuckled and laughed. She reached for the glass, but she changed her mind. Instead, she reached for the bottle and tossed her head all the way back. She could feel she was getting emotional, but she didn't want to cry. She would rather drink her feelings away and talk about the good times they shared with him.

"Yes, and I was right along with him doing the running man. We had a lot of fun that day."

"Yes, we did. You and Tana didn't leave my side, not once." Sydney said.

"Santana had myself beat for delivery. I always said he should have been a make-up artist." Meeka said.

"I knnooowwww, that boy had hands of an angel. I've seen him make some ugly people pretty.

Meek and Sydney laughed and continued to talk about Santana. It felt good to talk about the good times and share memories.

***

Today Meeka and Justice were finally meeting up today she told Meeka how she was depressed about Santana and needed to get away for a while. Justice forgot to mention how she was working with her brother against her. She tried her best to meet Meeka at her house, but Meeka insisted they go out for lunch. She lied and told Justice she hired a new cleaning crew to clean her home.

While Justice was on the phone with someone, Meeka sat at the bar in Sombreros. She was also on the phone talking to Hustle.

"Where is she?" Hustle asked.

"She's outside on the phone. She said she was talking to her new friend." Meeka dipped the tortilla chips into the salsa then took a sip of her Coke.

"Do you believe that?" Hustle asked.

"Do you believe that the earth is flat?" Meeka chuckled. She turned around to see where Justice was. She was still on the phone, but she looked tense.

"Not at all, she's probably on the phone with Austin. Be careful what you say, baby. I'm sure that wire is sitting between her breasts probably the center of her flat ass chest." Hustle laughed.

"That explains why she has on a crew neck t-shirt. As long as I've known her, she has never worn a crew neck shirt." Meeka sucked her teeth and rolled her eyes.

"Not even to Santana's funeral." He laughed.

"Right, the bitch had a low-cut dress on. I have to go, she's coming."

"Okay, I love you." Hustle said.

"I love you too." Meeka disconnected the call and slipped her phone into her bra. Justice walked to the bar jolly and with a big smile on her face.

"Did the bartender come back yet?" Justice sat on the stool and reached for the bowl of chips. She poured a little salsa on her chips and stuffed a chip in her mouth. Meeka stared at Justice with hate in her eyes. She was so disgusted with her. Even the way she chewed made Meeka angry.

"No, she was getting our food."

"Oh good because I'm starving," Justice said.

"You and me both, I'm glad you finally decided to get out of the house. We were missing you girl, and you had us worried." As Justice dropped her head, Meeka stared at her chest. She could see the print of the wire, and she laughed.

"Yea, this is nice. We haven't been here in a while." Justice said.

"I know and tomorrow is their drink special. I think we should come back tomorrow."

"Baby you know I'm down. I could use a few drinks in my system." Justice laughed.

"You and me both." Meeka gave Justice a fake smile and raised her eyebrows. The short blonde hair waitress approached the bar with a big black tray on her shoulder. The Chimichangas, Tamales, and fish tacos looked delicious. Justice was ready to grab the hot plates of the tray herself.

The waitress swiftly placed the plates in front of them and pulled two sets of utensils out of her apron. She set the utensils and asked, "Do you ladies need anything else?"

"No, I'm good," Meeka said, and she unwrapped the utensils and dug her fork into the Chimichangas.

"I need some extra pico and sour cream," Justice said.

"Okay, I'll be right back." She said and walked away.

"So Tameeka, so what's the next move? I know you're plotting to kill whoever killed Tana."

"What?" Meeka asked with a mouth full of food.

"When is the next killing Tameeka?" Meeka wanted to laugh, but she held it together. She knew Justice was saying her full name for a reason. She shook her head and swallowed the food she was chewing. Then she took a big gulp of her drink and wiped her mouth.

"I was thinking about taking Izzy to Disney World. Lord knows we're overdue for a vacation." Justice said.

"Speaking of Florida, do you still have those escorts in Miami? Isn't one of their names Misha or something like that?"

"I sure hope a hurricane doesn't form during that time? I do not want to get stuck in Florida."

"With the way you trick those hoes down there, getting stuck might be a good thing." She laughed.

"I was thinking we should put new floors at Santana's grave every month. Clean around the tombstone often, keep it clean and shit you know." Meeka said.

"Of course, Santana would kill us if we didn't. You know he was a neat freak." She laughed.

"His mom didn't want any of his things, go figure. I decided to donate his wigs to the hospital for the cancer patients." Meeka reached for a taco and shoved half of it in her mouth.

"Aaww that was a kind gesture Meek, what are you going to do with his clothes? He had some badass outfits." Justice said.

"I know I'll give them to someone who's in need of clothes," Meeka said.

"With all that money you make from pimping you can buy those people clothes." She laughed.

"You should try some of these tacos. They are waaayyy better than mines, but don't tell Brink that." Meeka continued to eat and ignore Justice. Meeka could tell Justice was getting annoyed at how she was ignoring her questions and comments. She knew she couldn't say anything because Austin could easily twist her words.

"Yea, I hear you." Justice turned away and rolled her eyes. Meeka slightly laughed.

"I wish you could have really met Santana's cousin Joseline. She's a cool girl, and she reminds me a lot of him. Crazy, loud, and silly, I need to visit her soon in Florida."

"That's where the money is," Justice said.

"Do you remember when that AKA was teasing you about your clothes? I think that was your second semester in college."

"Yea….you punched her in the nose for me. I didn't even know your name or who you were. You've had my back for a long time."

"I told you, you're the sister I never had and always wanted."

Meeka's phone began to vibrate, so she pulled it out of her bra. It was Roman, she was surprised. She hadn't spoken to him since the club, and it was rare when he called her.

"Who is that?" Justice asked and leaned to the side to get a better view of Meeka's phone screen. Meeka pretended she didn't see Justice looking and covered her phone. The text message on her screen was something serious. It was about Justice and Miami. Meeka knew it couldn't be anything good.

"It's Brink's mom, she needs a loaf of bread from the store. Ugh, she acts like I'm here child instead of Brink."

"You basically are her child. That lady loves you like you're her daughter. Does she know what you do?"

"The only thing I do is take care of Isabella and her son. I'm pretty sure she knows that." Meeka laughed.

"She would be heartbroken if she knew Tameeka was a pimp."

"The only thing you can call Tameeka is a mother. I wouldn't call myself a pimp because I played her son a few times. You can call me a playa, but not a pimp. Aw man, she's calling, let me take this." Meeka took a bite of her taco then jogged outside. Roman was calling her phone non-stop, and it started to scare her. On the six call, she quickly slid her finger across the screen and said, "Hello?"

"Tameeka, where are you?" Roman asked.

"I'm at Sombreros with Justice. Why what's up, is something wrong? Meeka asked.

"We need to talk in person. I got some information you may want to see."

"Your text message said it's something about Miami and Justice."

"Yea, but you need to see this yourself. When can we meet up?" Roman asked.

"We can meet up in a few minutes. Where are you now?"

"I'm leaving the gas station, I'll be home," Roman said.

"Okay, I'll see you then." As Meeka turned around Justice was walking out of the door, she kind of startled Meeka.

"Meek, do you want another drink?" Justice asked.

"Uhh, yea, a Sprite please that other drink taste watered down."

"Okay, but is something wrong? It looks like you saw a ghost."

"Yea, I saw Casper." Meeka laughed and walked into the building.

"Girl you're crazy, but seriously, is everything okay?" Justice asked.

"Yea, Brink's mom was giving me a damn grocery list. I have to go, girl, I'm sorry."

"It's all good Meek, I'll pass by later."

"Okay, I'll text you when I get home." Meeka reached into her pocket and handed Justice a twenty-dollar bill. Meeka gave Justice a hug and asked, "What's that in your shirt?"

"Oh, it's my bra. The mental wire is starting to pop out. Don't judge me or tell anyone." She awkwardly laughed.

"Baby it's time to buy some new bras. Matter of fact, when I got to Wal-Mart, I'll buy them for you. Just send me your bra size. You know Linda is sending me to three different stores." Meeka said.

"Okay, thanks, girl," Justice said.

"I love you Juju."

"I- I love you too Meek." Meeka waved and walked away. The grin on her face was priceless. She knew telling Justice she loved her would mess with her head.

Meeka got into her car and sped out of the parking lot. Traffic was light, and she would make it to his home in no time. She tried her best to focus on the road, but her mind couldn't stop thinking about what Roman needed to tell her. Justice had already crossed her, but to double-cross her would be messed up.

Meeka arrived at Roman's home and parked her car neatly behind Roman's F-150 truck. It was weird being at his house. Since she broke up with him, she hadn't been at his house. Her hands were a little sweaty, so she wiped them on her pants. We reached into her bra for her phone so she could call Roman, but he opened the door. He was shirtless, but his wife beater was in his hand. His semi-naked body brought her down memory lane. She and Roman would have amazing sex throughout his entire house. There wasn't a place in the house that her pussy juices didn't soak.

"Hello beautiful, you look nice." Roman waited for Meeka to walk in then he closed the door.

"Hey." She said. She stared at his toned back. She was ready to jump on him and fill his back with soft kisses. Being in the company of Roman wasn't easy for her. He always made her feel a certain type of way, and today he made her feel horny.

"Give me a second I was at the gym before I went to the gas station. I just got out of the shower."

"You're good, take your time Ro." Meeka exhaled and sat on the couch. Roman made a little change this house, but not much. It was the same burgundy couch and chestnut brown curtains Meeka picked for him. The six pictures she purchased from Kirkland's were still on the walls and in the same positions. She looked around the house to see any signs of a woman being here. She couldn't find anything and she happy. That meant if Roman was involved with anyone she couldn't leave of her belongings here.

A few seconds later, Roman entered the living room, but this time he had a shirt on. He smiled at Meeka and sat next to her.

"How are you?"

"I'm doing, that's all I can say." Meeka rolled her eyes and rolled her neck. Just thinking about Justice made her neck tense.

"I understand that, but if you need me you know, I'm here."

"I know Roman and thank you. What's up though, what happened?" Meeka asked.

"About an hour ago I was at the gym, and Miami was there."

"Okay, what does that mean?" Meeka asked.

"We talked a little, then we went on about our business. Somehow she forgot her phone in the bathroom, and I thought it was mines. I went to the text messages and saw some fucked up shit."

"What did you see?" Meeka asked.

"I'll let you read it yourself." Roman pulled the phone out of his back pocket and handed it to Meeka. She scrolled to the message, and the first name she saw was Justice. As she read the messaged between Miami and Justice, it felt like someone punched her in the stomach. Justice told Miami about the meeting with Austin, and she agreed about helping Justice and Austin. They even made jokes about Meeka going to prison and Hustle leaving her for another woman. Meeka was so mad that she couldn't continue reading the messages.

"These bitches get worse by the day. Justice is really showing her ass now." Meeka rubbed her face and handed the phone to Roman.

"What's going on Tameeka do you want to start from the beginning?" Roman asked.

"So I put this rookie cop on payroll a few months ago. You don't need to know his name. Two days ago, he told me he had some information for me, so we met up. He had a recording of Austin and Justice. Austin asked her to testify against me and Sydney." She said.

"What, are you serious man?"

"Yea, but she said no because she knew I would get her killed. He gave her another option to wear a wire, and she agreed to it. Today was my first time seeing her in about two weeks. She had the wire on her today. When I gave her a hug, I felt it. Just to apply some pressure to her, I asked her what that? She said it was the wire in her bra sticking out. The stupid bitch makes all that money and lied about having a ruined bra." Meeka chuckled and cried.

"What the fuck!" Roman punched the pillow that was next to him.

"I know right, but I played it so cool. She was asking me all kinds of questions and making statements just to get me to talk. I didn't say ANYTHING, I ignored everything and talked about other things. I've should have listened to Syd, she told me this was going to happen. In the back of my mind, I knew she was true. I was trying to give her the benefit of the doubt. That bitch made me look like a damn fool. Oh, but believe me when I tell you I have a cake baked for her. I trusted her and Miami and look how they're betraying me."

"Have you told Sydney about the conversation?" Roman asked.

"No," Meeka said.

"Okay, are you going to tell her?"

"No."

"Tameeka, are you telling her ANYTHING?" Roman stood to his feet and began to pace through the living room. Roman was stressing as if he was stressing over the problems.

"NO, I'm not Roman."

"Why not, what if she says something to Justice and they use it against her?"

"She won't, Sydney is in her own little world right now. She met some guy named Jason, and he's a teacher. Do you know him?" Meeka asked.

"Jason Thomas, does he have dreads?"

"Yea, he does."

"I know exactly who you're talking about. He's cool like a cat but isn't a tad bit young for Sydney. On of top that, doesn't she have a boyfriend?"

"Yea, but she caught him cheating in the house."

"Damn, that's fucked up. If you're going to cheat at least do it somewhere else. Not in the house where the woman lies her head. That's just downright disrespectful." Roman shook his head and sat down. He stretched his entire body out and gave Meeka a hug. She slightly chuckled and smoothed her hair with her hand.

"Did you ever cheat on me Roman and be honest? I won't get upset, it's too late now."

"No Tameeka, I never cheated on you. I never had a reason to cheat on you." Roman said.

"I guess all men don't cheat. Do you mind if I keep this phone? I want to show Brink these messages."

"Sure, be my guess."

"I also have the recording of Austin and Xavier. Before I know, I'm going to have box full of things like this. I wonder who's going to turn on me next."

Meeka shook her head, and the tears streamed down her slim face. Not only was Justice crossing her again, Miami agreed to work with Justice.

"Are you okay Tameeka?" Roman sat closer to Meeka and rubbed her shoulder. She dropped her head on his shoulder and wiped her face.

"You know I often think about how life would have been with you?"

"Really?" Roman was surprised.

"Yea, I know if I was with you I wouldn't continue to do this. Maybe it was a mistake, and I should have stayed with you. You're a wonderful guy Roman, and I hope you find a great woman."

"I can't lie Tameeka, I really haven't moved on from you. I've had relations with another woman, but not on the level we were on. You are truly something special. Brink is a lucky guy, and I've always been jealous of that."

"Jealous of what?" Meeka asked.

"That he has you, he had your heart, and he's the father of that pretty little girl," Roman said.

"I don't understand Ro, and I need you to explain this to me. You were the one who told me to be with him. I may have broken up with you, but technically you broke up with me. If you felt that way, why did let me go?"

"I let you go because I loved you. I wanted you to be happy, and I knew that's where your happiness was. It didn't matter how much I made you smile or laughed. You laughed and smiled more with him. From day one I told you I wasn't mad with your decision jealous, yea a little. I'm human, and I can't help it."

"Wwwooooowwww, I don't know what to say." Meeka turned to face Roman and slowly grabbed his face. She began to kiss him, and he kissed her back. She missed his touch and feeling his soft lips. She began to climb on top of him and pulled her shirt over her head. Roman unhooked her bra and tossed it behind the couch. He stared at her breast like they were a work of art.

"Man, I've missed you so much." Roman gently squeezed her breast and planted delicate kisses on them. Meeka could feel her panties were getting wet and she liked it. She reached for his zipper, but he stopped her. She stared at him and said, "What, what's wrong?"

"Trust me, I want you, but we can't do this. I know you're in your feelings and you aren't thinking straight." Meeka realized what she was doing and climbed off Roman. She was a little embarrassed that she was topless and had let her emotions get the best of her.

"Damn, you're right. I'm sorry Roman I didn't mean to get you all hot and bothered."

"It's alright Meek. I would be less of a man if I fucked you like this. You know I love to make love to you, not fuck." He laughed and reached behind the couch. He handed Meeka her bra, and she grabbed her shirt. She quickly put her clothes on and stood to her feet.

"Sometimes I wonder Ro, I swear." Meeka tapped his face and shook her head.

"Wonder what?" He asked.

"Why I didn't choose you."

"You didn't choose me because your heart didn't want you to." Roman shrugged his shoulders and smiled.

"Maybe or I let my mind do the thinking for me. I'm so lost right now Roman, it's crazy." Meeka slumped in the couch and pulled her hair.

"What are you going to do?" He asked.

"What do you think, kill them. It's crazy how I'm so comfortable telling you things like that."

"Why do you say that?" Roman asked.

"How everyone is crossing me, I don't know who's working with Austin." She sighed.

"You know that's the last thing you have to worry about. That nigga couldn't pay me to talk to him."

"I know you've always hated him." She laughed.

"Are you really going to kill her?"

"Hell yea, Justice has crossed me twice in less than six months. That bitch has to GO, her and Miami. Miami of all people should know better. That girl was dead broke when I found her slanging pussy in the Ranch Motel. I groomed her and made her start selling her pussy in the Holiday Inn. Look at the thanks I get Roman."

"I can't believe Justice, I'm shocked. You, Santana, and her were like The Three Musketeers."

"I know, we have memories that will last for a lifetime. My life is all messed up right now. I'm not when it got this crazy."

"You have to fix it Meeka and get everything in order. You have that little girl watching your every move." Roman said.

"I know Ro, I know." Meeka rolled her eyes and dropped her head.

"Thanks for calling me with this information. I owe you big time."

"It's all good Tameeka." Meeka took one more look at Roman and kissed him.

"I love you Roman, and I'm going to always love you." Meeka walked out of the house, and she could feel Roman was looking at her. For some reason, her heart ached. She left like she was telling him her last farewells.

As she drove off, she reached for her phone to call Hustle. She wasn't sure what she was going to tell him or who what kind of lies she would tell him.

"Come on baby, pick up," Meeka whispered.

He answered the phone and said, "What's up baby?"

"Brink I swear, if it's not one thing it's another."

"Oh Lord, what happened?" He asked.

"Someone gave me some information. Justice has Miami working with her."

"What?" Hustle asked.

"Just listen to me I have the text messages to prove it. I'm on my way home."

Chapter 5 (September 2015)

Sydney sat next to Jason on the park bench staring at the dark sky. The cloud seemed transparent, and the stars were shining brightly. Weeks had gone by, but she still wasn't ready to go back home. It seemed like Xavier wasn't asking her to stay anymore. It didn't bother her much. Her time was occupied with Jason, and she loved it. She didn't see a future with him, and she wasn't trying to settle. Jason made her feel young and free. That was two feeling she hadn't felt in a while.

"So, when are you going home?" Jason asked.

"I'm not sure, I don't know if I'm even going home. I feel like I'm single and I kind of like the way this feels. I went from a marriage to a relationship like it was nothing. I always said when I would get married I would never divorce my husband. I said I would stick by his side no matter what."

"So what happened, if you don't mind me asking?"

"Change, people change right before your eyes. He changed, and I changed as well. He was no longer the good cop, and I was no longer the pushover teacher who wasn't satisfied with not being happy anymore. He became this evil cop, and I couldn't take it anymore. I was no longer attracted to him anymore. My love was slowly fading away also. Once I saw Xavier, it was a wrap. I was ready to jump in his arms and be with him. I practically did, and I didn't care what anyone thought. He was so perfect, and I didn't see any wrong in him. I was a fool though I should have known perfect doesn't exist."

"Why didn't you tell him how you felt?" Jason asked.

"Trust me, I did. I tried several times, but he brushed me off. He was too worried about the wrong things. Literally, that man used his power for evil. I couldn't be with a person like that anymore. Lying next to him made me disgusted with myself Jason. For weeks, we wouldn't have sex, and I was fine with that. Seem like he was also, he probably was cheating. When I met Xavier, I became me again. I was happy again, I was happy with myself. I really thought we were going to build a future together. Now I'm sitting on the park with a twenty-six-year-old drinking beer. My life is slowly going down the drain." She laughed and raised her beer in the air.

"You say that as if it's a bad thing." He laughed and took a big gulp of his beer.

"I'm sorry Jason, it's not bad. I enjoy your company and conversation. You take my mind off all the bullshit I have going on. Thank God the judge denied Austin request for joint custody! The look on his face was priceless."

"Why would he want to put you through all of this?" Jason asked.

"Because he's a bitter old woman and he can't handle that I moved on. Then again I can't blame him, look at me." Sydney laughed and sized herself up and down.

"I don't blame him for going crazy. You are a beautiful woman, and both of those men were lucky to have you."

"Thank you, but too bad they didn't see it. Maybe you should tell them that." She laughed.

"Maybe I will, they were fools to treat you the way they did. If you were my girlfriend or wife, I would treat you like a queen. Nothing less than that, you deserve the best Sydney."

"Hopefully one day I'll get that. If not, I'll give it to myself. There is nothing wrong with being your own Superman, even if you're superwoman."

"You're right about that, but who do you want to be with, your husband or your boyfriend?"

"Oh my God, that sound so crazy, I have a husband and a boyfriend! I can't wait until this divorce is over. I'll be back to being Sydney Pope."

"That still doesn't answer my question. Who do you want to be with?" He asked. Sydney turned away and bit her lip. She was embarrassed to say who she wanted to be with. Sydney took a sip of her drink and said, "Xavier, my boyfriend. I want to be with him, but I don't know. Things are changing between us, and I'm not sure if I care."

"I can see it in your eyes, you do care. If you know you want to be with him go back home. Fix the problems between you and him. Get back to that happy place you were when y'all first met Sydney." Sydney tried to focus while Jason spoke, but she couldn't. She wasn't sure if it was the beer, but tonight he was looking extra handsome.

"Forget them both my happy place can be right here. I want you to make me happy, make me feel good Jason."

"How do you want me to do that?" He asked.

"Pleasure me, I'm all yours." She grinned and dropped her empty beer bottle. Luckily, the bottle didn't shatter into pieces and break.

Jason tossed his beer bottle and fell to his knees. Sydney was giving him a sexual look, and she was giving it back to him. Neither one knew what to do, but Sydney made a move. She wrapped her legs around his neck and slid her pants to her knees. He massages his penis to get it hard while he buried his face into her vagina. Sydney moaned and arched her back. Jason's tough was moving in every direction that was possible.

"Oooouuuuuuuuuuu, Jason slow down."

"Damn, that pussy taste good." Jason used his two fingers to massage Sydney clitoris. Then he licked his fingers and smiled. The sweet taste of water was all over his face thanks to Sydney.

Sydney covered her mouth and grabbed the back of his head. She wanted him to bury his face deeper into her vagina. This was something she hadn't done in a while, but she loved how she was being spontaneous. This was going to be a night to remember.

"Fuck me." Sydney reached for Jason's penis as he stood over her. He let her massage it before he shoved it in her. He was ready to break her back and show her age was nothing, but a number.

***

Sydney leaned against her car waiting for Justice to arrive. She wasn't sure what Justice wanted to talk about and why they were back here.

"Come on Juju where are you?" Sydney zipped her jacket and slid her hands into her pocket. The tropical storm was slowly making its way on land, and south Louisiana was feeling it. Her phone began to ring and it Meeka.

"Hey, Meek, what's up?" Sydney asked and looked over her shoulders.

"I'm cooking a beef stew, and I baked a strawberry cake. You should stop by and get some food when you leave from Juju."

"Oh you know I will. I'm in no mood to cook."

"I hear you girl. I barely wanted to cook, but Hustle ass was craving it."

"Did you say craving? It sounds like someone is pregnant to me." Sydney laughed and raised her hands in the air. Her tubes weren't tied, but she was done with having kids. She was patiently waiting for one of her friends to have a baby, mainly Meeka.

"Only in your dreams, Hustle must have gotten someone else pregnant. The last thing I need is another child right now. I would selfish and crazy to bring an innocent child in this world. At least not right now, maybe when this shit dies down." She said.

"If you are pregnant I'm so against abortions. Black lives matter Tameeka, they really matter." Sydney clapped her hands and laughed.

"Hashtag BLM all day and every day. By the way, what did Juju want to talk?"

"I'm not sure, I haven't talk to her yet. She needs to get here ASAP. She knows I have work in the morning, unlike her." Sydney leaned forward and squinted her eyes to get a better view of the road. At 7:45 pm the road was dark and creepy. The only lighting she had was the small light from her car. It was no traffic coming or going on the road.

"I wonder why she wanted to meet you back there? Hustle use to have a big lick back there, but I made him stop dealing with him. It's way too creepy back there. Are you strapped, just in case?" Meeka asked.

"I'm strapped like a dyke with a dildo." They both laughed.

"Girl, for a moment you sounded like Santana," Meeka said.

"Long live Santana!!"

"Long live King Santana, you are truly missed, baby." Sydney stared at the dark clouds and waved. She knew Santana was somewhere in heaven laughing and waving done at her.

"Knowing Juju, she's probably fooling around with someone on Cosay Road."

"I wouldn't be surprised. She's looking for any shoulder to cry on. On top of that, she's been acting extra funny lately. You already know what that means."

"New dick!" they said and laughed.

"She makes it sssooooo obvious every single time. Just like when she was fucking around with ole boy Terry. Juju was going back and forth to Mississippi like it was nothing." Meeka chuckled.

"No dick is that good to put that many miles on my car." Sydney joked.

"Hell no, but Juju has always been the type to be crazy over every guy she gets involved with. Thank God Pedro came into her life and calmed her ass down."

"I know, he is literally a gift from God. It's only so many times you can tag along with your friend to the clinic. They knew Juju by her first name." Sydney said.

"That doesn't make any sense. The only reason why the clinic knows us is because of WIC appointments and when the kids have to take their shots." Meeka ran upstairs and walked into her room. Hustle was sitting on the bed naked and rubbing lotion on his body. He was fresh out of the shower and was ready to get in bed. Seeing his naked body instantly turned her on, but sex was the last thing on her mind. She jogged to him and gave him a kiss. He held her face and kissed her again.

"I love you and be careful," he whispered.

"I love you too and I will." Meeka ran downstairs and slipped her tennis shoes on. Time was ticking, and she needed to hurry. Her shoes were barely tied, but she ran out of the house.

"Girl you are crazy, but it's the truth." Sydney could see bright lights approaching her, so she grabbed her gun. Her 22 was new, and she was itching to use it. It was only Justice, and she exhaled.

"There goes Juju I'll see you when I get there."

"Okay." Sydney walked towards Justice and disconnected the call.

"Who were you talking to? Let me guess master Tameeka?" Justice had a mean mug on her face her hands here behind her back. Sydney took a step backward. Something was a little off about Justice. Usually, she was dressed from head to toe with a face full of make-up, but tonight was different. Her hair was covered with a bonnet, and her face was bare. You could see the bags and dark circles under her eyes. It looked like she hadn't slept in days and she barely blinked her eyes.

"Master, what?" Justice asked.

"Yea that was her, why?" Sydney asked.

"Hhhmmm, I figured that. You can't ever make a move without informing Meeka."

"Yea and you either." Sydney laughed.

"Whatever maybe that's why Xavier cheated on you," Justice laughed and wiped her nose.

"Maybe, maybe not, but what's up? Why did we have to meet back here?" Is it top secret?"

"No it isn't, but you're going to do something for me." Justice pulled a wire out of her back pocket and handed it to Sydney. Sydney held the wire in the air and stare at it, but she was confused. She wasn't sure what kind of shit Justice was going to get her into.

"Ju, what the fuck is on your nose?" Sydney reached for Justice knows and wiped it. She pushed Sydney away and said, "Nothing!" Sydney stared at her hand and noticed a white powder.

"Juju, are you doing…POWDER?!" The cocaine odor was loud and strong. Sydney knew it was Hustle's work. She wiped her hand onto her pants and shook her head.

"That should be the least of your worries. Wearing this wire and not getting caught is the only thing you should be worried about."

"What why do you want me to wear a wire?"

SSSSSSSSSSSSSRRRRRRRRRRRCCCCCCCCCC CCCCCCCCCC

POW! POW!

"Aaaaahhhhhhhhhh," Sydney screamed and dropped to the ground. She wasn't sure who was shooting or where the bullets were coming from. Her hands were covering her face, but she still managed to see the shooter, and she couldn't believe who it was.

"What the fuck, Meeka how did-"

"Just get in the car and go, Syd! Go to my house, and I'll be there soon, GO!!" Meeka pointed at the gun at Sydney and waved it towards her car. Without questioning Meeka, Sydney jumped to her feet and ran to her car. She sped off and drove down the dark road without any lights on. She was beyond terrified.

Meeka squatted to the ground and moved closer to Justice. Her body jerked several times, and blood gushed out of her mouth. Meeka used her sleeve to wipe the corners of her mouth. She reached for Meeka's hand, but she pulled it away.

"M- M-M- Mee- Meeka, pl-easse don't let me."

"What, I can't hear you?" Meeka chuckled.

"P – P- Please don- don't this t-t-t- to me." She stuttered.

"Please don't do what? Let you die? Of course, I'm going to let you die! That's the whole reason I shot you. What I won't do is let you die alone. I'm not that heartless, and I love you waaayyyy too much for that."

"Meek, pl-" Justice's body jerked harder, and more blood gushed out seconds later blood started to fill her eyes.

"Ssshhh, you're using too much energy talking. Everything is going to be okay Juju. This is going to hurt more now. You're approaching death baby girl. You should be seeing the light soon. Just know that I'm hurting more than you. Sydney and I talked about this before, but I never thought it would actually happen." Meeka stared at Justice and realized her eyes were in the back of her head. She pressed her index and middle finger against Justice's neck and shook her head. She no longer had a pulse, and her body wasn't as warm. A single tear fell from her eye, but she wiped it away. She didn't care that Justice was dead. She still wanted to talk to her.

Meeka rubbed Justice's forehead and tucked her loose hair behind her ears. Then she moved a little closer to her. She wasn't bothered by the dead body at all. It wasn't her first time seeing a dead body, but it was her first time seeing a friend die so close.

"Even when you're dead you look peaceful and beautiful. I remember when I first met you. I was going to sell some college kids a few pills and spotted you in the student union. You were an ugly college student struggling in UL's dorm rooms. You said the only food you could afford was hot pockets and Ramen noodles. You didn't have a car or a decent shirt on your back. Within three weeks I changed all of that. I put you on and bossed you up. You were my favorite project. I literally made something out of nothing. I took care of you like a sister. Sometimes I felt like you were my daughter. I guess that's why motherhood is a breeze for me. You already had me prepped for motherhood. There wasn't anything you asked me to do that I didn't do! I guess that wasn't enough for you. It's okay Juju, I still love you. You were my girl, and I could never hate you. Take girl baby girl." Meeka blew a kiss at Justice and walked away. She could feel her heart sinking with every step that she took. The pain she was feeling was deeper than anyone could imagine. Killing Justice was hard, but it needed to be done.

Meeka got into her car, and the tears pushed out. All of her memories with Justice fluttered to her mind. The clubbing days, the laughs, the arguments, and deep conversations seemed like they happened yesterday.

"Why did you have to do this Justice? Right now, I need you more than ever." Meeka softly banged her head against the steering wheel and cried. Bright lights shined on her car and blew the horn. She became nervous, but it was only Hustle and Marlo. Meeka wiped her runny nose and got out of the car. She noticed Pedro was sitting in the back seat and she nodded her head at him.

"Get back into the car Tameeka."

"No," Meeka said. Hustle grabbed her by the arm and slightly pushed her into the car. He took one look at her, and he could tell she was destroyed. Hustle used his sleeve to wipe her nose and kissed her cheek. Meeka pulled away so she could get a better view of what Forty and Marlo was doing. They laughed and joked while they scooped her body from the ground. They tossed her into the empty trunk as if she was a piece of trash. The loud thump made Meeka shake. Forty slammed the trunk and laughed. Marlo reached into his pocket and pulled out a cigarette and a lighter. Even though she was the one who killed Justice, she was beyond pissed at how they treated her body.

"I gotta go I'll see you at home."

Meeka drove home in silence and was covered in blood. It was a long, silent, and painful drive. She could only imagine how they were handling Justice's body. She purposely drove slowly, and she was in pain. She never thought she would have to do something like this to her friend.

Ten minutes later Meeka arrived home and rushed out of her car. She could see Sydney's car was parked behind the house, so that meant she made it home. She felt sick and knew she would be vomiting soon. She walked into her house and found Jamie lying on the couch. Her kids were on one couch, and Jamie held Isabella tightly in her arms. Meeka tried to tiptoe, but she still managed to wake Jamie.

"I'm so sorry," Meeka whispered.

"You're good, but are you just getting back?" Jamie asked.

"Yea, I literally just walked in."

"Did you handle it?" Jamie was a little afraid to ask Meeka that question.

"Yea, it's crazy, and I don't think I have the heart to talk about it."

"Trust me, I don't want any details. Sydney is upstairs in your room. She threw up, twice!"

"Damn, I'm going to check on her in a minute. Thank you so much, Jamie, I owe you one."

"Nah girl, you're good. Every now and then it's nice to lie up in a nice house." She laughed.

"Yea, it is. You know y'all are welcome him anytime. We're family girl and family helps one another. Goodnight." Meeka walked down the hall and ran into Isabella's room. She lay across the bed and cried. Everything that has happened hit her at once. She couldn't believe she killed Justice and left her there. She left her in the middle of the road like she was road kill. Everyone she knew and loved was dying or betraying her. She had to often ask herself who was next. She couldn't take any more pain. She started to think about the shootout on I-10 and her tears transformed into laughter.

"Hhmm, did you ladies know that people with brown or green eyes are hyper and love to laugh?" Santana asked.

"Girl what?" Justice asked.

"Yes, it's a proven fact. They also tend to be quiet at first, but once you get to know them, they never shut up. On top of that, they make AMAZING friends."

"That definitely describes you, Tana. You green-eyed bandit," Justice laughed and gave Santana a kiss on the lips.

"Hell yea, I don't know what I would do without you, Santana." Meeka reached over and gave Santana a kiss on the cheek.

"Aww, you really like me! You guys really like me." He laughed.

"Of course we do. You're the most savage homosexual that I know." Justice said.

"You got that right. They better not let this beat face and handbag fool them. I'm quick to put a fuck nigga on his pockets. Believe and trust that."

Meeka's Desert Eagle 50 Caliber pistol sat oh so pretty on her lap. She constantly checked her watch so she could keep track of time.

"All my muthafuckin memmmmmoooorieeeessss!" Justice shouted and shuffled through her clear makeup bag.

"Aayyeee!" Meeka shouted.

"I-10 shawty," Santana held onto the steering wheel and started to pop his ass.

"BOW!" Meeka chimed in.

"I-10 shawty!" Santana said.

"BOW!" Meeka said.

"BOW! BOW! BOW!" Justice tossed her hands in the air, and everyone laughed.

"I swear you two keep me laughing," Meeka said. Justice reached for a cleaner sponge and blended Santana's highlight and contour.

"Really Santana, do you need to have your face beat for a shootout? Technically it's already beat," Meeka used her jacket to cover her face and laughed.

"Really Meek?"

"I'm sorry baby, too soon?" Meeka asked.

"Uuumm, yea," he said sarcastically and laughed.

"Hey, if Tana wants to be beat for the Gods and Goddess while terrorizing I-10 I'm with that. You know I support anything you do baby." Justice reached for a pair of eyelashes and glue. Santana pulled away and shook his head.

"What's wrong with you? You know you can't have a face full of makeup without eyelashes."

"Yes, I can. You know he doesn't like when I wear eyelashes."

"Uugghh, him? So that's the REAL reason why you're getting all cute?" Meeka said.

"Are you still dealing with him? I thought that was over two weeks ago?" Justice asked.

"Yea when his wife is back at home from her business trip then when she goes back, we're back on."

"I guess Santana. You deserve better than that. You don't need a half of man because a half man can't handle all of you."

"Just like Hustle deserves better than you." He laughed.

"Touché bitch, touché," Meeka cleared her throat and chuckled. She checked her watch again, and it was 4:10 am.

"Y'all, it is 4:10 am. Save all of that shit and let's get ready. We don't have time for the extra shit. We're not chasing these fools all the way to Houston. Especially you, Santana, you know you like to be all extra and shit. You know you can get all carried away during a shot out." Meeka said.

"Uuugghh, we can't even have fun this rip," Santana said.

"We sure can't. Hustle is coming over when he gets back in town. I can't cancel on him. You know he was upset I didn't go to Mississippi with him."

"Okay boss lady," Santana said.

Ten minutes later a 2013 black Infiniti QX50 sped down I-10 left's lane. Henry was robbing his head and listening to the loud music. He had no clue what was about to happen to him, and this would be the last song he would ever listen to. Everyone pulled their ski masks over their faces.

"It is show time baby," Santana started the car and rubbed his hands together. Things like this always made him excited. Without turning his blinkers on, he drove straight into the left lane.

"Santana don't lose him. I'm not in the mood to go to Houston or hear Hustle's mouth."

"I won't lose him," Santana increased the speed from 80 to 90 miles per hour. Meeka knew she needed to focus on what was currently going on, but she couldn't stop checking her phone. If Hustle called, she didn't want to miss it. The closer Santana drove to Henry, Meeka got excited.

"Get his ass, Santana, get him!" Justice shouted.

"Make it quick," Meeka tapped him on the shoulder. She spoke like a sassy Latina and snapped her fingers. Santana grabbed his gun and pressed the button on the door to let his window down. Justice grabbed the steering wheel as Santana hung out of the window. Mike was concentrated on the road he didn't notice the guy in the blonde wig hanging out of the window. The gun was pointed directly at Mike's head and he only going to shoot to kill.

POW! POW! POW!

The bullets glided directly into Henry's ear, temple, and the back of his head.

SSSSCCCCCRRRRRRRRRRRRR!!!!!

His car began to spin out of control.

"Got 'em!" Santana shouted and chuckled. He pulled his wig off and tossed it to Justice. The aggressive winds felt amazing on his skin. He was glad that he didn't put the eyelashes on.

"I feel like I'm in a music video. Take me aaawwaayyy, to beettteerrr daayysss," Santana's singing was horrible, and it made Meeka laughed.

"Girl get in the car," Justice reached over and pulled him into the car.

"Damn, can I have a little fun?"

"What did I tell you about the extra shit," Meeka pushed Santana's head. He flipped his imaginary hair and laughed.

"What did I do?" he asked.

"Take me away my ass," Meeka said.

"I got a pocket, got a pocket full of sunshine. I got a love, and I know that it's all mine. Oh, oh, whoa," Justice sang.

"Do what you want, but you're never going to break me. Sticks and stones are never going to shake me. No, oh whoa!" Santana sang.

Sydney stumbled into the room holding her stomach. She was in Meeka's sweatpants and a t-shirt. That explains why she was in Meeka's room without her permission.

"I needed some clothes Meeka and a bath. I threw up twice, well really three times. The third time I made it to the bathroom. What the hell happened out there?"

"Not right now Syd. My mind is on a hundred, and my stomach is doing flips."

"Excuse me, I just witness you kill our friend! I NEED SOME ANSWERS!"

"Don't you dare call that bitch a friend in my house or in my space when I have a recording of the friend plotting with her brother to take us down the bitch was wearing a wire."

"What?"

"Wendell recorded the whole conversation. It's all there if you want to hear it, but I don't think you should listen to it. It literally made me sick to my stomach Sydney. His exact words were that he wanted us on a silver platter. Not any one of us, not Pedro, Brink, or Hustle!! She wore the wire the day we were eating out!!! The same day Roman calls me with more information!! Just when I thought things couldn't get worse, they did Sydney!!"

"What happened??" Sydney asked.

"Miami left her phone at the gym, and Roman found it. He thought it was his phone. He went through the text messages and saw messaged between Juju and Miami. Miami agreed to work with Juju, she didn't hesitate at all. Justice had a plan for you."

"What was the plan?"

"She was going to get you to work with her. If you didn't agree to it, she was going to kill you." Sydney's eyes grew big, and she gasped.

"What?" She asked.

"You wanted to know what happened, so I told you. Deal with it and move on like me."

"I can't deal right now, this is too much. I'm going to sleep in the guest room with the boys." Sydney ran out if the room and Meeka rolled her eyes.

Hustle tapped on the door and startled Meeka. He slowly walked to her and asked, are you, okay baby?"

"Yea and no. It hurts like hell." Meeka cried harder and ran her fingers through her tangled hair. Hustle kicked his shoes off and climbed into bed with her. The bed was small, but it was big enough for the both to sleep in. He held her tight and rocked her from side to side. He wasn't sure what to say to her.

Chapter 6

Meeka stood in Pedro's neatly cut grass contemplating what to say to him. For the first time in a while, she felt bad because of her actions. She betrayed someone close to her, and she had to watch him grieve firsthand. Her phone was attached to her ear, and she was speaking in a whisper.

"I know he's in there being all dramatic," Meeka said.

"If he only knew the truth he probably would have pulled the trigger himself." Sydney laughed.

"Six shots and nothing less, you know, dumb shit."

"I swear Meek, you came out of nowhere. You were all in the ditch driving. I had never seen anything like that before." Sydney laughed.

"I'm glad Hustle brought that truck. I would have never done that in my Jeep Wrangler."

"I would have killed you if you would have done that. Oh shit, Issac just woke up. Call me when you leave."

"Okay." Meeka disconnected the call and placed her phone into her bra.

She took one more hit of her cigarette and tossed it into the grass. Meeka rang the doorbell and waited for Pedro to come to the door. She could hear him approaching the door, and she started to get nervous. She regretted tossing her cigarette and wanted to search for it in the grass. She scanned the lawn and spotted the cigarette, but Pedro opened the door. The sad look on his face gave Meeka the chills. She was tempted to get in her car and drive off.

"Uhh, hey Dro."

"Hey, Meek, what's up with you?" Pedro leaned against the door and stretched. He was shirtless, but he wore a pair of blue pajama bottoms. Last Christmas Justice purchased the pajama set as one of his Christmas gifts. His bread wasn't neat like it usually is and Meeka could smell a little sour odor coming from his mouth. Crust was in the corners of his eyes. His eyes were red, and the bags under his eyelids were deep.

"Can I come in?" Pedro turned around and motioned for Meeka to come in. She took a glance at his living room and mumbled, "Damn Dro." She closed the door and stood in front of the door.

"What was that Meek?" Pedro asked. He searched for the remote and found it under the pillow. He cleared his cluttered throat and flopped on the couch. Meeka moved the pile of clothes and sat on the suede lazy boy couch.

For minutes, no one said anything. Pedro stared into space and Meeka stared at the carpet. She knew they couldn't sit there and not say anything, so she started to talk.

"It's pretty hot outside. I can't wait until a cold front hits us."

"Yea, that was nice." A defeated look was all over Pedro's face. It seemed like he lost his best friend. Despite the petty arguments and disagreements they had, Pedro and Justice had a solid friendship. They were friends first, then lovers. Pedro was a laid back and a quiet guy. Justice was a wild tender, and he kept her well-rounded majority of the time. She loved how Pedro minded his business, focused on his money, and played everything cool. If you crossed him things could get ugly. Justice always had a thing for Pedro, and she made it known. He couldn't take her seriously because she was so wild and young.

Three years ago, she finally decided to slow down and go with her move. She always joked and said that was the best move she went with.

"How are you feeling today Dro?" Meeka asked.

"I feel…..exactly how I look a hot damn mess and an emotional wreck." Pedro rubbed his head and reached for the remote. He flipped through the channels then he stopped. The show Golden Girls were playing, and for some reason, Pedro loved that show.

"I know the feeling Dro, believe me. The past few months have been hard, and then this shit happens. I don't know what to do and how to move. First Santana then Juju, who is next, me?" Meeka dropped her head and pushed out fake tears. Her long hair draped over her face. She peeked through her hair to see if Pedro was looking and he was. Pedro stood to his feet and walked over to Meeka. He rubbed her shoulder and said, "Don't say that Meek!"

"It's true Pedro, and I'm pretty sure everyone is thinking it. The messed up part is that no one will admit it to me. If I die, what's going to happen to my baby Dro? I love that little girl so much. I love her more than I love myself."

"You don't have to think like that because that won't happen. We just have to play chess and not checkers." Pedro said.

"It's kind of hard to play chess with a cop. Austin isn't going to stop." Meeka wiped her runny nose and shook her head.

"I don't think he will either. It's time to do this Meeka."

"Time to do what?" Meeka played dumb, but she knew what he was talking about. Pedro said.

"Leave the game."

"That's funny Dro. I'm like Jordan right now, I'm in my prime, and you of all people that. You're sounding like Brink right now." Meeka said.

"It doesn't matter who I sound like. It's the truth Meeka. You must end it now so Austin can stop."

"Look, Dro, I didn't come here to talk about this. I wanted to check on you and make sure you're straight." She said.

"Thanks, but I'm not straight. This shit is hard, and I don't know how I'm going to get through it. How could Austin do something like this to his own sister? His own fuckin sister man!! Only a sick muthafucka could do that."

"Over the past few months, Austin has proven to must that he is a sick muthafucka. You have to stay strong Dro, you have to. You can't get caught slipping out here. You're weak right now, and they're preying on the weak."

"I know Meek, you're right. Man, I'm going to miss her so much that was my lil' baby. I love that girl and I always will. Who's going to feel her shoes now?" Pedro nibbled on his bottom lip and turned away. Meeka started to feel bad, but it didn't make her regret killing Justice. Killing Justice was the best thing for all of them. It saved them all from going to prison, including Pedro.

"I understand how you feel Pedro, I do. Both of my best friends are dead. It makes me feel naked and stripped of everything. We shared good times together good and bad. Our memories will last forever and a day. I want to break down and cry, but I have to be strong and figure all of this out."

"Anyone that looks at me crazy will get it. I'm telling you now Meeka. I'm not showing any mercy, fuck all that. I know Austin didn't pull the trigger, but I'm pretty sure he called the hit." Pedro said.

"Know your shooter baby, that's all I can say." Meeka exhaled and rubbed her thigh. Pedro didn't understand her words and that was a good thing.

"That's right you never know who's working with Austin."

"Speaking of Austin, did he come around here to question you?" Meeka asked.

"No, not yet what about you?" Pedro asked.

"Same thing here I'm just waiting for his arrival. The day of the shooting they pick up Sydney for questioning. She was the last person who spoke to Sydney on the phone."

"What about her trap phone? That could break the case big time. She used that phone more than anything." Pedro said.

"I'm not sure if she had it with her. The detectives aren't telling us much. Don't worry about Pedro. When I get any information, you'll be the first to know." Meeka said.

"Thanks, Meek, I appreciate it. I can't sleep at night not knowing anything. I've been popping Lortabs like Skittles."

"Well, hopefully all of this comes to an end soon. You won't have to hope pills, and you can get some rest."

"I have a question, Meek." Meek's eyes slightly grew big, but she didn't panic.

"Of course, what's up?"

"How?"

"How what?" She asked. Now she was starting to panic.

"How do I get over this? How am I supposed to move on? On some shit, when am I supposed to move on without feeling guilty? That girl was my everything man."

"Honestly, Pedro, I'm not sure. I haven't lost anyone like this before. I can tell you pray, and it's going to be okay, but I'm sure you don't want to hear that. In your heart, you'll know when it's time to move on. You'll can always talk to Forty about this. I know you too don't speak much, I'll holla at him for you."

"Thanks, Meek, I appreciate," Pedro said.

"No problem Dro, you know I got you. I'll see you later I have to pick up Isabella. She's at Brink's mom and tonight is Bingo. You already know what that means!" Meeka and Pedro stood to their feet, and she gave him a hug.

"That means come and get Isabella early. Bingo doesn't start until 6:00 pm, but she starts getting ready at noon." Pedro laughed.

"Right, that lady is crazy. Thank God Brink has his father's ways and not hers. Oh, don't worry P, I can let myself out. Go and try to get some rest. I'll call you later and check on you. I fully don't understand what you're feeling, but everything is going to be okay."

"I will Meek, thanks." Meeka smiled and walked out of the house. She deserved an award for the role she played. She got into her car and drove off. She suddenly burst into laughter and called Sydney.

"Hello, what up Meek?"

"I'm leaving from Pedro's house. He has no idea I killed Juju, but he's so hurt." Meeka frowned.

"Forget that Meeka and shake those emotions off. I rather him cry from home than a prison cell."

"That is true Sydney. He said neither Austin nor anyone else has come and question him yet."

"That's a good thing, but when are we going to handle that little situation?"

"At 7:00 pm, that's when Miami goes to work. Once we plant the phone on her, I'm going to call the tip hotline on that ass."

"Then what?" Sydney asked.

"I'm going to kill her, duh." Meeka laughed.

"Of course, the usual when people cross us. I'm not sure about you, but I'm not surprised that Austin got to her." Sydney said.

"Me either, but it still shocks me you know. She and Juju were the two pictures I took out the trenches. You can groom and clean a bitch, but they'll still bite the hand that feeds them." Meeka stopped at the four-way stop sign and sighed. Her head was in a million places, and she wanted to scream. Everything was hitting her at once and spinning out of control. The thought of killing another friend was messing with her.

"It's crazy how people turn on you, but can you blame them Meek? Justice wasn't built for prison, and neither is Miami. That's why they're switching sides on us. Who would put their freedom on the line for a friend?" Sydney said.

"That is true, and people aren't solid anymore. I know I killed her, but I'm hurt. She never had a chance to live her life because of me. She'll never experience marriage, having a career, or motherhood."

"You're not the reason for that, SHE is! She could have told you what Austin was plotting. Then she threatened me to do the same shit AND pulled a gun out on me. That bitch has been a snake in the making if you ask me."

"Maybe so, but I am human, and I have feelings I took her like a sister, and she backstabbed me like this! I swear she cut me to the core Sydney."

"I know Meek, and I'm sorry she you're going through this. I know you don't want to hear this, but Hustle is right. It's time to leave the game."

"Come on Syd, not you and not today with this shit. I don't have the energy for it at all."

"Well, Tameeka you need to find the energy. Shit is getting more real by the day, and you know it. We can't do it anymore Meek, I can't do it anymore!! I'm paranoid as hell, I'm always looking over my shoulders, and I'm always worried about my kids. I fear their father will hurt them just so he can get revenge on me. I'm tired of crying Meeka!! Every day it's something new Tameeka, and I don't know what's going to happen the next day. How can you live like this because I can't? Another state, shit, another country is sounding great right now."

"Please don't say Mexico because that is ssoooooo typical. The police will be waiting for you at the border." Meeka laughed.

"Tameeka it's not funny. None of this shit is funny. Once Philly is killed I have to go, I'm sorry."

"WHAT, YOU CAN'T BE SERIOUS!! Tell me you're in your feelings and talking just to talk!!!! Tell me you're not leaving me Sydney."

"I have to go Tameeka and should consider doing it as well. Think about it, Austin has no concrete evidence on us. I hate to say it, but eventually, he will. He's going to link up with the right person, and it's a wrap. We'll be in the parish serving time while some other bitches are raising our kids. I don't know about you, but I want to see my sons grow up."

"I'll talk to you later Syd, Rocko is calling me." Without letting Sydney finish her sentence, Rocko disconnected the call and answered Rocko's call. It was a lot of noise in the background and she could hardly her Rocko.

"Jupiter, hello?"

"I got him, Meek, I finally got him. He agreed to meet up in a few days. We are on our way to the states!"

"Are you serious?!"

"Yea, it's time to put an end to Philly. I'll see you when we get there."

"We'll meet up at the New Orleans airport and go from there."

Chapter 7

"It's been a long two months, but we're finally here," Rocko said.

"I know, but it's weird as hell. Do you think he's playing stupid and he knows it you? We all know Philly is fucked up in the headache."

"Don't think like that Meek you read the messages. Philly has no clue it's a setup or that it's me. All he saw was a nice ass and breast. He's already telling me that he loves me." Rocko rubbed her head and laughed.

"This town is so boring. I don't understand how people live here." Rocko said.

"They probably say the same thing about Opelousas." Meeka chuckled.

"That is true."

Rocko and Meeka sat comfortably on the hotel bed watching TV and Hustle and Kane were out getting food and probably talking shit together. Tonight was the big day, and everyone was nervous. For Rocko, it felt like the first day of middle school. For Meeka, it felt the day Austin approached her in the club a few months ago.

"I wonder how long those two are going to be?" Rocko grabbed a bottle of lotion and removed the top from the bottle. She poured a small amount into her hand and rubbed it against her legs. She lathered the lotion until he faded and waited for Meeka to respond.

"I'm not sure, but if Meeka comes across a casino, it's a wrap." Meeka laughed.

"I guess he's still addicted to that blackjack table."

"Yea and he's falling in love with playing poker. Before he hated dropping off guns to the Lopez Brothers. Now he loves it, girl. That gives him a reason to slide into Baton Rouge and hit their casino."

"That sounds about right. By the way, how is Pedro doing? I know he's taking it hard."

"He is, but he'll be okay. The love of his life was going to get all of us thrown in jail." Meeka said.

"What about that Miami girl? Did that get handled?" Rocko asked.

"Actually Pedro is handling that. The rumor around town is that Miami had something to do with Juju's death. I told him to go with his move, so he is."

"When we first moved to Opelousas, I had the biggest crush on Pedro. That accent and green eyes can sure drive a girl wild. Once I spotted Kane all of that went out of the window. I'll take Kane's chipped tooth over those green eyes any day." She laughed.

"Trust me, I know the feeling. My ex-boyfriend Roman was perfect! I swear he was literally perfect. I couldn't find one flaw in him, but that didn't make me love him more. I was loving on Hustle when he had the gap teeth." Meeka laughed.

"Hey, that's true love."

"It really is he's my baby."

"So why not leave the game, Meek? Give them want he wants. He's rare you find a man like him. Most of these niggas want to sell drugs forever, but not him. He's not perfect, but he's damn sure different. Don't lose him because of this bullshit because it won't last forever."

"So now you have all the answers. I'm usually the one giving you advice." Meeka stood to her feet and walked to the bathroom. She was tired of everybody telling her she needed to leave the game. Meeka knew she had to listen to Rocko since they were stuck in the room together.

Meeka stared at herself in the mirror and adjusted her bangs. Rocko walked into the bathroom and leaned against the door. Meeka rolled her eyes, and she knew Rocko had more to say.

"I swear Meek, the time Kane and I were separated it felt like I was in hell. I didn't know what country or state he was in. I didn't know if he was dead or alive. I didn't know if he was poor, homeless, or anything! Every second I was thinking about him. I felt alone, I felt miserable, and I felt weak. I experience pregnancy and birth without him. I use to dream about this shit, but he was always in the dream with me. That shit tore my heart into micro pieces. Every day I watched my daughter grow up without him. Don't be stupid, you're smarter than this. Don't let this bullshit be the reason you lose Brink. He loves you so much, and everyone knows it. The way he walks talks, and even breaths says he loves you."

"I'm scared to love Rocko. I really don't know how to give him my all. I love him with all my heart, but it's confusing at times. I've been through too much to sit back and be a hopeless romantic. If I ever find out Hustle is cheating on me, I'll kill him. I swear to God I would do it with my bare hands."

"Girl you are crazy for real. I'll never forget the day Kane, and I reunited. Kennedy and I were in the grocery store. I'll never forget it, I was on aisle three."

Rocko browsed through the variety of chips. She grabbed four bags and dropped them in the shopping cart.

Kenn-Kenn, do you want chips?" Rocko smiled and asked Kennedy. Kennedy only smiled back Rocko wasn't looking for an answer in return.

"I'll take that as a yes." Rocko grabbed another bag of chips and handed it to Kennedy. Kennedy wrestled with the bag, but she couldn't open it. Rocko laughed. The faces Kennedy was making, she looked exactly like Kane.

"Little girl, you are really your father's twin. Look at you, you are so beautiful." Rocko gave Kennedy a kiss on the cheek and continued walking. For some reason, she could feel someone staring at her. She turned around, but no one was there, so she continued walking and stopped in front of the milk. She wasn't sure what kind of milk she wanted to purchase since Kennedy's stomach wasn't tolerating soy milk.

"Kenn-Kenn, I think we should try 2 percent milk for that little tummy of yours."

"I need a thug in my life, and you ain't gotta be my life. Just hold me down when it's tight."

"What the hell?" Rocko turned around and searched the store for the person who was singing. She didn't find anyone, but she thought it was funny how someone was singing that song. It brought back memories of her and Kane when they were younger. She instantly became sad and was ready to go home.

"Let's go home baby girl. We can listen to mommy and daddy's song." Rocko turned around and screamed. Kane was standing toe to toe with her with a huge smile on his face. He looked more mature but better than ever.

"NO, this can't be! I must be dreaming." Rocko slowly placed her hands on Kane's face. Touching his smooth back made her jump back. She couldn't believe it was actually Kane. He smiled and kissed her hand. He stared at her ring finger, and his smile grew bigger.

"You're not dreaming baby. It's big baby in the flesh." He laughed.

"Oh my God, Kane, how? This can't be real, this can't be real this cannot be real!!!" Rocko whimpered and pulled Kane closer to her. She held him so tight that she could feel his rib cage. She could tell he was uncomfortable, but she didn't want to let him go.

"It's real, I'm here baby. It's all of me, right here."

"Kane, how did you get lost? We were supposed to meet up in Vegas."

"I was getting on my flight, and someone recognized me. I took off running and was hiding for three days. I had to catch whatever flight I could."

"Baby where were you?" Rocko asked.

"First I was in Cancun, and then I was in P.R. For some reason I couldn't remember what place you always talked about. Then it hit me, Bora, Bora. I left everything behind and came here. It took a while, but I finally found you. Man girl, I missed you. I'm sorry I put you through all this Diana. I swear, I thought about you all day. It drove me crazy, and I was ready to kill myself. I thought you moved on and was in love with someone else. The thought of you with another man messed my head up."

"My sisters told me I needed to move on, but I couldn't. Every day I wrote you a letter and sent them to random addresses. I know it would stupid, but I thought maybe someone knew you. Maybe they would have given you the letter."

"It wasn't stupid Diana. I would have done the same thing. Everywhere I went I looked for you. I showed people your picture, but no one knew you."

"Umm, it's no longer Diana, its Jupiter," Rocko said.

"Jupiter, what kind of stupid name is that?" Kane asked and laughed.

"I don't know, but it was the first thing that came to mind. I thought you were dead. I'm raising her without you." With wide eyes, Kane glanced at Kennedy then he glanced at Rocko.

"Diana, this little girl looks a lot like me were you-" Rocko shook her head and started to cry.

"Her name is Kennedy, and she's your daughter. Well, she's our daughter Kane."

"What, we have a daughter? Are you serious?"

"Yes, I'm very serious." Just as Rocko continued her story, her phone rang. She rushed into the room, and it was Philly. She waved for Meeka to come in the room and she did.

"Answer it!" Meeka shouted. Rocko answered the phone and placed it on speaker.

"Hello?" She said in a soft voice.

"What's up beautiful, I'm headed to the restaurant," Philly said.

"Okay, I'll see you in ten minutes."

"Bet." Rocko disconnected the phone. Her heart started to race.

"It's on now Meek. Let's get this shit popping."

Rocko slipped into her dress and pulled her bonnet off her head. She gave herself one look in the mirror and blew herself a kiss. She looked damn good for a killer.

"I'm going to text the guys and let them know what's up." Meeka pulled her phone out and called Hustle. Her hands were shaking, and she could barely hold the phone in her hand.

"Baby, it's time we're going to the restaurant."

Chapter 8

Meeka and Rocko sat in the car anxiously waiting for Philly to arrive. Rocko thought she was nervous, but she could hear Meeka's hurt beating loudly.

"Meek, are you okay?" She asked.

"Huh?" Meeka asked, but she continued to stare out of the window. Rocko could tell Meeka's mind was in another place. Nothing could break her concentration.

"I asked are you okay? I can hear your hearting from here girl." Rocko placed her hand over Meeka's heart and could feel it pounding.

"Oh, yea Rock, I'm good. What about you? Are you ready for this and to sit across the table looking at Philly's ugly ass?" Meeka laughed and scanned the parking lot with her eyes. She wanted to spot Philly before he spotted them.

Meeka sat lower in her seat and pulled her hood lower over her face.

"I'm good, but I can't wait to reveal who I am. He's going to shit on himself." She laughed and tapped against the window.

"It's going to be a sight to see." Meeka laughed.

"Look Meeka, he's pulling up." Meeka sat lower in the seat so Philly couldn't see her.

"Get out." She whispered to Rocko.

"Okay, okay." Rocko pulled her dress a little and got out of the car. She walked to Philly with a smile on her face. He rushed to get out of the car and grabbed Rocko. He kissed her lips several times, and she was disgusted, his breath smelled like cigarettes and cheap liquor.

He wore an oversized black t-shirt and a pair of Wranglers jeans. His black Air Force Ones were dirty and looked worn out. She was not pleased with his appearance.

"Hey, handsome,"

"Hello, sexy,"

Rocko and Philly walked into the Red Lobster restaurant holding hands. Her red leather dress and six-inch black heels made everyone stare at her. Men were getting a hard-on while their wives and girlfriends were feeling uncomfortable.

"It's a little chilly in here. Do you want me to run and get my jacket out of the car?" He asked.

"No thank you, I'm fine." She said.

She was shocked at how he was a gentleman, but she wasn't fooled. Philly pointed to the first table he saw, and they walked to the table. Philly wasn't going to wait for anyone to sit them. He pulled her chair out and helped Rocko sit down.

"Damn all eyes are on you I see. You do look good though, I don't blame them for staring." Philly laughed.

"Thank you."

"You're welcomed beautiful you look nice too." Rocko lied.

"Thank you, I brought this shirt just for our date." Rocko wanted to laugh. Instead, she rubbed his arm.

A man who seemed to be in early thirties came to the table. He held a notepad in his hand and had a frown on his face. Rocko could tell he was going to be a problem.

"Hi, I'm Todd, and I'll be your waiter. Can I start you two off with drinks?"

"I'll take a Coke, what about you baby?" Rocko asked.

"I'll take water with lemon." Philly smiled at Rocko. She started to blush and turned away.

"Okay, I'll be back with your drinks. Here are your menus." Todd dropped each menu in front of them and walked away. Rocko used her leg to rub against Philly's thigh and bit her bottom lip. He smiled and laughed. She could feel his penis getting hard. She couldn't believe she was rubbing against the penis he fucked Santana with.

"You are a naughty girl." He grinned.

"Yea I am, and you like it." Philly and Kane stared at the menus in silent. She was nervous and thinking about all kinds of crazy things.

"I was thinking, after this, we should do something," Philly said.

"Do something like what? Go back to your place?" Rocko pulled her hair back and pushed her breast out. She wanted Philly to get a better view of her breast. Philly's eyes were glued to him, he was in love.

"Yea, I want to explore those breasts of yours. I love a woman with big breast." He smirked.

"Well get ready to love all over me. I'm a 36 double D." Rocko grabbed Philly's hands and placed them on her breast. She caressed and squeezed breast and stomped his foot. His sexual facial expressions told her all she needed to know. Philly was clueless to who she was and cared about her appearance.

"Damn girl, I'm going to tear you up." He shook his head and pulled away." Todd came back to the table and placed the drinks in front of them, and Rocko fumbled into her purse and secretly pulled the Rohypnol pill out.

"Are y'all ready to order?" He asked.

"No, can you give us a few more minutes?" Philly asked.

"Sure, I'll be back." Todd rolled his eyes and walked away. While Philly wasn't looking, she quickly dropped the pill into his drink.

"We don't need dessert because I'm sweet like candy." She laughed.

"Can I have seconds?" He asked.

"You can whatever you like baby." Rocko was gasing Philly so much, it was crazy. She knew Meeka was listening on the earpiece and laughing.

"So, I saw on your profile you're from Arizona," Rocko asked as she flipped through the menu.

"Yea, born and raised," Philly said.

"That's crazy." Rocko took a sip of her drink and batted her eyes. She could hear Meek in her ear laughing and making jokes.

"Ask him if he was fucking Tana or if Tana was fucking him!" Meeka laughed. Rocko cleared her throat and crossed her legs. She was trying her best not to laugh.

"What's crazy?"

"You have a Louisiana accent, but you aren't from here," Rocko said.

"Oh, well I spend a lot of time in Louisiana basically every summer and the holidays with my dad. Before I knew it, I sound like I was from Baton Rouge."

"225, dumb shit." She laughed.

"Hell yea, but enough about me. Tell me more about you. I'm all ears." Philly reached for his drink and took a few sips. For a second she thought Philly was a good guy, but an image of Melissa's cold body appeared in her head.

"Hhmm, let's see, I'll be returning to school in the fall to finish my degree."

"Oh really, what school were you attending?" Philly asked.

"I was attending UL in Lafayette for professional writing. My dream is to own my own magazine company. I want to build something like the magazine *Sixteen*. You're a guy, so I'm sure you're not familiar with it." She laughed.

"Uuuhhh, don't judge a book by its cover. I pick up that magazine from time to time in the supermarket."

"Hey, I'm not judging you." She said.

"Philly is playing a damn good role. Don't you fall for that shit Rocko!!"

"I won't." She whispered.

"What was that?" Philly asked.

"Huh?"

"It sounds like you said something."

"Uh, yea I did. I asked when are you going back to Arizona?"

"Maybe next Tuesday, but I'm not sure yet."

For an hour and thirty minutes, Philly and Rocko talked and ate. They basically told one another numerous lies to keep the conversation going. His conversation was terrible, and she couldn't understand how Santana was interested in him.

"How was your food?" Philly asked as he wiped his mouth.

"Everything was delicious. I think we should do this again." Rocko smiled.

"We will, I'm always free for you."

Philly repeatedly rubbed his eyes and yawned. She could tell the pill was starting to work.

"For years you damaged our lives, you're the only person I hate."

"Huh?" Philly raised his head and asked.

"Didn't you hear what I said? For years you damaged our lives, you're the only person I hate. The way you killed Kane's family members was brutal. Tonight you're going to feel the pain we all felt."

"Wait who are you?" Philly tried to squint his eyes, but he rubbed them instead. He was feeling drowsy and antsy.

"It's Rocko, I'm sure you remember me." She laughed.

"Rocko?"

"Yea nigga Diana, Kane's girlfriend," she said.

"What the fuck, it can't be you."

"Yea, it is and don't think about running. The pill I slipped in your drink will have you feeling good!" Rocko said.

Philly ran out of the restaurant, but he stumbled majority of the way outside. Rocko laughed and walked behind him. Several people stared at Philly as if he was crazy.

"I'm sorry, my boyfriend is drunk." Rocko smiled and waved as she walked out of the restaurant. Philly's pill fully kicked in, and he couldn't function. He tried to run, but he fell. Meeka got out the car and laughed. She stood over Philly and said, "Surprise bitch, it's me!"

"Tameeka?" He asked, but his speech was slow.

"Duh, it sure isn't Santana Clause. Rock, help me get him in the car."

***

"Leave the car running, we can't waste any time," Meeka said and got out of the car. Philly was still sleeping even though they were pulling on his body. Rocko climbed to the back seat and used her feet to push Philly's body out of the car. Meeka struggled trying to pull him out, but she still managed to.

"Hold him against the truck. I'll come around and help you." Rocko said as she got out. Meeka pinned Philly against the truck and said, "Okay, but hurry." Rocko shook her head and ran around the truck. Meeka was struggling to keep him against the truck. She was disgusted by the drool that was falling out of his mouth.

"Eww, he's saliva smells like ass." She laughed.

"I can imagine." Rocko tossed Philly's arm around her shoulder and did Meeka. They slowly walked towards the house, but they were getting tired already.

"Man, he is heavy," Rocko grunted. Philly's dead weight was killing her shoulders and back.

"I know, someone is eating good this nigga weighs a ton!"

Meeka and Rocko struggled bragging Philly into the house. It felt like they were trying to drag a bag of bricks into the house. Rocko was hot and aggravated. The plastic trash bags they wore over their clothing didn't make her feel any better.

Rocko and Meeka approached the house and exhaled. The little house was basically falling apart and was sitting in the middle of high chairs. They could tell no one lived in the house for years and maybe even decades.

"I swear Meek, it feels like I'm walking down Plank Road with a human on my back." Rocko laughed and wiped her sweaty forehead. Meeka laughed and said, "Plus Lobdell, the car is literally like three feet away." Meeka heavy breathing only made her mouth dry. Right about now she needed a gallon of ice cold water.

She fully stretched her leg out and kicked the door open. Dust flew everywhere causing Meeka and Rocko to cough.

"What the hell?" Rocko waved the dust away and rubbed her eyes. Meeka scanned the living room and found a chair in the wall. She used her head to point at the chair and said, "Rocko I'm going to need you to hold him against the wall. We can tie him to that chair. Get the rope out."

"Okay." Meeka slowly released the part of Philly's body and Rocko held him against the wall. Her arms instantly began to shake. His wide body was no match for her arms.

Meeka ran across the room and grabbed the chair. She quickly ran back to Rocko and grabbed a portion of Philly. She carefully placed him in the chair, and Rocko immediately started to tie the rope around his body. There was no way Philly could run away.

"WAKE UP MOTHERFUCKA!" Rocko shouted. Rocko and Meeka sat in the other wooden chairs staring at Philly. It was 2:45 am, and the wind was blowing heavily. Rocko felt like she was on top of the world. After trying to kill Philly on several different occasions, he was finally captured.

He tried to raise his head, but he was dizzy. His black eye was dripping a clear liquid and getting swollen by the second. He still managed to open one.

His bottom lip was split wide open. You could see the white meat showing. Rocko didn't care how bad he looked. Her eyes were glued to him, and he had all her attention. It was kind of awkward to be in his presence and staring him in the eye. She felt like she was finally facing her issues head-on.

"I swear, I never saw this day coming. You gave me nightmares. When I thought about you, I would get sick for days. If I looked in the sand or ocean for too long, I would see your ugly little face. What you took from Kane I, I will hate you forever. All of this started because of you! You always gave me bad vibes. I wish we would have never got into that car when you. One wrong move damaged our lives forever!!" Rocko stared at Philly with a disgusted look on her face. His head was spinning, but he still managed to laugh. It made Rocko furious, and her blood started to boil. She jumped to her feet and slammed the muzzle of the gun into his chin. Blood splattered everywhere, and a piece of his chin fell to the floor. Seeing a piece of human flesh on the floor made Rocko's stomach weak. Rocko held her stomach and tossed her finger in the air. She hadn't seen a dead body in years or this much of blood.

"I'll be right back Meek." She said and rushed out of the house. Meeka followed Rocko with her eyes and said, "Unlike her, seeing your shit busted open doesn't bother me. I've seen way worse than this. Anywho, you and I, we're going to have a nice little chit-chat.

"Oh, we are?" He asked.

"Yea, we are Philly." She said.

"I ain't saying shit." Philly spit out a large amount of warm blood and laughed.

Meeka glanced at the blood on the floor and laughed with Philly. Meeka sat closer to him and sat with her legs wide open. The smell of blood lingered heavily in the air. Meeka thought the odor was stay on her clothes.

"You're going to talk, trust me, Philly."

"If not, what the fuck are you going to do with me? You're going to kill me? I've seen everything besides death."

"You and me both, do you want a cookie? I am going to kill you though. Since I'm a good person, I'm going to let you choose how you what to die." Meeka laughed.

"You can die a slow and painful death if you don't tell me what happened. Or you take one shot to the head if you tell me the truth. My aim is perfect, so I know exactly where to shoot you."

"Why should I tell you what happened it doesn't make a difference I'm going die anyway, but I'm taking what happened to my grave."

"That's true, but let me tell you something else. You have caused sooooo much pain and heartache. You don't know the half of it. So many people want your head, it's ridiculous. We both can agree that you will not be missed. Your mom in California left you behind for a person, and the rest of your family don't even know you exist. Your dad is on some island now on vacation with his new family. He doesn't give a fuck about you either. No one in your family cares about you because of all the pain you have caused. We can also agree that you are better dead than alive." Philly's wide smile slowly faded away and became a frown. Meeka was ready to gloat, but she didn't. She knew talking about his family would break him down.

Rocko walked into the house and stood by the door. Meeka signaled for Rocko to stay at the door. She shook her head and placed her hands on her hips.

"I didn't want to kill him, but I know you don't believe me. I'm not sure if it was the drugs or if I like him. I can't lie and say I was hurt that I killed him. I've have been knowing Kane's family for years, but I didn't think twice about killing his sisters and grandparents. Since you want to know the truth, I'll tell you;

Santana arrived in Scottdale, Arizona with a huge smile on his face. It's been a month since he had seen Philly and he was missing him like crazy. It took him two hours to get dressed because he wanted to look perfect for Philly. His crimson red wig was parted down the middle and was bone straight. His nighttime makeup made his face seem slim, and his all-black dress exposed his figure.

Santana sped walk down the hotel halls searching for Philly's room. When he realized he was standing in front of room 202, he became more excited. He knocked on the door twice and waited for Philly to answer.

"Who is it?" Philly asked.

"It's Santana, open the door."

A few seconds later the door swung open. Santana stood with his arms out and a huge smile on his face. Philly nodded his head and sat on the bed. He didn't seem too happy to see Santana.

"What's wrong with you?" Santana asked. He walked into the room and closed the door. Santana was flaunting his new hair around, but Philly ignored him.

"Nothing, I'm just tired." Philly rubbed his ashy face and laid across the bed. The hotel room was full of empty pizza, dirty clothes, and crushed beer cans. The hotel room was so dirty Santana didn't want to sit on the bed.

"Are you sure? You seem a little….off." He said. Philly barely made eye contact with Santana when he spoke. Philly didn't want to admit it, but Santana could sense that something was wrong it seemed like he was high and in a daze.

"I said I'm good. How was your flight?" Philly asked.

"Besides the woman sneezing the entire time and the crying baby, it was okay." He giggled.

"Oh, okay, let's go and get something to eat. I'm starving, and I'm pretty sure you are too."

"Yea that's cool. Do you want me to drive? You seem tired."

"I'm not tired. I'm not on any drugs today, and I'm sober."

"Baby how is your auntie?" He asked.

"Baby, now, call me by my name. She's doing well, thanks for asking." Santana walked side by side with Philly quietly. He tried to hold his hand, but he means mugged him and pulled away.

"What are you doing?" He asked.

"Nothing, I was trying to hold your hand."

"Why?" Philly asked.

"Because I always hold your hand, what the hell is your problem today?"

"Nothing is my problem. Just stop all of that gay shit!" Philly shouted. His loud outburst startled Santana and the front desk worker. He was a little embarrassed, so he gave her a fake wave. She smiled back and walked away from the desk.

This was Santana's first time seeing Philly act in this manner and he was a little hurt. He was usually a nice, caring, and affectionate person.

Philly pointed to a red 2008 red Jeep Cherokee and said, "That's our ride right there."

"Okay." Santana and Philly got into the Jeep and drove through the empty hotel parking lot. Philly pointed left, so Santana turned left and drove down the road. It was dark and a little creepy. The awkward silence between them was bothering him, so he began to talk.

"I've been keeping my ears close to the streets like you said. No one is linking you to the robbery. Miami heard they picked up some guy from Eunice for questioning."

"Oh, that's what's up. I wasn't worried anyway."

"Good, that means you can come back home. I've been missing you like crazy." Santana smiled.

"I'll think about it, but I highly doubt it." Philly yawned loudly and covered his mouth. Santana made a left turn and asked, "What's to think about?"

"Maybe I don't want to go back home ain't shit there, but thots, trouble, and potholes."

"You should know. You're the one fucking the thots and causing the trouble." Santana laughed, and it made Philly angry. Philly raised his right hand and slapped Santana across the face.

BAM!

Santana slammed his foot on the brakes and held his warm cheek. He caught his breath and pulled off.

He was shocked that Philly hit him. He was puzzled and wasn't sure how to handle Philly's attitude.

"Don't ever say some stupid shit like that again! If you do, it's going to be way worse than a slap across the face."

"Ba-ba- baby I'm sorry. I was only joking with you, and you know that."

"What the hell did I tell you about calling me that dumb shit!" Philly slammed his hand against the airbag and shouted. His loud shouting made Santana serve to the shoulder of the road. He quickly regained control of the wheel and made his way back onto the road. Philly pulled his gun out and buried the muzzle into Santana's stomach. Santana gasped and asked, "Philly, what are you doing?"

"What does it look like I'm doing? It's time for you to go!"

"Go where? Philly please-"

"Philly please what?" He laughed.

"Philly please don't kill me. I'm literally begging you. I- I- I'll get in the middle of the road and beg you."

"Get out of the car, NOW." Without replying, Santana got out of the car. His legs felt numb, and he could feel butterflies in his stomach. For a moment, he thought about running, but he changed his mind. He knew Philly would gun him down and leave him in the middle of the road like road kill.

"WALK!" Philly shouted and hit Santana in the head with the gun. He staggered to the ground, but he managed to regain his balance. As he walked in the middle of the road, Philly shot Santana in the back.

"UUUUGGGGHHHHHHHHH!" he moaned.

Santana begged for his life, but Philly didn't care. He continued to send shots into Santana's body. Once again, Philly took another body, and he wasn't bothered by it. Santana's body hit the ground, and Philly ran the other way. He jumped into the Jeep and drove off. He rolled over Santana's body and laughed.

"That nigga is still wearing that purse."

"No, no, no!" Rocko's hand and lips trembled.

Meeka and Rocko gasped. Hearing how Santana was killed made Meeka light headed. She wanted to break down and cry, but she had a job to do.

"I killed him because I was hired to. Not because he was gay. I don't know who made that dumb rumor. He told me if I did it he would clear my criminal record of everything. It didn't matter what I did in the streets, he would get me out of it."

"Who is he?" Rocko asked.

"Maybe I'm gay, shit, I don't know. It doesn't matter to me. As we all can see, I don't have nothing to lose or to gain." He chuckled.

"What? Who paid you to kill him?" Meeka shouted through a tight mouth. Philly laughed and spit blood out of his mouth. His mouth was running like a faucet. She poked his face with the gun and waited for him to give her an answer.

"Who do you think, Tameeka? You're on the top of HIS hit list."

"Austin?" Meeka asked. She could feel her heart starting to race, and she was becoming nervous. He's been plotting against you for a while now. He's been jealous of the relationship between you and Sydney. He knew by killing someone close to you would break you. That's why he chose Santana."

POW! POW!

Meeka let two bullets go, and they entered his chest. His body and the chair fell backward and he hit the dusty floor. Rocko was ready to throw up, but she held herself together. Rocko ran to Meeka's side and asked, "Is he dead?"

"If this nigga took two bullets to the chest and isn't dead, I'm killing myself." Meeka raised her gun to Philly's head and let four shots go. Pieces of his head started to fly off.

Rocko didn't care that Philly's head was blown off. She continued to shoot until his head was completely blown off. She cried and sobbed, she felt like she was finally free. Apart of her past that she hated so much finally vanished.

"Okay Rock, that's enough. Let's get the hell out of here!" Meeka snatched the gun out of Rocko's hand and pulled her by the arm. They ran out of the house, and no one looked back. Philly was finally dead.

They ran outside and got into the car. The car was still running so they sped off. Meeka tried her best to control how her hands were shaking, but she couldn't. She swerved from left to right trying to get out of the high grass.

Her heart was pounding so loud, she thought Rocko could hear it.

"Rocko, call Brink and tell me what's up," Meeka said.

"Okay." Rocko quickly dialed Hustle's number and waited for him to answer. On the first ring, he answered and said, "What's up?"

"The plan went through, and we're leaving now," Rocko said.

"Okay, we're on our way." Hustle said and disconnected the call. Rocko closed her eyes and rest her head against the window.

"Meeka, I feel free now, he's dead, Philly is finally dead!" Rocko shouted and clapped her hands.

"Yea, he's finally dead. Rest in Peace, Philly, you won't be missed."

Are you ready for part 3? It's the finale!

CPSIA information can be obtained
at www.ICGtesting.com
Printed in the USA
BVHW042249250321
603492BV00002B/7

It's Up To Us!
a brief guide to
community leadership

Tom O'Connell

with contributions by Colleen Callahan

It's Up To Us!
a brief guide to community leadership
by Tom O'Connell

Graphic concepts and content contributions by Colleen Callahan.

Layout and design by Wendy J. Johnson of Elder Eye Press – a design and concierge publishing house dedicated to designing with the best design practices for legibility and clarity, to benefit all eyes, of all ages.

First Edition

O'Connell, Tom G.
It's Up To Us! A brief guide to community leadership / by Tom O'Connell

ISBN–13: 978-1984167927 (alk. paper)
ISBN–10: 1984167928 (alk. paper)

Elder Eye Press, PO Box 142, Crystal Bay, MN 55323 USA
www.ElderEye.com

Manufactured in the United States of America by the CreateSpace Independent Publishing Platform.

Dedication

To Becky, Artist, Leader,
my Love and Foundation.

Acknowledgements

This may be a brief book, but I owe a village full of people for getting me to the finish line. My students in the Community Leadership Theory Seminar at Metropolitan State University were the inspiration for the book in the first place. Colleagues Dave Mann, Sandy Heidemann, and Marcia Avner—all community leaders in their own right—reviewed the manuscript and made helpful suggestions. Thanks as well to my friend and copy editor, Richard Steven, and my co-teacher, Colleen Callahan, who assisted and persisted on this project from the beginning. Colleen's help and gentle insistence made this book possible. Finally, to Wendy Johnson of Elder Eye Press, thank you for converting my scribbles into book form. I learned so much from you about the brave new world of custom publishing. Let's do another book soon!

Contents

Introduction

This is a book for people who are leaders, whether they call themselves that or not.** It is for people who are already making a difference in their communities, or aspiring to make a difference. It is for the humble ("What me, I'm not really a leader"), for those who could use a little humbling ("I already know all there is to know about leadership"), and most of us who are in between.

The core idea is simple: leadership is an activity not a position. It happens when people gather to take action on shared goals and values. You don't have to be a "big shot" or have a fancy title to be a leader. Leaders come in all personality types: extrovert, introvert, soft hearted, and hard headed.

My perspective on leadership was shaped by personal experience as a leader and participant in a variety of community organizations and public campaigns. I have drawn on and deepened this experience through my work teaching community leadership at Metropolitan State University, a school that serves working adults from the Minneapolis–St. Paul area.

My approach to teaching leadership is built on the Greek notion of Praxis: the integration of experience with theory. Good theory depends on rich experience—experience that is expressed through stories; the ones we tell ourselves and share with others.

My focus here is on community leadership. Just as there are almost as many definitions of leadership as there are leaders, community itself is an elastic concept. For me, the term "community" relates closely to the concept of civil society; that space between government and the market where people come together to act on shared interests and values. Community leadership takes place in neighborhoods, churches, clubs, nonprofits, and social action groups. It takes place in organizations large and small; in groups that have enough money to hire staff and in those that are all volunteer.

I do not approach community leadership as a political neutral. Many of the stories I share come from a broad commitment to social justice. I understand that readers will have differing ideas of exactly what social justice means. Good! Whatever your starting point, reflective leaders develop the capacity to refine, revise, and reconsider their own values over time. The leaders I most admire, not only understand how to get things done, but are willing to assess the social and moral consequences of what is done.

This is a short book. I have tried to distill a limited set of concepts that can be useful both in real time and as points of reflection over time. I have also written it as an invitation. Democracy is more than elections, legislation, and political debates. A strong democracy depends on active citizens, coming together in neighborhoods, churches, workplaces, and service organizations. Whether you chair the fund raising committee of your neighborhood association, help organize volunteers at the local food shelf, educate your neighbors about climate change, or lobby for criminal justice reform, you are engaged in community leadership.

So get on board. The ride can be bumpy, but the view is great; and discoveries—about yourself and your community—are guaranteed!

❦

Chapter 1
Community Leadership:
Key Concepts and Dimensions

There are dozens of definitions of leadership. Many have important things to say about what being a leader really means. But the definition I find most helpful comes from the author and social commentator, Garry Wills:

> *The leader is one who mobilizes others toward a goal shared by both leaders and followers.... Leaders, followers, and goals make up the three equally necessary components of leadership.*

This definition is elegant in its simplicity, yet comprehensive enough to include all the critical elements in real world leadership. Leadership happens when there are one or more leaders, a band (large or small) of followers and a goal embraced by both leader and follower.

This definition is also especially helpful when we consider community leadership. Community leadership often takes place in voluntary associations. Members are not coerced to join. They cannot be fired if they refuse to go along with the group. Community leaders must bring people together around the shared motivation to tackle common problems or advance common agendas. That doesn't mean *all* community leadership must take place in voluntary groups. It does mean that the stronger the relationship between leader, follower, and shared goals, the more powerful the leadership.

Here it is important to distinguish between leadership as activity and leadership as position. Positional leadership is about titles and rank. Examples include the grade school principal, bank president, director of the local social service agency, and bishop. Think of the people you know in positions like these. How many of them actually engage their employees, clients, congregants, and customers in common action toward shared goals? How many would have followers at all if it weren't for the coercive power inherent in their position? It is very possible to have a position AND be a leader in the sense of the definition we are exploring here. However, not everyone who has a leadership title actually leads.

And what about followers? Isn't the term itself a little demeaning? Aren't followers by definition passive, unwilling, or unable to take initiative? First, there can be no leadership without followership. For example, mounting a one-person campaign to renew your local neighborhood is hardly an act of effective leadership. If we think of followers as participants rather than mindless automatons, we can get closer to the true meaning of an effective leader/follower relationship.

Second, in dynamic organizations and groups, the leader/follower relationship is constantly shifting. In one context, I may be the leader—in another, the follower. A former student of mine, Andy Driscoll, started a nonprofit public affairs media organization called Civic Media. Every Monday morning he produced and hosted an interview show on local community radio. In his role as leader, he convened an informed and creative cast of on-air guests, recruited volunteers to run the control board, and inspired people who shared his interest in community media to join the organization. In all these roles, Andy personified leadership. He had a passion. He attracted others who shared his passion; and together they created a weekly radio program and audio documentaries. Yet, Andy was not the leader in

> "Not many of us will be leaders; and even those who are leaders must also be followers much of the time. This is the crucial role. Followers judge leaders. Only if the leaders pass that test do they have any impact. If the leader takes his or her followers to the goal, to great achievements, it is because the followers were capable of that kind of response." – *Garry Wills*

all aspects of the organization. Others convened the nonprofit board and committees, raised money to maintain Civic Media's website, and lined up support for new public affairs initiatives. There would be no Civic Media without Andy. But the reach, impact, and sustainability of this spunky community media outfit would be severely impaired without the leadership of others in the organization as well.

In many of the strongest community organizations, the leadership/ followership dichotomy is modified by a leadership team approach— or what people in leadership studies refer to as *distributive leadership*. Notice the "ship" in leadership. The captain has an essential role to play, but acts of leadership throughout the crew are necessary to keep the ship afloat. Back on land, when I ask students to list the characteristics of effective leaders, the adjectives come tumbling out:

- Visionary
- Decisive
- Strategic
- Principled

- Persuasive
- Fair-minded
- Motivating
- Courageous

- Good Listener
- Organized
- Results oriented

The sheer length and substance of this list make the case for a shared approach to leadership. Leadership traits are not evenly distributed and certainly no single leader can possibly possess them all. I am a good listener and talented strategic planner. I am also indecisive and, at times, fail to follow through on commitments. You may be a powerful speaker but less mindful of supporting the growth of the very people you have inspired. Effective followers, joined as they are by a common purpose, take up the call as time, potential, and life circumstance allow. In strong organizations and communities, the leader/follower relationship looks much more like a continuum than a chasm—and a dynamic and shifting continuum at that!

Community Leaders: Some Key Characteristics

None of us possess all the qualities of successful leaders—at least not in equal proportions. However, I do believe that there are four qualities that characterize strong community leaders. First, effective community leaders are **reflective.** They work hard at getting to know themselves and the groups they are leading. This means being open to self-criticism as well as the feedback of others. Really good community leaders learn how to lead by leading and then reflecting on the experience. They understand that, without honest reflection, learning from experience can't happen.

Second, effective community leaders are **active.** Leadership is something people **do.** You would think this would go without saying. But actually, many people in community leadership positions do very little. Unfortunately, because we often mistake a leadership position for actual leadership activity, the real leaders may get overlooked.

Take the example of Sage Holben, a resident of the Dayton's Bluff neighborhood where my institution, Metropolitan State University, is located. Sage participates in a variety of community organizations *and* she builds community every day through the weekly films she shows in her backyard during the warm summer evenings, the mini-book lending library she organized with friends, and the simple act of getting to know her neighbors and then introducing them to each other.

Sage doesn't do these things alone. She involves others. But the way she involves others is *through* the doing. As they used to say in the Civil Rights movement, *she walks her talk.* Seeing leadership as an activity, reminds us to broaden our gaze when we are looking for leaders. Informal leaders (leaders without titles) weave communities and organizations together.

In addition to being reflective and active, powerful community leaders are motivated by deeply-held **social values.** Some are very clear about what those values are. They can articulate them clearly and are conscious of the relationship between what they do and what they believe. Others hold their social values less consciously. An important characteristic of effective community leadership is an understanding of the values that motivate us as leaders and the organizations in which we participate. In evaluating our own and other's leadership, it is important to ask both if the leader is helping the group achieve its goals and how valuable the goals are themselves.

Was Hitler an effective leader? Did he mobilize followers to accomplish shared goals? Did he get stuff done? Some might argue that Hitler was indeed an effective leader until he overreached by invading the Soviet Union. After all, his policies helped lift Germany out of the Great Depression and the military he built up went on to conquer most of Europe. However, when we assess the social values that animated his leadership and (sadly) motivated his most ardent followers, we reach another verdict entirely.

What does this have to do with community leadership? Aren't those who work to make our communities a better place doing the work of angels? Not always—or at least not without tensions and moral complexities. A nonprofit organization might do a great job of feeding the homeless but fail to confront the underlying policies that contribute to homelessness in the first place. An inner city neighborhood group might do heroic work building a sense of neighborhood identity, but oppose the nonprofit that wants to locate a shelter for abused women in their neighborhood.

The value-based leader works with others to understand the deep social values that underlie the most profound community-building work. And the value-based leader works hard to develop an awareness of the value conflicts and ethical conundrums that inevitably accompany public work.

Finally, effective community leaders develop other leaders. They understand that the ability to reach shared goals depends on the collective effort and capacity of the group. Far from hoarding power, community-based leaders work hard to develop it in others. They are participatory leaders; they lead *with* rather than *for*. The great labor leader Eugene Debs put it this way:

"I would not be a Moses to lead you into the Promised Land, because if I could lead you into the Promised Land, someone else could lead you out of it."

Dimensions of Leadership

So these are the characteristics of effective community leaders. But what are the key dimensions of effective leadership? I like to divide the leadership universe into four quadrants: Process Leadership, Task Leadership, Ethical Leadership, and Strategic Leadership. All four are necessary for effective and authentic community efforts over time. Few of us have the capacity to do excellent leadership work across all four dimensions but all of us have the capacity to grow in each. There are other ways to organize the leadership universe, but these four dimensions have helped me reflect on my own leadership work—specifically, where I need to grow and where I need to get help from others.

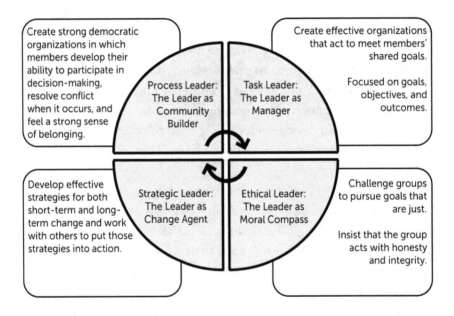

Process Leader: The Leader as Community Builder

The process leader creates strong participatory organizations in which members develop their ability to participate in decision-making, resolve conflict when it occurs, and feel a strong sense of belonging. Process leaders are attuned to the feelings of group members. They listen and pay attention. They take the time to find out what members are thinking. They understand the connection between group identity and effective collective action. They understand that group solidarity has both an emotional and instrumental component. If we imagine groups as living in a continuum of being and doing, the process leader remembers not to lose the being in pursuit of the doing.

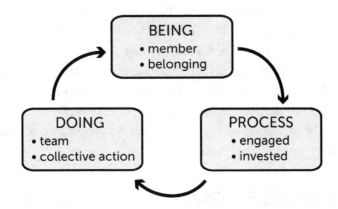

Take the volunteer coordinator for a political campaign. The work is time-sensitive and quantitative. The candidate's name and message must get out to thousands of voters by election time. Enter the phone-bank or door-knocking volunteers. Does the coordinator take the time to give a greeting, find out the volunteers interest, and foster some connection between the volunteers? Are the volunteers treated as part of a leadership relationship or simply "bodies" to get the work done—cogs in the campaign juggernaut? Or consider the volunteer coordinator at the local elementary school. Does he or she get to know the parents and community people who come to tutor the kids?

Does she or he foster a sense that "we" are part of a team with the common purpose of educating our children?

How many of you have ever been part of a book club? Most of the ones I know about feature good food and plenty of opportunity for the participants to share what is going on with their families, work, and personal lives. When it is time to select the next book, the process leader makes sure that everyone has a chance to get their ideas into the mix. Actually, book clubs that are sustained over time have developed an effective process culture. It is not only one person, but most (if not all) of the members who create an environment of inclusion and are able to work through the inevitable conflicts that come when people differ over what book to read next.

But what if members of the book club never read any books? What if the group never got beyond eating the good food and sharing life stories? Two things might happen. First, the group might realize its mission really isn't books at all and that was OK. Second, some members might become frustrated because they really want to discuss books, but the group rarely gets around to that. Put another way, the *doing* in the being/doing continuum is either socializing OR socializing AND discussing books. If the purpose is the latter, the group will need at least one person to remind people to put down their coffee cups and pick up that book!

Task Leadership: The Leader as Manager

The task leader is focused on supporting and at times challenging the group to meet the group's shared goals. He or she is results-orientated and focused on outcomes. Effective task leadership, as we suggested above, is not in contradiction to strong process leadership. The two depend on each other. The effective task leader is able to clearly define what the phone-bank volunteer needs to do to deliver a clear message to the desired number of potential voters. She is able to provide a time, place, and necessary resources to that volunteer tutor so that the learning relationship can happen. The effective task leader makes sure that members of the neighborhood association have a clear sense of the tasks they agreed to take on before they leave the meeting and develops accountability systems to reinforce the commitments that were made.

If the lack of effective process leadership results in members feeling unheard, under-appreciated, and not included; a lack of effective task leadership results in members feeling ineffective and frustrated. Members start to feel that the group is spinning its wheels—or to use another car analogy, that the air is seeping out of the tires. Soon there is discord (that is often not stated openly). Joe Smith said he was going to arrange a meeting with our city council representative but he never did. Francisco promised to see about having our next meeting at the Latino center but he forgot. Sue was going to ask Louisa if we could have our spring fundraiser at her home. Now it's May and she still hasn't gotten around to asking. Joe, Francisco, and Sue may all enjoy the neighborhood association meetings. They may feel like they belong. But if the mission of the organization extends beyond being a social group, some effective task leadership is in order—and quick!

Strategic Leadership: The Leader as Change Agent

Strong process and task leadership keep a group running. Strategic leaders determine where the organization is running *to*. Perhaps the most important characteristic of strategic leaders is that they believe in the possibility of change. They are "yes, we can" people, rather than "no, we can't." But what distinguishes mere optimists from genuine strategic leaders, is their ability to develop effective strategies for both short-term and long-term change, and put those strategies into action. Strategic leaders are often catalysts for starting new groups and/or helping existing organizations develop new approaches to old issues.

Over the years I have met and worked with dozens of excellent strategic leaders. Larry Hiscock, for example, was director of a neighborhood organization representing a mixed-race, mixed-income neighborhood in North Minneapolis. Like too many neighborhood associations in center city neighborhoods, the group Larry worked for functioned mostly as a white homeowners association. Absent, for the most part, were renters. And although there were a few African-American home owners on the association board, neither the participants in the group nor the issues the group addressed, were reflective of the broader community. As a result, the organization had minimal power and was only a marginal force in the community.

When Larry was hired, he developed a team of effective leaders with strong connections to a much wider cross-section of the neighborhood. He brought in skilled trainers who could help the staff and board develop a deeper understanding of the racial and class dynamics of the community. Together, they recruited a much more diverse group of board and committee members. Moving beyond simple inclusion (a necessary step in itself), they fashioned strategies for neighborhood change and identified concrete action steps to get there. From the environmental justice movement, they learned about the negative impact of industrial pollutants on many inner-city neighborhoods, including their own. They demanded—and won—cleanup of the most polluted sites. They developed more effective approaches to affordable housing.

In addition to looking forward, the neighborhood association, at Larry's suggestion, also looked back. They studied the history of racist policymaking in Minneapolis, stretching back to the 1930s. They developed a mini-history curriculum to educate both residents and city leaders on the political and policy dynamics that resulted in the economic and racial segregation of North Minneapolis. Armed with this historical perspective, neighborhood leaders could more effectively create strategies going forward.

I mentioned that Larry is an example of a strategic leader. He actually helped build a strategic leadership team. He and the team developed the strategic capacity of their organization to make change over the long haul. When I ask students in my leadership seminars if they have the capacity to become strategic leaders, many say no.

They are confident in their ability to lead a work group or facilitate a meeting, but to figure out how to make change, seems like almost a magic quality to many of them. It takes vision, the ability to analyze forces for and against change, an aptitude for planning, and an orientation toward the future, to be a powerful strategic leader. But experience has taught me that many people have the capacity to develop strategic thinking skills and participate in strategic change processes.

Ethical Leadership: The Leader as Moral Compass

If the strategic leader helps the group or organization figure out what is to be done and how to do it, the ethical leader asks the group to consider the moral implications of the actions themselves. He or she is the person who raises their hand to ask, "But is what we are doing right?" or "If we take this action, how will it impact others?" It is easiest to recognize this form of leadership in the lives of those who are widely perceived as great moral leaders, like Martin Luther King and Mahatma Gandhi. One of my favorite examples from Minnesota history is William Whipple, an Episcopal Bishop who spent much of his life crusading for justice toward the disinherited Ojibwa and Dakota people. In the aftermath of the bloody Dakota uprising in 1862, Whipple appealed to an enraged Minnesota frontier population to put aside feelings of revenge and recognize the causes of the conflict: the theft of Dakota land and the long trail of broken treaties and unmet obligations that reduced native communities to impoverishment and dependence. In a period of intense hatred, Bishop Whipple called white Minnesotans to a higher sense of justice. Through persistent advocacy, he convinced President Abraham Lincoln to spare 264 Dakota warriors from the gallows, although in this largest mass execution in U.S. history, 38 Dakota were hung.

Given the climate that existed in 1862, you can imagine the reception that Whipple's call to a higher moral understanding received. Although history remembers him as a man of high principle, his fellow citizens weren't so kind at that time. Many citizens would have loved to put him on the first steamboat heading back East. You don't have to be a William Whipple to feel the irritation of group members when you raise an uncomfortable moral question. Ethical leadership requires moral courage. When you question an action or a practice as a matter of justice, it implies that members of the group have been acting unjustly. And that makes people uncomfortable. This is particularly true with nonprofit and community-based organizations. Aren't we the good guys here? Aren't we the ones who are providing a needed service or trying to make our communities a better place?

I believe that every group, and therefore every leader, is engaged in actions that have moral consequences. And sometimes those consequences can be negative. Moral courage is that trait that allows a person to raise the issue despite the backlash that might result. Moral sensitivity is the ability to recognize the issue in the first place. Like strategic leadership, both moral courage and moral sensitivity can be cultivated, and just as importantly, incorporated as part of a learned group culture.

> Moral courage is that trait that allows a person to raise the issue despite the backlash that might result. Moral sensitivity is the ability to recognize the issue in the first place. Like strategic leadership, both moral courage and moral sensitivity can be cultivated, and just as importantly, incorporated as part of a learned group culture.

Saul Alinsky, the father of community organizing, established his reputation in the years following the Second World War by creating a powerful organization in the Back of the Yards neighborhood of Chicago. Back of the Yards was a working class, largely white, ethnic community. Like many older urban communities, it suffered from poor public services, lack of job opportunities, and declining home values. Most residents felt powerless—strict adherents to the old adage, "You can't fight city hall." Alinsky taught them that they could fight city hall, by coming together to exercise their own power. For over a decade, they used this power to promote the common good. But in the 1960s, when Black Chicagoans found their power and demanded integrated neighborhoods, the good people of Back of the Yards resisted. Who was there to raise the moral issue? The social justice issue?

Moral issues are endemic. They pop up everywhere, if you have the eyes to see them. They include the nonprofit that serves the poor, but underpays its workers; the chamber of commerce that sponsors employment readiness programs for youth, but lobbies against the minimum wage; and the environmental group that fights for wilderness protection, but ignores the destruction of urban habitat. The resolution of some moral and ethical issues, raises new issues. Naming the issue is not the same thing as resolving the issue. But it is a necessary start and a critical function of leadership.

Chapter 2
The *Community* in Community Leadership

Community is a word with multiple meanings. We experience community as an emotion, as in *sense* of community; as a physical place such as a neighborhood or town; as a set of shared interests or pursuits, like the environmental community or legal community; or as common ethnic or cultural identity, such as the Somali community or Catholic community. We often think of community as something fixed—something that just is. In fact, from a leadership perspective, communities are made and maintained through human relationships. People create community.

The principles and skills of effective community leadership are applicable in business, government, and the military. What makes community leadership unique is the context. Community leadership most often takes place in civil society—that large space between the market and government where citizens come together to pursue shared interests, confront common problems, and knit the fabric of society that makes both commerce and democracy possible. Civil society is Little League Baseball and Girl Scouts, the church social action committee, the volunteer fire department, the neighborhood improvement association, and Black Lives Matter. Community happens in physical space (living rooms, church basements, and union halls) and virtual space (social media, cyber activism, and on-line affinity groups.)

Civil Society is as joyous as a community choral group, serious as the local library board, and as contentious as a sit-in or protest march. It can be deeply conservative or intoxicatingly transformative. It is through the communities of interests, values, identities, and

places that make it up, that our common life is stretched and
restored. Although he didn't use the term, Alexis de Tocqueville,
described America's genius for civil society when he visited the newly
emerging United States in 1838. As a member of the old world French
aristocracy, de Tocqueville was struck by Americans' willingness to
join together in voluntary associations to accomplish an amazing
array of common projects.

"Americans of all ages, all conditions, and all dispositions
constantly form associations. They have not only commercial
and manufacturing companies, in which all take part, but
associations of a thousand other kinds, religious, moral,
serious, futile, general or restricted, enormous or diminutive.
The Americans make associations to give entertainments,
to found seminaries, to build inns, to construct churches, to
diffuse books, to send missionaries to the antipodes; in this
manner they found hospitals, prisons, and schools. If it is
proposed to inculcate some truth or to foster some feeling by
the encouragement of a great example, they form a society.
Where ever at the head of some new undertaking you see
the government in France, or a man of rank in England, in the
United States you will be sure to find an association."

– *Democracy in America* (Book II, Chapter 5)
by Alexis de Tocqueville

To de Tocqueville, this penchant for association was as fundamental
to democracy as representative government itself. It was through
association that Americans protected themselves from the twin
dangers of excessive individualism and centralized power. The first
makes society impossible and the latter snuffs out the initiative and
ultimately the freedom of the people. Americans, de Tocqueville
believed, overcame their tendency to imagine that "their whole
destiny is in their own hands," through the constant experience
of mutual association. In turn this regular exercise in common

action nurtured the skills and attitudes necessary for genuine self-government.

We most often experience civil society at the local level. But with the explosion of the internet and other modern communications technologies, it is more possible than ever to participate in civil society at the global level. Through global civil society, leaders connect communities of culture, values, and interests on activities ranging from religion to athletics and human rights to environmental justice. Not all links are virtual. Volunteer and social justice travel is a growing phenomenon. Whether a two-week volunteer trip to build a community center in Uganda, or the Diaspora connections that link communities in Mexico, Somalia, or Haiti with friends and family members now living in the United States; global civil society is a growing—and vital—arena for community leadership.

Dimensions of Community

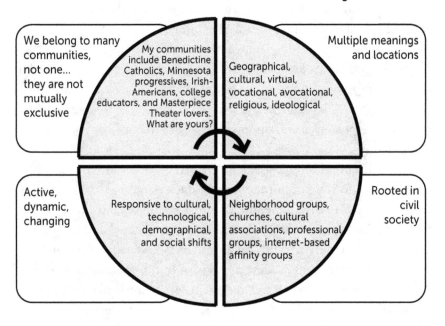

Communities and Cultures: Bounded or Bridging?

Communities and the organizations that flow from them, can have strong boundaries or they can be permeable, outward-looking, and diverse. Bounded communities tend to emphasize commonality, feature a strong sense of belonging, and a well-developed radar to identify who is "in" and who is "out." Bridging communities value diversity, base their sense of belonging on shared interests and purposes, and have permeable borders. The European-American ethnic neighborhood is an example of this dynamic. At its best, the Italian-American or Irish-American neighborhood offered a strong sense of community, local institutions to support the community, and a vehicle to defend the interests of the community against those who were hostile or indifferent. At its worst, ethnic communities discriminated against outsiders, stifled the individuality and creativity of its members, and failed to make common cause with potential allies outside their neighborhood.

The dynamic for African-American neighborhoods and other ethnic communities, often was, and is, more complex. Socially isolated and economically disadvantaged, movements for neighborhood control were at best only partially successful in gaining the necessary power and resources to flourish. Historically, race and class inequalities have shaped American community life and continue to shape the obstacles and opportunities for effective community action today.

Strategic community leaders, motivated by a passion for justice, view the relationship of borders and bridges as critical to community empowerment. For example, the Dayton's Bluff neighborhood in St. Paul's East Side was once a white ethnic neighborhood with Swedish, German, Irish, and Italian-Americans sharing place and livelihood in peace and modest prosperity. In the wake of World War 2, all that changed. The GI bill and the freeway construction boom made suburbia possible. The closing of Hamm's Brewery and several major industrial employers in the 1970s and '80s completed the change process. Today, Dayton's Bluff is a mixed-class, multi-ethnic neighborhood where African-Americans, Hmong, Latino, and more recent immigrants from Africa, share space with the white, mostly home-owning residents. Old identities are being reshaped. New identities are being formed. You can see Latino businesses on the neighborhood's main commercial strip and hear the voices of new arrivals reflected in churches, cultural groups, political groups, and social service organizations.

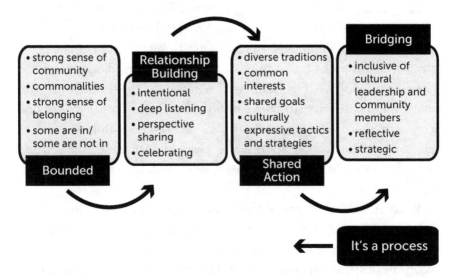

Dayton's Bluff is a neighborhood of loose boundaries and fragile bridges. Here a discussion of culture is critical for understanding organizations. Organizations, and the communities they represent, are cultural creations. Often we use the term "culture" as a synonym for race or ethnicity. But organizations also have cultures: values, rules, and norms that leaders and participants learn and, when appropriate, learn to challenge. A labor educator I knew wrote an article called, "The Politics of Furniture." In it, she pointed out how important it is to understand the meanings behind apparently innocuous things, like how the furniture is arranged for a meeting. If the chairs are arranged in straight rows with space up front reserved for the organization's leaders, it tells you something about power and participation. How much it tells you will be quickly revealed if you suggest changing the arrangement of chairs to a circle in which the leaders with the titles have the same locational status as the rank and file.

Reflective community leaders pay close attention to the relationship between bounded and bridging communities. How tightly does a particular ethnic group or community organization patrol its boundaries? How tightly should it patrol them? Several years ago, I attended the founding convention of a group called Somali Action Alliance. The food was Somali (itself a mix of pre-colonial and Italian influences). Given its strong tradition of poetry, it was fitting that the invocation was given by a revered Somali poet. The poet was followed by elders who represented the traditional identity and authority structures of Somalia. Several other presenters were women—itself an expression of cultural change. But most telling of all, the keynote address was given by Mee Moua, the first Hmong person elected to a state legislature anywhere in the United States.

What did this event reveal about the organizational culture of Somali Action Alliance? The event signified a cultural dynamic that preserves identify (this is a Somali organization after all) through incorporating diversity and change. The leaders were reflective and strategic. They built on a deep connection with their community while bridging to others. They didn't just sweep in and re-arrange the furniture. They incorporated traditional leaders and community members in a gradual and intentional process of continuity and change.

Community Leadership: Organizational Contexts

I previously noted that community is not static. It is not simply a thing. Community is created, challenged, deconstructed, and reconstructed through action. And since we are talking about social action, as opposed to simply individual action, community leadership requires form and purpose. The form can be as simple as a block club or as complex as a large agency or global coalition. But form itself is not what determines the nature of community leadership. Rather, form follows mission—or, more accurately, form *should* follow mission. Too often what starts as an empowering endeavor, ends up as a self-perpetuating institution: a form without an animating purpose.

Community leadership takes place in a multitude of community settings and far too many to list here. Taking our cue (again) from de Tocqueville, we can begin to imagine the breadth and depth of leadership settings by calling to mind the almost limitless variety of associations that give form and meaning to community life.

Creating a typology of community organizations is only a slightly more manageable task. What does a city planning commission have in common with the Little League or the Lions Club with a GLBT coalition?

What follows is far from a complete categorization. Each category focuses on a broad but distinct purpose and approach to community engagement. And each presents specific leadership challenges.

Direct Service and Charitable Volunteering

In my community leadership seminars, I have found that this category describes the most common form of community engagement. In fact, many students conflate direct service and charitable giving with community engagement itself, rather than understand service as one of many arenas in which leadership takes place. The organizations and networks through which this multitude of good works take place reflect the breadth and diversity of American society: From disaster relief to food shelves, homeless shelters to tutoring programs—millions of community people offer their time, skills, and money to support those in need.

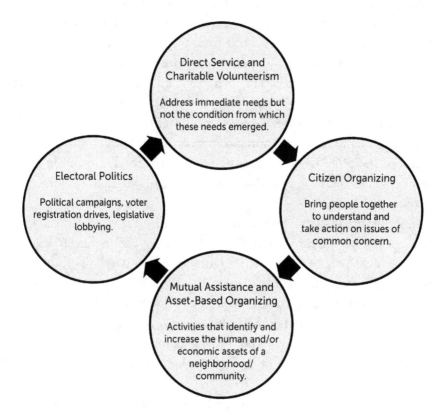

The most visible strength (and attraction) of this approach is powerful: millions of people in America and around the world receive life-sustaining support. Perhaps not as obvious is the transformation in attitudes and awareness that can result from engagement in service activities. Service volunteers (and staff) often develop new skills, as well as the confidence that comes with successfully organizing a charitable event and seeing the positive impact on the lives of others. Service volunteers also experience new insights into the lives of others and the personal impacts of social injustice.

But charitable giving also has its limits. Service programs generally fail to address the underlying social causes of individual problems. The volunteer energy that leads to a well-stocked food shelf is a direct response to a family's need for food today. It does not address the lack of income that leads to the need for food shelves in the first place. The massive donations for earthquake relief in Haiti saved thousands of lives. But most people in Haiti were desperately poor before the earthquake and remain so today. At their best, direct service programs combine immediate aid with education and action to address causes and create solutions—but too often they don't.

Two stories illustrate this dynamic. The first is about a mother who attended her son's graduation from college. Like many colleges and universities in the U.S., this school encouraged its students to volunteer. Her son had a very meaningful experience volunteering in a homeless shelter. According to the story (it has been told so many times that I really can't vouch for its accuracy in every detail), the mother went out of her way to thank the college's volunteer coordinator. She thanked him for making her son's experience possible and she expressed her hope that when his children were old enough to go to college, they too would have the opportunity to help the homeless.

The second story is really a parable. Some friends were having a picnic near a river. Suddenly they heard a young child crying for help. They rushed to the river and pulled him out. No sooner had they saved the first child, than another appeared thrashing about in the water. After another successful rescue, a third child came into view. Rather than wade into the water for yet another rescue, one of the group members bolted up the river shore. "Where are you going?" her exasperated friends demanded. "I am heading up river to find the source of the problem in the first place," was the wise response.

Some people prefer to wade in and pull the child out of the water. Others, like the college graduate's mom, believe there is something noble in doing service. At their core, good service organizations are effective in mobilizing volunteers and staff in carrying out the shared purpose of service provision. In many organizational settings, probing too deeply into the causes of social problems or advocating too strongly for approaches that inconvenience the "haves" while empowering the "have not's," has real risks. For example, the manager of a corporate-sponsored inner city tutoring program might look unfavorably on their employee tutors organizing the kids to appeal for increased public spending on urban education; and the campaign to aid hurricane victims might lose support if the effort included demands for restructuring the economic relationship between Haiti and the U.S.

Even if there is no organization-threatening pushback from constituents and funders, the effort to research, educate, and come to agreement about causes and effective responses can be daunting. It is much easier to send that donation to the food shelf than figure out your position on the farm bill! And, on a deeper level, when volunteers and staff are asked to transform their relationships with clients from service provider to community organizer, the process can be disorienting for both.

Citizen Organizing

Citizen organizing takes up where direct service and charitable volunteering leave off. Citizen organizers bring people together to collectively address common problems. A citizen in this context is a member of a group who is taking collective action in pursuit of common interests and values. Neighborhood organizations, environmental groups, labor unions, anti-poverty coalitions, civil rights, immigrant rights, women's, and global justice movements are all citizen organizations in this sense of the term. So are the powerful libertarian and social conservative movements that collectively assert their values and interests.

Citizen organizing has played a decisive role in the development of democracy and economic justice in the U.S. and around the world. Imagine what the United States would be like if there hadn't been citizen organizing. No American Revolution. No end to slavery or legal segregation. No voting rights for women, or economic protections for working people. All of these came from a combination of pressure from below and skilled (if often reluctant) leadership from above.

If the charitable volunteer asks, "How can I help that homeless person today?" the citizen organizer asks, "How can I bring homeless people together with allies to challenge the policies that lead to homelessness in the first place?" While the food bank volunteer scores yet another crate of donated food from the supermarket, the citizen organizer brings together low-income people and allies to fight for living wage jobs so families won't need the food bank in the first place.

The strength of the organizing approach is in its emphasis on mobilizing collective power and, at its best, nurturing new citizen leaders and influencing institutional change. But the process of change is often long and complicated. The task of building genuinely participatory and effective organizations takes great skill and perseverance. The fight to change institutions runs into deeply entrenched patterns of power and privilege. Have you ever tried to change a university, a corporation, or a public agency from the outside? Often the people who most need changes in policy are the least well positioned in their lives to fight for it. Immediate needs trump the long and winding path of institutional change. Being at the bottom of the heap can just as often lead to feeling powerless: "Positive change doesn't happen for people like me!" as often as it leads to creative indignation: "I am sick of getting stepped on and I am not going to take it anymore!"

Mutual Assistance and Asset-Based Organizing

The citizen organizing tradition, rooted in the protest and social reform movements of past and present, engages members in campaigns to change laws, institutions, and social practices that are (to its participants at least) unfair or unjust. The mutual assistance/asset-based approach shares a commitment to member engagement; but rather than leveraging power to *change* institutions, proponents of this approach enlist members to create their own institutions. Like the citizen organizing tradition, the mutual assistance tradition runs deep in American culture. Ben Franklin started the first volunteer fire department in 1736; there are over 20,050 in existence today. From burial societies to food cooperatives; community gardens to threshing bees; book clubs to Little League—members come together as peers and equals to create and manage their own groups and institutions. The object is not to take care of other people's needs, but to meet each other's needs.

Neighborhood Problems	Neighborhood Assets
Unemployment	Local business
Truancy	Green spaces
Lack of affordable housing	Schools
Achievement gap	Libraries
Illiteracy	Churches
Crime	Willing volunteers
Mental health issues	Community gardens
Poor health	Food co-ops
Environmental hazards	Neighborhood associations
Lack of healthy food	Elders

One of the most vital expressions of this very old tradition is Asset-Based Organizing, a perspective having significant impact on the field of urban and rural development. Asset-based and mutual assistance approaches start with affirming the power and resources that every individual and community possess, regardless of income and social position. John McKnight, a noted advocate of asset-based approaches, asks us to imagine a two-sided map of a low-income urban community. On one side is the Neighborhood Needs Map. The human topography it sketches is bleak: unemployment, crime, school drop-outs, dilapidated housing and other deficits that shape the common view of the inner city neighborhood. But McKnight urges us to flip the map over to see the other side. Sharing terrain with deficits are assets: schools, local business, energetic youth, gifted elders, churches, and informal networks. The businesses may be surviving on a shoestring, the parks may need tending, the gifted residents may lack professional degrees, and the churches may not be as grand as those found in more affluent neighborhoods; but all of these exist and contain the potential for neighborhood renewal.

The vision that underlies McKnight's maps (here presented as a list), helps us contrast the asset-based approach to direct service and citizen organizing. The direct service leader sees the first side of the map as a set of needs to respond to and clients to serve. The citizen organizer looks at the issues facing the neighborhood and attempts to organize the community to demand policy changes. The asset–based leader looks for change from *within* the community by engaging residents directly in mutual assistance projects. These approaches are not mutually exclusive. The direct service provider might see the connection between establishing a food shelf, organizing a lobby campaign against reduced public assistance allowances, and organizing a neighborhood food cooperative. In fact, strong strategic leaders look across the boundaries of their specific organizational approaches to find points of synergy and perspective.

Like direct service and citizen organizing, the mutual assistance and asset–based approach has limits as well as strengths. In low income and working class communities, the approach works best when problems can be addressed without the need for substantial financial resources. That often means that the scale and pace of change will be slow. For example, it is possible for neighbors to create a housing rehab cooperative and, like the barn raisers of an earlier era, work together to repair and maintain homes. But the financial capital needed for new or large numbers of substantially repaired housing is often beyond a community's reach. Put more generally, disparities of wealth and income that lead to poor neighborhoods and poverty in the first place, will not be overcome by collective bootstrap methods alone. It takes a village and *more* than a village to create deep and positive change.

Electoral Politics

The place to which communities most often look to find that *more than a village* is electoral politics. The goal of electoral politics is to elect people who represent the interests and values of their constituents. In the electoral arena, community leaders (campaign officials and active volunteers, as well as the candidates themselves), engage fellow citizens in collective action to meet shared needs and express shared values.

At its best, electoral politics achieves community representation on city councils, state legislatures, and Congress. Through their representatives, citizens have a place at the table where laws are passed and resources are allocated. Funds become available for housing and community development projects in the neighborhood. Laws are passed to protect victims of domestic violence, clean up polluted industrial sites, support clean energy development, and reduce barriers for ex-offenders to become productive citizens. As is true with all forms of community engagement, participants in campaigns can develop leadership skills and learn that they indeed can make a difference. Successful engagement in electoral politics expands the old adage: Not only *can* we fight city hall, we (in coalition with others) can *take over* city hall.

What more do we need than results like the ones listed above? Is there more to the picture? First, the ability of elected officials to "deliver the goods" for low-income and working-class communities is in decline. This is hardly a reason to give up. That would only leave the field to those who don't believe government ought to provide public goods in the first place. However, it does point to limitations in electoral politics as an approach in itself. For example, modern campaigns too often take a marketing—rather than relational— approach to communication with voters. Too often the emphasis is on "getting the name out there" rather than engaging in a leader-to-community-member conversation. Even in local elections, where it is possible to have a face-to-face conversation at the door, emphasis is on the 30-second interaction. Identify your base, so the common wisdom goes. Touch it four or five times and make sure they get to the store (election booth) to buy your brand on Election Day.

I sympathize. Elections are like the harvest. They are seasonal and time sensitive. You have to get your seed in and your crop out. Effective task leadership is key. But as a strategic approach to change, politics alone is inadequate. A community leadership approach connects politics to community, and political representation to community building. That requires a vision of politics that is year round rather than seasonal; one that both recognizes the division of labor between the different approaches to community engagement, as well as explores ways to bring them together.

> A community leadership approach connects politics to community, and political representation to community building.

As noted earlier, community leadership takes place in a multitude of settings. It is not limited to the four categories discussed above. In sketching out this basic typology, I have tried to highlight the fundamental purpose, leadership dynamic, and effectiveness of each as an approach to social change. Much of the work we do as community leaders comes in hybrid form. It is not all one thing or another. What is important is the awareness and intentionality with which we approach the work. Who is being served by our group's efforts? How are members involved? What difference are we making? Are there other approaches we could be taking?

The leadership choices we make are reflections of our personal passions, comfort level, and value commitments. Not all—or even most—community organizations are focused on major community problems or social issues. The church liturgy committee, on-line affinity group, lawn and garden club, or a Girl Scout group do not make a revolution. They do, however, bring joy or purpose to people's lives. And most fundamentally, they are expressions of every-day democracy necessary for society to flourish.

Chapter 3
Personal and Social Power

Power is an essential aspect of leadership. Many people think of the term as a negative one. People who have power, they believe, usually end up using it *over* somebody else. And if we don't feel we have much power ourselves, then the fear of *power abuse* by others is all the greater.

A more helpful way to look at power is to remember that it derives from the Latin, *poder,* which simply means "to be able." People with power are *able* to do things; to act on their own behalf or the behalf of others. People without power are not. All of us have some power in our lives. But how do we identify that power and build on it? How do we become more power*ful?*

In order to understand the relationship between power and leadership, I find it helpful to make the distinction between *personal* and *social* power. Personal power is what I do as an individual to meet my goals. Its scope is private. I exercise personal power when I go to school to further my education, pull myself out of bed to get to work and earn a living, and in general accept my individual responsibility for getting ahead in—or at least getting on with—life.

We Americans are great ones for personal power. We worship individualism. We believe that each one of us is responsible for our own successes and failures. We built an economic system that is modeled on personal initiative and choice.

In a larger sense, of course, none of us can really claim that we are autonomous individuals, solely responsible for all the good or bad things that happen to us. For one thing, we were raised by one or more parents. We were born into varied economic circumstances.

Race, class, and gender influence who we are as well. But still, most of us imagine ourselves as individuals. Whether we succeed or fail, it really is up to each of us as individuals.

Or is it? Leaders understand that to meet many of our goals, collective action is required. Social power is that power we exercise with others when what we want or value as individuals can only be attained through group action. The farmer who gets up every day at the crack of dawn to milk the cows is exercising personal power. When he joins with other farmers to fight for a pricing system that will save him from bankruptcy, he is exercising social power. The parents who work hard to balance career and family responsibility are exercising personal power. When they join with others to organize a child-care cooperative, they are exercising social power.

When I was six years old, I had polio. To this day, I walk with crutches and a brace. When I assumed a positive and hopeful attitude about my life, got a good education and became a college teacher, I exercised personal power. But when I park right up front next to the ball park or concert hall or grocery store in a specially marked handicapped parking spot, that is the result of social power: disabled people and their supporters working together to secure access to workplaces and public spaces.

Feeling unsafe in your neighborhood? You can buy a watchdog and install an alarm system. That's using personal power. You can help organize a neighborhood watch program. That's one of many possible exercises of social power toward making neighborhoods more secure.

Can't afford health insurance? Quit smoking, get lots of exercise, and watch out for those fatty foods. That's personal power. But, if you join a group advocating affordable health coverage for all—that's social power. Or, if you form a committee to educate others about healthy life styles, that is a form of social power aimed at helping others exercise personal power more effectively.

Power: Social Capacity in Action

Community leaders engage followers in the effective use of power to achieve common goals. Understanding power as the ability to act (to be able) means that we all have power, and through study, reflection and purposeful action we can gain more. But it is not that simple. Power is not distributed equally. All of us live in a web of power relationships: parent/child, worker/manager, student/teacher, working class/upper class, renter/landlord, lender/borrower, expert/novice, among many others. Appreciating power as a positive force does not diminish the need to be realistic about pervasive power imbalance. Indeed, effective leadership requires a realistic assessment of power relationships as they exist and a clear-eyed strategy to tip the scale when possible; to move in ways both little and large from the world as it is, to the world as we want it to be.

From a community leadership perspective, the most important thing to understand about social power is that it is based on capacity. A group can't accomplish shared goals without capacity. The good news is that most groups have far more capacity than they imagine. However, members often fail to recognize the capacity they have. The exercise of social power is rooted in the ability to *see* the multiple skills, assets, and resources that make up the collective capacity of the group. And how do we do that? We can begin by simply asking, making a list, and creating an inventory.

> From a community leadership perspective, the most important thing to understand about social power is that it is based on capacity.

For example, imagine that you belong to the community outreach committee of an urban church. You notice that your community lacks recreational facilities for the increasingly diverse group of kids in the neighborhood. You decide that you want to start a community center. Achieving this goal will require power. What sources of power do you have? What capacity do the members of your committee have?

Imagine that you engage committee members in making a list. If you really get a creative process going, it might look something like this:

- Jose can coach soccer.
- Lydia has written grants for the nonprofit she staffs.
- Nimco speaks Somali.
- Karen loves to organize parties.
- Bill is a social media geek.
- George always follows through.
- Chris has friends in city hall.
- Taylor is comfortable asking people for donations.

The exact mix of skills you will need depends on the nature of the project. Will the church provide the space for the recreational center? Will it be staffed by volunteers? Will the church join others in demanding that city government re-open the center they just closed because of budget cuts? Understanding that social power is based on capacity doesn't substitute for a clear mission and effective planning, but it is an essential element.

But how do we understand capacity on a deeper and more general level? Here are a few of the most important categories:

The power of relationships

Most of you have heard the old saying, "It's not what you know, it's who you know." Actually, both what *and* who you know are critical sources of social power. Relational power is the *who* part of that equation. Think how important relationships are to our example of the community center. Most committee members share a good intention. They want to provide recreational opportunities for kids in their neighborhood. Fortunately, Nimco speaks Somali. She can communicate with Somali families in the neighborhood. She can develop relationships. No one on the committee is a city council member, but Chris has strong relationships with council members and those will be important as the project develops. Church attendance has been dwindling, but Bill's extensive list of Facebook friends can connect this project with hundreds of potential supporters.

In our public or community life, like our private life, relationships don't just happen. They require active communication, the discovery of mutual interests and, above all, intentionality. Nor do all public relationships serve the same purpose. I find it helpful to think about relationships in a concentric circle. In the center are relationships with family, friends, neighbors, and group members. Expanding to the second ring of the circle are relationships with allies and those who can offer specific skills or resources. At the outer circle are power holders and decision makers in government, nonprofit agencies, and the business community. The exact nature and scale of these relationships depends on the project. A neighborhood recreation program is one thing; organizing a state-wide effort to develop community-responsive health care exchanges is another. Neither project can succeed without the power that comes from strong relationships mobilized to achieve common goals.

Social Power Relationship Inventory

Who do you know? Take a few minutes to make a list.
You might be surprised at just how broad and deep
your relationships actually are.

Institutional Power Holders

- ❏ Elected officials (local, state, national)
- ❏ Members of boards and commissions
- ❏ Heads of foundation and charitable organizations
- ❏ Business owners and managers

Relationships with Allies

- ❏ Church leaders and members
- ❏ Social justice organizations
- ❏ Neighborhood associations
- ❏ Public interest journalists

Relationships with Friends and Associates

- ❏ Family
- ❏ Neighbors
- ❏ Social groups and clubs
- ❏ Co-workers

Knowledge

One of the most important functions of relationships is the ability
to connect people who don't know, with people who do. Often we
imagine knowledge as something we don't have. "Don't look at me;
I'm not an expert at that." No, maybe you are not an expert at that.
But, somebody is, and perhaps you or someone in your group knows
who that person is. Failing that, Google it! What kind of knowledge
does it take to develop a community recreational program? Jose
knows how to coach soccer. Lydia knows how to write grants. Nimco
knows Somali. George always follows through, so let's assign him to
research church-based recreational centers in other communities.

Effective community leaders understand the power of knowledge and help build knowledge organizations. The nature and complexity of knowledge varies with the task. Knowledge can be physical (how to plaster the wall in our meeting room); legal (how to structure our nonprofit organization); social (what are the dynamics of racism in our communities today); political (what steps are necessary to get our legislation passed); and programmatic (what are the most effective approaches to literacy education for immigrants and refugees). Knowledge can be big picture or mini-focused. However, in itself, knowledge is not power. But knowledge—effectively understood, shared, and deployed—*is* power.

Collective Action

Community organizers and social movement leaders often contrast the power of big money with the power of the people. That is what Occupy Wall Street captured so well in their slogan, "We are the 99 percent!" Grassroots mobilizations often focus on petitions, marches, and rallies, increasingly organized and amplified through social media. The creative use of conflict is often a key element of people power. One organizing response to the housing foreclosure crises, for example, has featured sit-ins and public campaigns to pressure banks to extend relief to borrowers facing default.

In taking group action, individuals express a collective power that transcends that of individual action. The Land Stewardship Project, an organization that promotes sustainable agricultural practices and family farming, won an important victory in Minnesota in 2012 when it convinced the state legislature to defeat legislation that would have limited the power of local governments to regulate corporate farming and mining operations. Combining group and one-to-one personal communication with the power of social media, Land Stewardship proved that an organized network of small farmers and their urban supporters could defeat corporate interests. Whether creating a volunteer literacy program, organizing urban gardens, establishing an on-line advocacy campaign, or rallying for criminal justice reform; the capacity of organized people to accomplish shared goals is the essence of social power.

Organization

People Power involves action guided by knowledge and based on strong public relationships. There is one other essential source of social power: effective organization. Effective organization provides the structure and channels to facilitate action. Organizations can be built to last (sustainable) or designed to self-destruct (time-limited), after a specific purpose has been achieved. Too often the second type of organization lingers on, creating drift and confusion. The goal of sustaining the organization replaces the shared purpose that brought people together in the first place. Somebody *please* hit that self-destruct button! But more often, organizations are built to last—at least long enough to accomplish goals that require ongoing action.

Effective community organizations channel power by creating space for members to share their hopes and grievances, deliberate together, come to decisions, and carry out actions. Effective organizations nurture accountability in members and leaders and offer clear paths for members to *become* leaders. One way to appreciate the power of effective organization, is to reflect on what it looks and feels like when it is lacking. Have you ever participated in a group in which communication with members is inconsistent or the decision-making process unclear? Have you had a good idea, with no place in the organization where you could bring it? Disorganized organizations dissipate power, like air seeping from a punctured tire. But effective organizations multiply power. And fortunately, the skills necessary to create and maintain effective organizations are able to be learned through participation, observation, and training.

Power Over

I began with a definition of power that is purposely... *empowering!* This is in contrast to many analysts of social power who emphasize the limits of "ordinary citizens" to change society. A realist view of power must take into account this broader (and bleaker) understanding. At a societal and institutional level, power is often exercised through *force* (power over) rather than *mutuality* (power with). Force can be deadly and deeply exploitative. Here in the United

States we have eliminated some of the most egregious forms of power abuse: slavery, legal segregation, second-class citizenship for women, among others. But economic inequality is near record levels, the incarceration of young African-American males is re-creating Jim Crowe in communities around the nation, and millions of families are just one health care emergency away from bankruptcy. We don't burn witches anymore, but in tens of thousands of families, women and children fear for their physical safety.

Stepping back, it would seem that all these forms of coercion should be roundly condemned. And indeed many do roundly condemn them. Yet, the extremely coercive power relationships embedded in each example continue because they have some legal or cultural legitimacy. Prisoners are in jail because the criminal justice system represents the legitimate (in most white people's eyes at least) power of the state. Income inequality persists, because most Americans accept that capitalism has its winners and losers. Although a majority of Americans are critical of our private insurance-based health care system, it retains residual legitimacy because it is private. And while the United States has made great strides in criminalizing (delegitimizing) domestic abusers, in too many cultural corners of our society, relationships of power based on male domination stubbornly persist.

In most power relationships force is exerted subtly and even benignly. The lines between coercion and compliance blur. Coercive power (power over) can be gentle or abusive. It can mix rewards as well as restraints. More subtly still, our daily experience of power is muffled by taken-for-granted customs, rules, and laws. Often these expressions of power are unconscious to those on the receiving end and, when they are seen, are accepted as legitimate. It is only when a benign or invisible power relationship is reinterpreted as harmful or unjust, that change becomes possible.

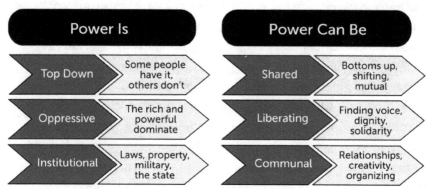

Power Is			Power Can Be		
Top Down	Some people have it, others don't		Shared	Bottoms up, shifting, mutual	
Oppressive	The rich and powerful dominate		Liberating	Finding voice, dignity, solidarity	
Institutional	Laws, property, military, the state		Communal	Relationships, creativity, organizing	

Adapted from Paul Francis DuBois and Frances Moore Lappe, *The Quickening of America: Rebuilding our Nation, Remaking Our Lives,* Jossey-Bass. 1994.

A Sense of Power

Since community leadership depends on empowered participants, it follows that effective community leaders nurture the capacity of members to exercise power. But how do leaders do this? We begin by understanding that power is not simply a "thing" out there. All of us have received empowering or disempowering messages based on family, social position, and personal circumstances. Whether consciously or not, we bring our own "sense of power" to group situations.

When I was in high school, I was voted *most optimistic.* I really wanted to win the prize for *most popular,* but alas that went to another student. However, looking back on it, I am glad that my classmates saw me as optimistic, because optimism is one of the key ingredients for exercising personal or social power. If you don't believe things can change or people can make a difference, you probably won't take action in the first place.

But how does a person become hopeful about working together for change? How does one develop a sense of power? Is it a matter of individual personality? Are some of us born optimists and others pessimists? There is evidence that personality traits do influence attitudes toward change. But developing a sense of power is primarily a *social* process. We learn about our own relationship to power through the messages we receive and the quality of our interactions with others.

Perhaps your sense of power came from family and early social experiences. Were you encouraged to express your opinion? Were you supported in your studies at school, your extracurricular pursuits? Did you get the message that you "were somebody," a person of worth and potential? Did you hang out with peers that had similar reinforcement? Did you experience the world more as a set of opportunities or a series of obstacles?

This certainly was my family experience as a middle class, Irish American Catholic surrounded by successful people who encouraged me to be successful as well. But my sense of social power was also influenced by larger political and cultural currents: the election of our own Catholic prince, John F. Kennedy, the inspiration the Civil Rights Movement, and my introduction to the student power movement sweeping across college campuses around the nation. *Power to the People,* was the slogan of the day. We were going to change the world, and looking back on it, in many ways we did.

In teaching about social power, I emphasize the importance of relationships and networks. Simply put, if you hang out with powerful people, you are more likely to feel powerful yourself. In one class, I tried an experiment. I went through my personal contact book and found that almost everyone in it was active in one or more public issues. My little book included local elected officials, neighborhood organizers, and public policy advocates on issues ranging from affordable housing and urban education, to human rights and the global environment. Some students may have thought I was bragging. "Look at me, I'm connected!" Actually, that was precisely the point I was trying to make. I am an optimist about people's potential to exercise social power, because that view is being reinforced every day by those I interact with. Some exercise positional power, albeit mostly at a local level. Most exercise power from the middle and power from below—power that my students can at least imagine. Acquiring power is a choice—a choice we can make.

Don't get me wrong. I don't always feel powerful. My attempts to make a difference are limited by my own personal shortcomings, personal conflicts, pesky regulations, and (if there is enough at stake) determined opposition. For every power surge, there are multiple power outages! But after a good night's sleep or a long weekend, my sense of power usually reasserts itself. Why? Because it continues to be socially reinforced.

Power Within and Power With

But time out! There are many people who haven't experienced either the personal opportunities I have or the connections I was inspired to make. Many people have little sense of agency either as individuals or members of groups. For many, powerlessness is reinforced on a daily basis and over a lifetime. Although I often stress leadership as linking power to action, developing power is often a psychological, social, and even spiritual matter. The sense of power or powerlessness we internalize as individuals, influences the degree of power we feel as members of community groups.

I began this chapter with a distinction between personal and social power. I noted that both are necessary for community action. Powerless people cannot create or effectively participate in powerful organizations. Since power is interactive (we learn it from others), both forms of power depend on each other. The antidote to Coercive Power (*Power Over)* is combining *Power Within* and *Power With*.

> The sense of power or powerlessness we internalize as individuals influences the degree of power we feel as members of community groups.

This connection was made most memorably for me in two speeches I attended by the civil rights champion, Reverend Jesse Jackson. The first was in an inner-city community center. Jackson was addressing a crowd of mostly African-American youth. He challenged them to work collectively to continue the legacy of Martin Luther King, but his main message was about personal dignity and responsibility. Go to school, study hard, believe in yourself and in what you can accomplish. You can do this, because you have worth. You are a human being. He ended by leading the assembly in a chant,

"I am somebody." Over and over again, the audience chanted, "I am somebody." And they were.

Years later, on a cold Saturday during Easter week, Jesse Jackson addressed a very different group. Over a thousand farmers came to hear him in Glenwood, Minnesota. They and their families were members of Ground Swell, a rural movement that was formed to fight the epidemic of farm foreclosures in the late 1970s. At the time, Jackson was building his "Rainbow Coalition" to unite farmers, workers, environmentalists, women's groups, and people of color into a powerful political coalition. It was social power writ large. At one point, he asked the farmers to join him in the *"I am somebody"* chant. I looked on in amazement as usually laconic Minnesota farmers slowly picked up the beat. By the end of Jackson's speech, the farmers had given public voice to the dignity they had reclaimed through the Ground Swell movement.

Let's look a little closer at the dynamics of the movement that brought Jesse Jackson to Glenwood. I first heard about the group when I was asked to tag along with a friend of mine who was doing a documentary on rural poverty. The movement started when members of the woman's club at the local church began sharing stories of tension at home. Something was clearly bothering their husbands, but the men weren't sharing it with their wives. Armed with a newly formed sense of shared understanding, the women encouraged their husbands to talk about the terror and shame of losing the family farm. As the conversations grew, isolated people with individual problems discovered they weren't alone. In discovering each other, both the women and the men transformed a deep sense of personal powerlessness into a shared sense of purpose: into social power.

Implications for Leadership

Friedrich Nietzsche famously wrote, "Where I found the living, there I found the will to power." Nietzsche was not writing about some innate need for humans to dominate one another. Rather, he was proclaiming that each of us longs for personal significance. We struggle to **be.** Later, humanist psychologists like Rollo May would refer to this personal quest as the search for self-realization— a concept that is similar to what I and others call the Power Within. There is more than one path to developing our individual sense of power: deep reflection, spiritual practice, creative expression, and education, to name a few. A sense of personal power is based on a foundation of self-worth, expressed through the give and take of reciprocal actions and reinforced by the recognition of others. Above all, power has to be earned and owned. As Rollo May put it, "Power cannot, strictly speaking, be given to another, for the recipient still owes it to the giver. It must in some sense be assumed, taken, asserted. For unless it can be held against opposition, it isn't power and will never be power and will never be experienced as real on the part of the recipient."

Nurturing the sense of power in others is a central leadership task. For those engaged in service, this means developing relationships that transform the helper/helped power dynamic. For the citizen organizer, it suggests creating opportunities for members to develop skills, confidence, and decision-making capacity. Whatever the context, the wise leader is a student of power dynamics, beginning with oneself. What is your motivation for taking or avoiding leadership? Do you seek leadership because you have a need to be recognized? Do you wield that gavel as a club to silence others? Or do you avoid leadership positions from fear of conflict or failure? Do you prefer to shine your light brightly or keep the dimmer on?

The late leadership educator, Robert Terry, developed a parable that challenged his students to think deeply about their own relationship to power. His insights came from his experience working with civic leaders on issues of race and gender discrimination. He noted that the privileged (the "ups"), didn't much understand the "downs;" and the "downs," often lost touch with other people's down-ness when they became "ups." Once they got into power, they went, as Terry put it, *"Dumb Up."*

I remember a vivid example of this process. Years ago, a community organization I was with in South Minneapolis sent a

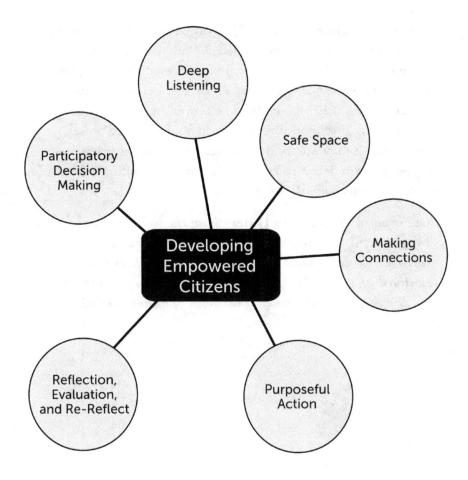

small delegation to discuss affordable housing with our newly-elected alderman. George *(name made up as an act of charity)* was clearly enamored with the trappings of power. Just a few months earlier he was a "nobody." Now he was a "somebody!" Once we were seated, he leaned far back into his expensively upholstered executive chair, clearly sending a message of his newly-found superiority. I thought he was going to take out a cigar and plant both feet on the desk! Unfortunately (for him) he leaned back a bit too far and his chair tipped over. I still remember the image of him flat on his back with his feet sticking up over the desk.

I have had my own pratfalls in understanding and displaying my relationship to power (though none as embarrassing as the alderman's). Developing a sense of individual and collective power in self and others, is a lifetime challenge. With discipline and practice we can get better at it. Far from being a dirty word, power is as essential as the air we breathe. Power can indeed corrupt, as Lord Action famously said. Perhaps he is even right that absolute power corrupts absolutely. But in a world of unbalanced power relationships, it may well be that the near-absolute powerlessness many people experience every day is the more corrupting influence. As political philosopher Elizabeth Janeway put it:

There is nothing inherently **better** *about the weak or worse about the powerful, as human beings. What is* **better** *is, first, that a relative balance should exist between the members of a power relationship, simply because one-sided relations are unstable or else deeply oppressive and wasteful of human abilities.*

And to that I say, "Amen."

Chapter 4
Value-Based and Ethical Leadership

Effective leaders are good at engaging with others to "get things done."** Value-based and ethical leaders don't stop there. They take care to assess the *value* of what is being done. What underlying values motivate us? Does the work we do serve people? In the process of working together for noble ends, do we sometimes forget to fairly treat those with whom we are working? What happens when the values of our group conflict with the values of others?

Social Values:
What are they and where do they come from?

Social values are deeply held, but often unconscious, beliefs about how society ought to be. Part of either the "mainstream culture" or counter-cultural, social values are individually experienced but collectively influenced. That is why we call them social. When listed as a series of words, values seem pretty abstract. When asked to define them, most people stumble. Values have to be experienced in order to be felt. And when that experienced value is given a name, it becomes conscious, something we own, and something we can reflect and act upon.

Imagine the world, nation, and community as you would like it to be. I would like a world where all people have their basic needs met, where wealth is widely shared, where diverse religious and cultural traditions are honored, where peace making replaces violence, where the dignity of all people is recognized, and where the natural environment that supports all life is preserved for future generations. These are social values.

Now imagine the world as it is. There is a gulf between the world as I would like it to be and the world as it is. My guess is that this would be true for you as well. Why encourage folks to articulate their deepest social values in the face of what often seems is to be unyielding resistance? Why not stick to what we CAN accomplish: the kids we can help read, the candidate we can get elected, the homeless shelter we can get funded, or the renewable energy group we can organize?

Actually, there is no contradiction between value-based and pragmatic leadership. Values inspire action and action in turn reinforces values. Value-based leaders work for realizable change, even as they recognize the liberating power that comes from naming and celebrating the underlying values that motivate people to take action in the first place.

What motivates people to act? Often it is a combination of material and ideal interests. Both are connected to social values. The individual pursuit of wealth is reinforced by deeply held values that are prominent in (but not exclusive to) American culture. It is not simply that many like the big houses, fancy cars, and gourmet meals that money can buy. Consumerism is a material practice reinforced by a cultural ideal. Though challenged by economic hard times, most Americans continue to articulate the American dream as financial independence marked by home ownership and the increasingly fleeting hope for a secure retirement. Many admire the rich for their accomplishments and resent them for their excess. Again, social values underlie each response.

Different aspects of community work are often motivated by different social values. The volunteer tutor is motivated by an ideal of service. The community organizer who fights against home foreclosures is motivated by a vision of social justice. The chair of a congregation-based social action committee is motivated by the belief that the scriptural command to "Love thy neighbor as thyself" ought to be reflected not only in our individual relationships but also in the laws and public policies that impact the world we live in.

For me—and for many others—the central social value that underlies community work is *social justice.* The term itself challenges us to look beyond individual acts of compassion and ask challenging questions about how society is organized. Are all people treated equally or are there second-class citizens in America—or other parts of the globe? Why is there a growing gap between the rich and the poor and, for that matter, the rich and the middle class? And is that OK? Does social justice require us to advocate policies that extend access to quality health care, education, and housing to all our citizens?

Solidarity and Social Justice

While there is a working class, I am in it.
While there is a criminal element, I am of it.
While there is a soul in prison, I am not free. – Eugene Debs

An individual has not started living until he can rise above the narrow confines of his individualistic concerns to the broader concerns of all humanity. – Martin Luther King Jr.

Do not oppress the stranger; you know the feelings of a stranger, for you were strangers in the land of Egypt.
– from the *Parashat Mishpatin*

Affirming the value of social justice is only the beginning. Deciding what actions are socially just, can be challenging. Is it socially just to tax the wealthy to fund programs for those who can't afford them? How effective are the government programs that are supposed to address social justice issues? Does solidarity require middle-class residents to accept a homeless shelter in their neighborhood? Is it fair for public schools in affluent neighborhoods to have more resources than those in low-income communities?

Because community members have different interests and
perspectives, their answers to questions like these will not be the
same. Value-based community leadership often leads to value-
based conflict. However, when value-based leaders invite members
to connect with their own values, they are tapping into a powerful
motivating force. In fact, the power of values fully realized and
effectively directed is, in itself, a transforming resource.

In order to actualize the power of values in action, it is first
necessary to make the invisible visible. Rule one: go to the source.
The two most powerful sources of social values are civil and religious.
Without thinking very deeply about it, most Americans share a
general belief in political democracy. Many social values promoted
through religious traditions influence our secular culture as well.

America's civic values are powerful, even if not always conscious.
There are two major currents that run through America's civic
culture: individual freedom and social solidarity. Our founders
envisioned a nation based on liberty from autocratic government.
After all, we fought a war of independence to rid ourselves of
King George. Even more profoundly, the founders affirmed the
revolutionary belief that individuals had the right and the capacity
to pursue life, liberty, and happiness without undue interference
from the state. This idea of liberty was at the heart of the American
Revolution and remains a powerful ideal to this day.

However, the revolution was more than a collection of individuals
fighting for personal freedom. It was also a collective event. The
framers of the Constitution formed a model of government they
hoped would balance individual liberty with some form of the
collective good. There is a reason the preamble to the Constitution
begins with the words, "We the people." As the decades passed, the
definition of "We" expanded beyond the narrow band of property
owning white males envisioned by the founders. It expanded because
of social movements determined to affirm and expand upon the
revolutionary ideal that all men are created equal.

America's Sacred Texts

WE hold these truths to be self-evident that all Men are created equal, that they are endowed by their Creator with certain unalienable Rights, that among these are Life, Liberty, and the Pursuit of Happiness.

From the Declaration of Independence, July 4, 1776

We the People of the United States, in Order to form a more perfect Union, establish Justice, insure domestic Tranquility, provide for the common defense, promote the general welfare, and secure the Blessings of Liberty to ourselves and our Posterity, do ordain and establish this Constitution for the United States of America.

Preamble to the Constitution of the United States, adopted September 17, 1787.

These currents remain vital today. Flowing from the first is the American value of individualism with its emphasis on self-reliance, individual responsibility, freedom from government regulation and a market economy. Flowing from the second is the value of social solidarity with its emphasis on interdependence, collective responsibility and strong public institutions. These traditions can express themselves as polar opposites. Yet the core values of each are critical to a healthy political culture. Just as *No man (or woman) is an island,* a collective is only as strong as the individuals who make it up.

As noted above, widely held religious values also influence society—whether or not all individuals are believers. Most religious traditions teach some version of the golden rule. For instance, the practice of *Zakat,* giving to the poor, is one of the five pillars of Islam; ancient Hindu society was based on the equality of all human beings; and Gandhi's embrace of the lower castes in Indian society was a return to those first principles.

Various versions of the social gospel inspired generations of American Christians to oppose slavery, affirm the rights of working people, and fight for civil rights. I was personally inspired by Catholic social justice theology with its preference for the poor and its insistence that Catholics are called to witness their faith in God through creating a just society here on earth. Perhaps this is why I feel such a common bond with so many of my Jewish friends who practice the tradition of *Tikkun Olam*—the responsibility to "repair the world."

Asserting that religious faith and tradition are major sources of social values, is not the same thing as saying that all religious values are above scrutiny or that all religious people and institutions act consistently with their values. Just as there is often conflict about what civic values should define our public life, there is—and always will be—value-based conflict within and between religious groups. As I write this, Pope Francis just issued his encyclical message on global climate change. Many will disagree with the Pope's approach to the issue, but by calling attention to the devastating impact of climate change on the world's poor, the Pope is stimulating dialogue and action on a critical issue facing humanity. He is asking all of us to *examine our conscience*—a process that is at the heart of value-based leadership.

Because we are social beings, all of us are members of value communities. Most of the time these values are latent and taken for granted. For example, when asked if we believe in democracy, most Americans would answer "of course!" As a religious people, most Americans would also nod positively when asked if they believed in the golden rule—an idea that transcends any one religious tradition. Yet, how powerful are these values? Do they transcend the 4th of July barbecue celebrating the Declaration of Independence? Do they extend beyond exhortations at the church, synagogue, or mosque? How do communities transform social values from soulless abstractions to powerful ideas and affirming emotions? How do leaders—and leadership teams—nurture value-based action?

Two Key American Values: Personal Responsibility and Social Justice

I believe the best idea of the conservative political philosophy is the call to personal responsibility: choices about individual moral behavior, personal relationships like marriage and parenting, work ethics, fiscal integrity, service, compassion, and security. And the best idea of the liberal philosophy is the call to social responsibility: the commitment to our neighbor, economic fairness, racial and gender equality, the just nature of society, needed social safety nets, public accountability, and the importance of cooperative international relationships. The common good comprises the best of both sides—we need to be personally responsible and socially just.

– Jim Wallis, from *On God's Side: What Religion Forgot and Politics Hasn't Learned About Serving the Common Good*, 2013

From Latent to Active: Nurturing Social Values

Imagine you decide to attend a meeting to promote sustainable energy in your community. You expect the meeting will include discussion programs to support home insulation, encourage solar power, and recycle waste. Maybe there will be talk about joining a state-wide coalition campaigning for major public and private investments in renewable energy technologies. You find a chair in the back of the room and get ready for some active listening. Instead, the meeting facilitator asks everyone to write down the values that brought them to the meeting and to be ready to discuss them.

Based on my own experience in a setting like this, many of the meeting participants will likely be comfortable with this exercise. There are millions of people in America, and the world, who are moved by values like sustainability, environmental justice, and stewardship. This meeting might simply be a local manifestation of that global value. Starting with a collective naming of these values might indeed be an effective prologue to the nitty-gritty details that will follow.

However, there may also be people in the meeting who are simply there to see if energy conservation can help them save money on their utility bill. They are motivated by material self interest and may not identify themselves as environmentalists. Others might be at the meeting because their neighbor asked them to come, or because they are worried about the strange weather and wonder if it might be connected to climate change. The question about values might be confusing or, even worse, a turnoff. Perhaps there would be a better way to start the meeting.

Value-based leadership is a learned skill. Like leadership in general, it requires intentionality, experimentation, and evaluation. Value-based leaders nurture organizations that make room for story, tap into and celebrate underlying values, and take action consistent with those values. Value-based leadership is not the same as inspirational or charismatic leadership. Great public speakers like Martin Luther King or labor leader Eugene Debs, are just two examples of gifted orators who inspired followers to act on powerful social values. But their effectiveness as leaders was rooted in the lives they led. They *walked their talk* and they were intentional about turning words into action.

> Like leadership in general, [values-based leadership] requires intentionality, experimentation, and evaluation.

Values often manifest themselves through stories. Values like honesty, respect, and compassion are widely held personal values. Many of us can remember how we learned them. From parents perhaps, a special uncle or aunt, an inspiring teacher, a coach, or a minister, rabbi, or cleric. Sometimes we learned the hard way just how important those values were. Have you ever been to a gathering of family or friends where the conversation turns to stories about getting caught telling a lie, or called out for acting like a bully, or found out stealing the change from mom's purse? Sometimes these transgressions were treated with a kind, but firm, talking-to. Other times the punishment was more severe. But we *remember* them.

But can we tell stories about where we got our social values? My grandfather bequeathed to me the value of public service. I don't remember his exact words, but just two days before he passed away from kidney disease, he called me to his bedside and gently informed me that I had a calling for public life. When I was in eighth grade, Father Murray (my parish priest), reinforced that call when he invited me into the rectory and rolled out a map of St. Paul. "See that area on the map that is marked in gray?" he asked. "That is the neighborhood where Negroes (the term of use in those days) live. They are not allowed to live in other neighborhoods in our city. This is wrong—and I know that someday you will do something about it."

I am not sure what Father Murray thought that something should be. He did tell me about a new organization he was working with – the Catholic Interracial Council. I couldn't imagine they would let 8th graders participate in their meetings. Looking back, I don't think he expected me to take any specific action then. If he did, I would have needed a lot more guidance. Rather, I think he was conveying his belief that I would in some way make that value my own and take it with me into adulthood.

I first told that story many years later at a meeting of an organization committed to building sustainable urban and rural communities. The organizer started the meeting by asking us to share a story about what motivated our involvement in this or other community projects. I didn't really know the other folks all that well, so sharing my story and listening to theirs created a bond between us. It gave us a sense of who we were and gave energy to the rest of the day's more technical discussions. Personally recalling the sources of our own values is a mark of reflective leadership. Collectively sharing these stories can bring a powerful sense of motivation and renewal to an organization.

The leadership educator, Robert Terry, introduced me to the power of sacred texts in bringing deep social values to consciousness. Bob would encourage participants in his seminars to bring poems, quotes from scripture, maxims, songs, speeches, political declarations—even a personal letter from a mentor or family member—and share what made their text especially meaningful. I have continued this tradition in my own leadership seminars.

Although students bring a range of texts, the broad patterns reflect the currents that underlie social values more generally. For many, texts that celebrate the personal virtues of hard work, integrity, persistence, and hope are especially moving. Values like these are reflected in the maxims of Ben Franklin, the "never give up" messages that come from influential people in our lives, and the inspirational sayings that end up as magnets

Ben Franklin on the Virtues of Individual Responsibility

- By failing to prepare, you are preparing to fail.

- An investment in knowledge pays the best interest.

- The U.S. Constitution doesn't guarantee happiness, only the pursuit of it. You have to catch up with it yourself.

- He that is good for making excuses is seldom good for anything else.

- Well done is better than well said.

on the refrigerator door. They reflect the American value of personal responsibility and are a celebration of the individual's ability to pursue life, liberty, and happiness even against the odds.

Other participants bring texts that more directly express themes related to neighborly compassion or social justice. Most common are variations of the scriptural injunction, "Love thy neighbor as thyself," and quotes from political or social movement leaders. Occasionally, participants will bring in the U.S. Bill of Rights, International Declaration of Human Rights, or Declaration of Independence. One text I share is the South African Freedom Charter—a moving vision of the democratic and just society, born in the struggle against apartheid.

The text most often shared is the Serenity Prayer:

> *God grant me the serenity to accept the things I cannot change;*
> *the courage to change the things I can;*
> *and the wisdom to know the difference.*

The prayer was developed in its current form by the most prominent Protestant theologian of the twentieth century, Reinhold Niebuhr. Niebuhr began his career as a social justice advocate and a pacifist. During the Great Depression of the 1930s, he was a strong advocate for the rights of labor and the unemployed, and the Christian message of peace. Then along came Hitler and the concentration camps. Forced by history, Niebuhr developed the tragic awareness that evil exists and human progress advances in fits and starts. Often read as an acknowledgement of the limits to individual action, the prayer also reminds us to keep the faith even as we face the gap between the expansiveness of our dreams and the limits of the possible.

Our social world is full of examples of groups and institutions that have lost, and then re-found their core values and the convictions that got them started in the first place. Renewal of our schools, community organizations, religious faiths, and democratic institutions often begins with questions like:

- Why did we become educators in the first place?
- Whatever happened to our sense of community?
- Are we really practicing the principles of our religious faith?
- Is this the best America can do?

Over time, posing provocative questions like these with patience and skill is a fundamental task of value-based leadership.

Martin Luther King once said, "Deed leads to creed." He meant that values are often discovered through action. He was right. My qualifying point—one that King's own life personified—is that creed illuminates and sustains deed. Ultimately, the goal of value-based leadership is to connect values to action, or to use the vernacular of the civil rights movement: to "walk the talk."

Leading with a Moral Compass

In Chapter 1, I introduced the concept of ethical leadership. Is that different than value-based leadership? Not really. Both ethical and value-based leadership are concerned with "right and wrong." Ethics, as a branch of philosophy, provides principles that help us apply our personal values in the work place and in the broader society.

Ethical leadership requires *ethical consciousness*. Before a community can act on an ethical issue, it must become aware that an ethical issue exists in the first place. Flowing from that awareness, ethical leaders bring the issue to the group and hopefully find ways to resolve it. Ethical practice is only as strong as the shared values of the group. Often there is a conflict between professed values and daily actions—between the words we speak and the actions we take. Often individual group members are in ethical conflict with themselves—wanting to do the right thing, but afraid of losing friends, being shunned by group members, or suffering economic harm. Often people aren't even sure what the right thing is!

> Before a community can act on an ethical issue, it must become aware that an ethical issue exists in the first place.

Facing value-based conflict is one of the toughest leadership challenges. Value-based conflicts are pervasive. And even though that is a hard thing, it is also a good thing. A society that doesn't experience the tug and pull of new values interacting with and refining traditional values is, by definition, inert. Conflict is necessary for change and change (along with continuity) is necessary for a society to flourish. The same goes for our churches, community organizations, public institutions, and businesses.

One development that set off value conflicts around the country, flowed from society's changing attitudes toward the mentally ill. Beginning in the 1970s, advocates begin to identify an ethical issue: Was it right to confine our mentally ill for years on end in large, prison-like treatment centers? A growing number of citizens thought not. In my state, Minnesota, laws were passed and programs established to move the mentally ill to smaller, community-based group homes where those who were able, could lead a fuller and more satisfying life. In the Minneapolis suburb of Brooklyn Center, that value ran headlong into opposition from nervous residents who felt that the values they placed on community—family, autonomy, and, yes, property values—were under threat. What followed was a case study in real-world ethics and a bracing look at just how difficult it is to exercise value-based ethical leadership.

The conflict began when in 1986, when Henry Norton decided to establish a group home for mentally ill adults who also were chemically dependent. Years earlier, Norton, himself a recovering alcoholic, left a lucrative career in the financial services industry to start the Bill Kelley House in an inner-city South Minneapolis neighborhood already saturated with group homes. Both residents and city officials had grown weary of being the "treatment mecca" for the entire state, and Norton agreed to move Kelley house to a first ring suburb close enough to the city for easy access to transportation, jobs, and social services. He found what he was looking for in a residential neighborhood off Drew Avenue in Brooklyn Center. He purchased a ten-unit apartment building with space for 23 residents and sent a flier to neighbors in the immediate area, inviting them to an informational meeting.

Jill Sherritt was one of the neighbors who received the flier and what she saw made her nervous. The group home would be located right across from where the bus stopped to take her kids to school. Jill, and neighbors like her, were working class and middle class people: plumbers, electricians, construction workers, nurses, and teachers. Their neighborhood wasn't especially grand and their houses were modest, but they had worked hard for what they had. They prized their independence and the community they had built.

As a result of deinstitutionalization, over 9,000 people were released from state mental institutions. With a severe shortage of adequate community-based facilities, middle-class suburbs like Brooklyn Center were under pressure to do their fair share. Norton expected some opposition. There had been a heated skirmish just a few years earlier when the city council refused to issue a permit to the first group-home applicant. The council's decision was overruled by the court and the home was located in the city anyway. Norton believed he had the law on his side. He wasn't asking permission. He felt he didn't need to.

He underestimated the organizing skills of Jill Sherritt. When Norton arrived at the informational meeting, the meeting hall was packed and TV cameras on the ready. As Norton talked in soothing generalities, community members seethed. They wanted to know who would be in the facility, was it secured, were their kids in danger, and would their property values decline. When the meeting got heated, Norton's lawyer got blunt. Neighborhood approval, he told them, is not required. The Bill Kelley House is coming whether they like it or not.

It soon became clear that Norton's confidence was misplaced. Two years of hearings, city council votes, and mutual recriminations would follow. The conflict was a case study in just how difficult it is to resolve competing ethical claims when people feel threatened. The neighborhood opposition simply refused to believe Norton's assurances that group homes do not result in higher crime rates or danger for children. They refused to believe studies showing that group homes do not decrease property values. For his part, Norton was befuddled and increasingly frustrated. He really believed that his project would not hurt the community, but he had no idea how to convince the residents.

Meanwhile, neighborhood residents were collecting "facts" of their own. They visited with residents of other communities who had negative experiences with group homes. They gathered crime statistics that seemed to indicate that group homes really did lead to higher crime. Alarming stories circulated with little regard for their accuracy. One resident claimed that she had talked to a psychotherapist who informed her that the chemically dependent were highly prone to sexual violence. When a rumor of a drug bust at a group home in a neighboring community turned out to be false, it kept circulating anyway.

As often happens, the conflict got personal. Norton, opponents said, was a rich guy from the affluent suburb of Wayzata. They charged that Norton was using the plight of the mentally ill to make money for himself. Some referred to him as "Snortin Norton, the Wall Street Junkie." Friends of Norton pointed out the irony in the claims of profiteering. Norton had been making far more money in the financial business. Whatever his flaws, he was genuinely committed to the people he served.

After two years, Norton realized he was defeated. Time was running out on his South Minneapolis location. In order to save the Bill Kelley Home, he needed to make a move. Ironically, Kelley House would remain in Minneapolis, relocating to an area of low-rise apartment buildings with nary a single-family home in sight. Learning from the Brooklyn Park experience, Norton dispatched staff to talk to residents one by one, inviting those who might be interested to serve on a community advisory board for the home. When the informational meeting that caused such uproar in Brooklyn Center was held, there was only one opponent. The Minneapolis City Council granted the permit on schedule.

Soon after the relocation in Minneapolis, lawyers negotiated a legal settlement and a solution of sorts was reached. Brooklyn Center granted a permit for a smaller group home to serve either the mentally ill or chemically dependent, but not both.

Separate from the settlement, Jill Sherritt lobbied Hennepin County to approve an audit of group homes like the Bill Kelley House. The report articulated a middle ground that neither side could find in the heat of conflict. It substantiated some of Sherritt's concerns. Residential treatment centers often fail to provide adequate mental health services to its residents. The report also showed that 74 percent of residents who lived near group homes, described them as good neighbors despite initial reservations. The authors concluded, "We didn't find anything that would lend credence to the theory that it is dangerous to have them in the neighborhood. Yet, no one should take neighborhood concerns lightly."

What are the lessons here for ethical and value-based leadership? What values were at stake? Is ethical leadership even possible when conflicts over opposing values become so heated? Could there have been a way to resolve those differences either before or during the conflict itself? More specifically, how are we to evaluate Jill Sherritt and Henry Norton as ethical and value-based leaders?

The search for ethical principles goes all the way back to Aristotle, or, in respect to Eastern and indigenous traditions, even further. College courses in applied ethics are available and most professions require some attention to the principles of ethical behavior by their practitioners. But most of us don't reason our way through conflicts with a checklist of ethical principles ready to be pulled out of our pocket. Fortunately, the Harvard-based leadership educator, Ronald Heifetz, has developed a simpler approach. He suggests ethical dimensions to consider *ethical process* and *ethical content*. Ethical process is about how we treat each other, and involves such principles as honesty, respect, and the participation of those who have a stake in the decision. Ethical content involves the action itself. Is what we are seeking to do, just? Does it conform to positive social values?

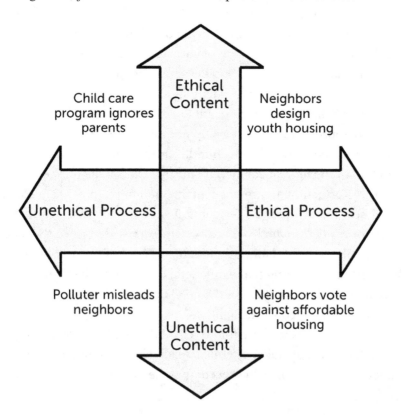

It is possible to use ethical processes toward unethical ends. It is also possible, and quite common, to use unethical processes to reach ethical ends. Heifetz uses the example of President Lyndon Johnson—one of the most powerful legislative leaders in U.S. history. As both majority leader and president, Johnson was skilled and ruthless in his use of power to get things done. He was known to cajole, threaten, intimidate, and ridicule senators in pursuing his goals. One could evaluate him as unethical in his process. But what about his domestic agenda: civil rights, Medicare, support for the poor, consumer protection, and the first environmental legislation in decades? Was the content of his agenda ethical? Was it based on righteous social values? Did the ends justify the means?

Naming these two dimensions is not the same as agreeing on what constitutes them. But this approach does invite leaders to stop and think. Are we treating each other with respect? Are the actions we are taking consistent with the values we believe in? Are those values in need of modification in light of changing circumstances?

Take the case of Henry Norton and Jill Sherritt. Norton believed he was communicating honestly (ethical process) but he really wasn't willing to listen to the concerns of the neighborhood. More basically, he had decided in advance to locate the group home regardless of the neighbors' wishes. One could argue that overriding a neighborhood's concerns is coercion—another violation of ethical process. On the other hand, Jill Sherritt involved neighbors to take collective action. She facilitated a neighborhood voice—an affirmation of ethical process. However, when she (and others) amplified rumors, distorted facts, and personally attacked Henry Norton, one could reasonably say that she too violated ethical process.

What about ethical content? Wasn't Norton's sincere commitment to some of the most isolated and demeaned members of society an affirmation of compassion and social justice? Even if he did profit, there were certainly less strenuous and more lucrative things a man of his skills could have done for a living. As for the neighborhood residents, is there something wrong with wanting to preserve a community to feel secure for yourself, your children, and your neighbors' children? Is there something wrong with concern for the property value of your home? And is there something wrong in insisting that the neighborhood itself should have a genuine say?

Both Norton and the neighborhood had strong value-based claims to their positions. The problem was that they became *incompatible* value claims. Would things have been different if Norton had asked the community rather than dictating to them? Would a longer and more open advisory process have helped resolve the conflict? What if neighborhood leaders committed to accepting a modified group home proposal? And what if public officials acted as problem solvers rather than reflecting the fears of their constituents?

Building Morally Courageous Organizations

Asking the questions isn't the same as successfully implementing effective answers. It is especially difficult to act as our best selves when a conflict reaches full boil. I do believe, however, that it is possible to nurture organizations where ethical challenges can be confronted, if not always completely resolved. As noted earlier, this takes moral courage. Is moral courage rare? Does it require the heroism of a Bishop Whipple? Can we expect leaders to risk the wrath of neighbors, the anger of co-workers, or the loss of member support when raising uncomfortable ethical issues?

I can certainly think of day-to-day examples of moral courage: the pastor who lost his congregation when he

Moral Courage

Cowardice asks the question—
  Is it safe?
Expediency asks the question—
  Is it politic?
Vanity asks the question—
  Is it popular?
But conscience asks the question—Is it right?

And there comes a time when one must take a position That is neither sage, nor politic, nor popular But one must take it because it is right.

Martin Luther King Jr.

spoke up for gay marriage; the teacher union leader who called for more meaningful evaluation of teacher performance; the suburban city council member who supported mixed income housing in the face of resident opposition; the chamber of commerce member who dared suggest that raising the minimum wage was a matter of economic justice; and the farm organization leader who questioned the equity of the current agricultural subsidy system knowing that some of his members benefited from those very subsidies.

Moral courage is virtuous—and exhausting. Some may be capable of consistent moral heroism, but if we rely on heroes to build and maintain ethical, value-based organizations, we are bound to be disappointed. Effective ethical leadership includes building ethical organizations. And, since values and ethics are socially influenced, that means working with others to support organizational cultures that reinforce ethical action. We need courageous leaders, yes. But even more, we need courageous organizations—organizations that make individual moral heroism less necessary, because moral/ethical leadership is reinforced rather than resisted by the group itself.

How can leaders make that happen? First, remember that leadership is a social, not individual, activity. You may have the moral stamina to be the lone prophet raging against the darkness, but you will be more effective (and suffer fewer personal consequences) if you go into action with others who share your concern. At some point calling individuals or groups to moral account requires a public voice. But before you take the rostrum, it is wise to find others who share your perspective. Or, as Winston Churchill advised, "Courage is what it takes to stand up and speak. Courage is also what it takes to sit down and listen."

When Rosa Parks refused to leave her seat to make way for a white man, she demonstrated the moral courage to challenge the deeply entrenched system of Jim Crow in Alabama. We remember that as an individual heroic act and it was indeed, heroic. But Rosa Parks knew she had an organized and committed community behind her. She did not act alone. Her courage—and effectiveness—was reinforced by hundreds and then thousands of civil rights activists who found ways to be courageous together. The Civil Rights movement, like many movements before and after, formed a moral community; a collective and mutually reinforcing body that made ordinary people into extraordinary heroes.

Building Morally Courageous Organizations

- Create a culture of reflection—build in times for the group to assess their work in relationship to their social values.
- Create forums for respectful conversation when moral issues or value-based conflicts emerge.
- Don't go alone: find out who else might share you concern.
- Listen!
- Avoid self-righteousness; respect difference.
- Illustrate principles with stories.
- Remember, change takes time

It does not require history-making actions to build organizations that sustain an ethic of moral and ethical awareness. It does take *intent*. Leaders can encourage members to reflect on the relationship between professed values and everyday action. When ethical issues do come up, leaders can create forums for their discussion and set a tone for open and self-critical consideration. Leaders can also check their own personal self-righteousness meter. Don't assume your fellow members are moral midgets. In fact, a willingness to raise ethical issues ought to be balanced with a belief in people's willingness to change, even if that change takes time.

We will always need our moral heroes—people who are willing to pay a high price for the principles they defend. But ethical, value-based leaders, are not prophets, nor need they be saints. Whether challenging external powers to act with justice, or calling on members of their own organization to live up to their own highest principles, they are artists of the possible.

Chapter 5
Organizational Leadership

Leadership is essentially a group activity. Whether the group is a tiny block club, mid-sized social service organization, or broad-based coalition, leaders interact with participants to achieve common goals. It follows then, that a key aspect of leadership is organizational dynamics. In this chapter, we will explore these dynamics—moving from the level of a specific organization to exploring how leaders help create change in the broader society.

Organizational Leadership: Know Thy Group

Organizational leaders know how to build and maintain strong groups. An effective organizational leader is like a good car mechanic who can pull up the hood and see what is happening inside. The mechanic not only can identify the parts, but understands how they work together. The engine might be working fine, but if the battery is low or the spark plugs need to be replaced, the car will just sputter along or not run at all. Human organizations, like automobiles, have identifiable parts. Sometimes the parts move in harmony and sometimes they don't move at all. It's the job of organizational leaders to identify what needs fixing and work with group members to make the necessary repairs.

> It's the job of organizational leaders to identify what needs fixing and work with group members to make the necessary repairs.

69

Of course, a car isn't much good if you don't know where to drive it. That requires both a destination and an ability to navigate. Effective organizational leaders develop a clear sense of direction for, and importantly *with*, the organizations they lead. In so doing, they engage members in finding the paths to reach the destination. They ask questions like:

- Where are we going?
- Is this really where we want to be going?
- What are the road blocks keeping us from going there?
- How do we navigate around and through those obstacles?

Organizational leaders understand both the dynamics of the groups they lead and the external environments that affect their groups. They believe in the possibility of change and understand how change actually happens. In Chapter 1, I noted that the most important characteristic of strategic leaders (a particular form of organizational leadership), is a belief in the possibility of change. The best strategic leaders are skillful optimists. They are hopeful about change *and* knowledgeable about how to make change happen. They know what to look for under that hood, and if there is a problem they can't fix, they know who to ask.

Four Elements of Effective Organizations

So what is under that hood? What are the moving parts that make an organization hum—or reduce it to a stall? The leadership educator Robert Terry, introduced me and thousands of others to his answer to that question. Terry believed all human organizations can be at least partially understood through looking at four key dimensions: Mission, Power, Structure, and Resource. Taken together, these represent four corners of a diamond. When all four dimensions are functioning at a high level, the diamond—the most durable element in nature—is strong. But when problems arise in any of the dimensions, the entire organization is affected.

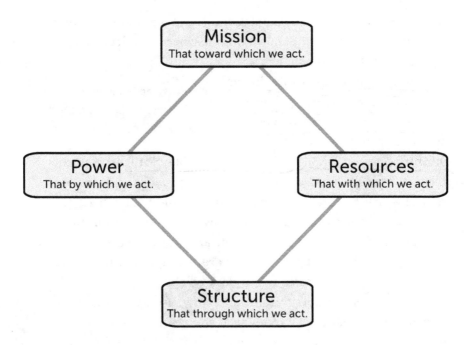

As a teacher, I have often used the diamond model to help me be conscious of what is going on in my classes. In my role as teacher/ leader I state the mission of the class in the course syllabus and in my opening remarks at the first class meeting. For example, in my introductory political science class, I convey my hope that students will develop a clear understanding of how our political system works, and how they can act individually and collectively on issues they care about. That hope—my purpose—is the mission of the class.

But who has the power in my class? My ability to accomplish the mission is dependent on the willingness of my students to embrace it. I do have some coercive power, some power-over as we discussed in Chapter 3. If a student doesn't demonstrate knowledge of how the political system works through tests, papers, and class presentations, I can always give them a bad grade. But genuine learning—and therefore successful teaching—requires that both students and teacher embrace a common mission. That requires *relational power*— in this case, the ability to engage, persuade, and inspire students to embrace a common purpose. And contrary to traditional notions of the student-teacher relationship, that relational power works best when it flows in three directions: from teacher-to-student, student-to-teacher, and student-to-student.

Power is energy. Structure directs energy. For example, our political science class meets on Monday, Wednesday, and Friday from 9:00 to 9:55. It begins on January 5th and ends on May 11th. Assignments include three short papers, a field assignment, and a mini-research project—each due on a specific date in the semester. Each assignment has a certain point value. Behavior is also structured. Both students and teacher are expected to be on time and stay until the end. Norms of active and respectful participation are encouraged. All of these expectations are articulated in my class syllabus.

Power is energy. Structure directs energy.

Agenda

In the modern university, there are many resources to support learning. Think of the classroom itself as a resource. There are desks and chairs, whiteboards, and lighting. With the advent of the "smart classroom," I can bring the world into my classroom through video and the internet. Textbooks, laptops, pens, and notepaper are all resources. But resources are not just *stuff*. The real currency of education is knowledge and expertise. In that sense, I, as the teacher, am a resource. But I also invite other *resource people* to my class as guest speakers; and *structure* (there's that word again) assignments for students to interview resource people on their own.

A successful class happens when all four corners of the diamond—mission, power, structure, and resource—support each other. However, often this is not the case. A careful look under the hood is in order. Let's imagine that my political science class was only a partial success. Although there were some students who clearly engaged, many simply did what they needed to do to pass the class. Was the problem the mission itself? Is there something about the purpose of the course that is intrinsically uninteresting to a significant percentage of students? Perhaps no amount of skillful teaching can motivate (empower) some students to want to learn about how the political system works.

Or maybe there is nothing wrong with the mission itself but the problem was my failure to motivate the students. Perhaps it was a power issue. Or perhaps, despite my mild manner and encouraging demeanor, I intimidated some of the less academically-prepared students. Maybe the academic jargon that crept into my vocabulary made some feel ignorant. Or maybe my power to issue grades encouraged students to try to figure out the answers I was looking for, rather than puzzle through the issues for themselves. Or conversely, maybe my emphasis on small group discussion and problem solving, placed too much power in the hands of the students—leading to confusion and uncertainty, rather than engagement and insight.

Perhaps the (partial) failure of mission had something to do with the way the class was structured. Meeting three times a week is often difficult for working students who have multiple obligations. Maybe it would be better if the class met for three hours, one night a week. Classes that are structured to meet for fifty minutes per session can also create pedagogical problems. Fifty minutes might be enough time to view a political documentary, but not enough time to discuss it.

What about resources? Was the text book engaging? Did I assign too many supplemental readings or too few? Was the photocopier always breaking down? Were the magic markers dry? And how about that community resource project I assigned? Were the resources actually helpful? Could the students actually access them?

Reflective teachers ask questions like these and are courageous enough to ask the students for their perspective on the learning experience. They are acting as organizational leaders—looking under the hood, identifying why the engine is sputtering, and figuring out what repairs need to be made. They are courageous because, unlike the car engine, students can talk back. Some of what they say might sting. Genuine leadership involves vulnerability and a supple strength that allows for adaptation based on honest encounter.

If you have been involved in community work over the years, you know that not all groups function at full capacity all the time. Effective leaders understand this and are able to recognize the forces that keep an organization humming and those that slow it down. Using the diamond model as a guide, here are examples from my own experience that illustrate the range of functionality.

High Functioning: The Legacy Project

In the autumn of 2003, about thirty Minnesota progressive activists gathered in a church basement to make plans to elect Democrats to the state House of Representatives. Their goal was modest: recruit and support two candidates in "swing" suburban districts where Democrats had a chance to win. The passion—as well as the name of this project—came from a deep sense of loss that many progressives were feeling that year. On one hand, their deeply held social and political values were not shared by the newly-elected Republican majority; and on the other hand, their beloved leader, Senator Paul Wellstone, had been killed in a plane crash a year earlier. The group wanted to honor the legacy of those who had struggled to make Minnesota one of the most progressive states in the union and they wanted in particular to honor the memory of Paul Wellstone.

The plan they developed was elegant in its simplicity. Based on careful research:

- target two promising legislative districts,
- seek out candidates who shared the group's values and had the potential to win, and
- commit volunteer energy to help put the candidates over the top.

Each Legacy project member would pledge 24 hours of campaign volunteer work during the election season—about six hours per month. A wide range of activities would be available to suit the interests and comfort level of each volunteer. All members of the project were empowered to vote on what candidates to endorse. Campaign training sessions were organized for those who had never participated in a political campaign before.

The result? Both of the candidates endorsed by the project were elected and attributed much of their success to the volunteer efforts of Legacy Project members. As it turned out, Democrats were

successful in other districts as well and the legislature returned to
DFL control.

What were the reasons for the group's success? First, the
mission was clear and understood by all the participants. Members
understood that electing two candidates was a "mission possible" and
drew on a deep reservoir of shared values. The power of the group
was vested in its highly-motivated members with a shared belief in
the mission. The power was distributed through clear structures
and an approach to decision making that included both small and
larger group deliberation. The actual campaign work was well
structured. Volunteers knew what was expected and how to carry out
their commitment. And the project made excellent use of resources
as the skills of the members were enhanced by contributions from
experienced political campaigners.

In short, the power of participants committed to a shared mission
flowed through clearly delineated structures and drew on the
resources of the members themselves, supplemented by additional
expertise as needed. Like a well-tuned vehicle, the organization
hummed along, undeterred by the occasional bump in the road.

South Side Community Enterprises: Disputed Mission/ Power Outage

Back in the early 1970s, an idealistic group of South Minneapolis
residents decided to create an organization to develop community
and worker-owned businesses in their neighborhood. The
organization, Southside Community Enterprises (SCE), was one of
the first Community Development Corporations (CDCs) in Minnesota.
As hybrid organizations, CDCs combined a commitment to
community representation with housing and business development.
Ideally, projects would respond to community needs, while still being
economically-viable enterprises.

The pioneers who started SCE had four things in common: they
were in their mid-to-late twenties, radical in ideology, inexperienced
in business, and white. Although they reflected neither the values nor
social background of most of the neighbors they sought to represent,

through their political connections, they did have access to start-up funds from the federal government. They used those funds to hire a staff, recruit a board of directors that was more representative of the community than themselves, and rent an office above a gun shop in the neighborhood.

From the very beginning, the leaders of the South Side Community Enterprises faced two major problems...

First, they lacked the expertise to start up community-based or worker-owned enterprises. The food cooperative movement was in its infancy at that time and frequented mostly by members of the '60s era counter culture ("hippies"). These cooperatives didn't generate nearly enough revenue to provide living wages for its workers. Then, as now, the vast majority of businesses were created and owned by private corporations and individual entrepreneurs. That was the system that people knew best.

Second, and even more basic, there was a mismatch between the mission of the organizers and the will of those board members who most clearly reflected the neighborhood. To the average South Minneapolis resident, the most important priorities were jobs, affordable housing, and a revitalized private business sector. To most residents, the idea of community or cooperatively-owned businesses seemed like a pipe dream at best, and a strong minority of the community board felt the same way. It wasn't that these board members were opposed to alternative ways to organize businesses, but that their first priority was to support business development in the most practical way possible.

Leadership as Diagnosis

At the beginning of this chapter, I stated that organizational leaders know how to diagnose what is going wrong—or right—in an organization. Just as doctors ask patients about symptoms in order to make accurate diagnoses, effective leaders listen to participants for what is working well and for problems that need to be addressed. For example, a problem with mission might be expressed through participant concerns about lack of direction or confusion about what constitutes success. Power problems are indicated when members feel that decisions are being made without their input, or conversely, when no one is making decisions at all. Problems with structure manifest themselves when participants complain about poor organization or confusion about where to go to in the organization to get problems addressed. And resource problems become visible when members feel they lack the knowledge to do the job.

Issues are indicated when a leader hears...

Mission
- I don't know if we are successful.
- We are not clear about our future direction.
- We've lost our way.
- There's nothing to hope or dream for anymore.
- People operate on selfish, narrow interest.

Power
- People who have no right to be involved are in on the decision.
- Why doesn't someone just do something?
- The decision making is by fate.
- All decisions are already made; it's a sham.
- My energy level is really low.

Structure
- The job is not clearly defined. I don't know what I'm supposed to do.
- The organization is poorly organized.
- The place is so loose, anything goes.
- There is no coordination among jobs.
- The organizational chart doesn't reflect the way things happen.

Resources
- We are not sure what we need to complete the task.
- I don't have the skills or knowledge to do the job.
- We can't make do with what we have.
- We can't create from nothing.
- I don't know what we need.

Often problems are interconnected. Taken together, they add up to what sociologist Herbert Ganz calls a ***disorganization***—an organization where members are confused and inactive, rarely come to meetings, and don't follow through on tasks between meetings. Ultimately, disorganizations are caused by a breakdown in the critical connection between leadership and followership. Effective group leaders can't do it alone. In fact, doing it alone is not leadership. Leadership only happens when leaders and members connect around a shared purpose.

However, it is the responsibility of leaders to point the way forward. Leaders must identify and name what is not working and present a vision for what a well-functioning organization really looks like. Pointing out the contrast between an ineffective disorganization and a well-functioning organization, can be bracing and even restorative.

Disorganizations

- They are *divided.* Factions and divisions fragment the organization and sap it of resources.
- They get *confused.* Each person has a different story about what's going on. There is a lot of gossip, but not very much good information.
- They are *passive.* Most "members" do very little. One or two people do most of the work.
- They are *reactive.* They are always trying to respond to some unanticipated new development.
- They are *inactive.* No one comes to meetings. No one shows up for activities.
- They *drift.* There is little purposefulness to meetings, actions, or discussions as things drift from one meeting to the next.

Organizations That Work

- They are *united.* They have learned to manage their differences well enough that they can unite to accomplish the purpose for which they were formed. Differences are openly debated, discussed, and resolved.
- They share *understanding.* There is a widely shared understanding of what is going on, what the challenges are, what the program is, and why what is being done had to be done.
- People *participate.* Lots of people in the organization are active—not just going to meetings, but getting the work of the organization done.
- They take *initiative.* Rather than reacting to whatever happens in their environment, they are proactive, and act upon their environment.
- They *act.* People do the work needed to make things happen.
- They share a sense of *purpose.* There is a purposefulness about meetings, actions, and decisions; and a sense of forward momentum as work gets done.

From Herbert Ganz, "Organizing and Developing New Leaders," the New School. 2002.

Developing Leadership-Rich Organizations

Effective organizational leaders understand that developing the leadership skills of members will increase the capacity of the group as a whole. This may be especially true in civic organizations, where much of the work gets done by members and volunteers. If members themselves are not involved or don't reach out to involve others, little will get done. But how do leaders support and develop other leaders? Herbert Ganz suggests that you take a look at the "leadership quotient" of your organization. Is there one leader, with everyone linked to him or her, like spokes on a wheel? Or are there many leaders, working together throughout the organization? Are some members followers only, or do leaders and followers trade roles depending on the task or activity? Is your organization blessed with a cornucopia of leaders, or is the cupboard bare?

The identification and development of leaders, is one of the most important functions of group leadership. Fortunately, leadership development is a skill that can be learned through reflective practice. It starts with an explicit commitment to put leadership development at the center of the organization's practice as opposed to it being an afterthought. Understanding that leadership development is both a means to an end AND an end itself, elevates it to a core element of an organization's mission.

Leadership development requires that leaders get to know the skills, interests, and motivations of members. Making an investment in relationship building (maintenance) is essential to identifying what members are willing to contribute to an organization's work (task). It also requires a clear understanding of the difference between delegating tasks and developing leaders. Asking a member to make twenty fund-raising calls, is delegating a task. Asking a member to put together a team to plan and carry out the annual awards banquet, is delegating leadership. Asking two of this year's phone callers to organize the banquet planning team for next year, is an example of creating ladders of leadership opportunities over time.

Imagine you have just moved into the neighborhood and decide to join the community association. You show up at your first meeting, pick up an agenda, and find a place to sit. No one greets you or asks what brings you to the meeting. There are committee reports that you find only mildly interesting. The coffee is bitter and the cookies taste like they are a week old. You leave the meeting feeling unwelcomed and, frankly, a little useless. If you are the assertive type, you might take matters into your own hands and offer your volunteer services to the association president after the meeting. Or you might walk away and never come back again.

Now imagine that the chair of the organization does greet you on your way out the door. She introduces herself and you have a friendly chat. She wonders if you would like to get together during the next week or two, to discuss what the community association is all about and where you might fit in. You agree and suddenly decide that maybe that coffee wasn't so bad after all. Two weeks later you sit down and have a conversation. You start with the usual things: where you grew up, the town you lived in before moving into the neighborhood, what you do for a living, and how your kids are doing in school.

Eventually the conversation turns to the community association. The chair, let's call her Jane, explains a little about the history of the group, how she became involved, and what the big issues are for the year. She asks you how you might want to be involved. You confess that you really don't like calling people to show up at events, much less ask for money. But you do like to do research and write, and are very interested in affordable housing issues. You also note that you have had experience chairing a housing committee and might be interested in doing that, if the opportunity should arise. When Jane asks if there are skills you would like to improve on, you are taken aback. No one since college has ever asked you a question like that! You share how nervous you were a few years back when testifying at a city council hearing and that you would welcome the opportunity to practice your public speaking skills.

As the meeting nears a close, Jane suggests that you join the association's housing and community development committee. They could use the help, she admits. The committee chair has served three terms and is ready to move on. There is a big development opportunity in the heart of the neighborhood and your research skills could be put to good use. She offers to arrange a meeting with the committee chair and sit in herself just to make sure the expectations are clear. The committee chair, we'll call him John, is a very nice man, but isn't particularly good at delegating tasks or developing leadership opportunities for committee members. Jane thinks that is one of the reasons he is burning out but she doesn't share that information—better to let you and John start your relationship fresh.

Clearly, Jane understands how important it is to develop leadership in the community association. I know I would appreciate the time Jane spent with our imaginary member. She is, after all, a volunteer. I would hope there are others similarly involved in taking the time to get to know their members. Perhaps the association has a staff member charged with this role. Perhaps each member of the group's executive committee takes on this responsibility. Maybe there is even a leadership development team. Regardless of how the process is structured, the key elements include conversations like the one imagined above, careful delegation, continuing communication and support, ongoing leadership training, skill development opportunities, and accountability.

A Leadership Development Check List

❑ Is leadership development a conscious practice that is understood as a priority throughout the organization?

❑ Do leaders have intentional conversations with new (and old) members about how they want to contribute to the group?

❑ Are tasks widely delegated or do a few people do all the work?

❑ Are there clear opportunities for members to move into leadership roles?

❑ When leadership is delegated is there ongoing support or are new leaders left on their own?

❑ Are members held accountable for volunteer tasks and leadership opportunities they volunteer for?

❑ Are the organization's officers, committee chairs, and other leadership positions rotated among members or do the same people fill those positions year after year?

❑ Does the organization offer opportunities for members to participate in leadership development workshops and seminars or create its own?

❑ When members step into leadership roles, are they recognized and thanked?

Strategic Leadership: Navigating Change

When I think about my own involvement in community organizations, I can see that each is like a snapshot in time. Some of the groups I helped start still exist, though almost always in altered form. Others streaked across the horizon and quickly disappeared. Organizations change and, more importantly, the social context changes. Strategic leadership takes place in specific organizations, but the strategic leader sees beyond the specific time and place, and understands how things change over time. Strategic leaders are organizational leaders with vision. Strategic leadership takes place when a group moves from maintenance (the way we always do things) to navigating—and ultimately embracing—change.

When I use the term "strategic leadership," I am not referring to an individual, although an individual often plays a catalytic role. Rather, I am referring to a collective capacity developed by at least some in a group or coalition of groups. Strategic leaders foster strategic groups that learn to understand social, political, and cultural contexts, and make adjustments over time.

Following, are five stories that illustrate the development of strategic capacity and, ultimately, community power over time.

The Praxis Project: From Women's Shelters to Systems Change

Although we seldom think about it this way, the evolution of cultural attitudes about violence against women is one of the most impressive examples of positive cultural change in recent history. The movement began when small groups of women set up private homes as shelters for battered women. One of the first, Women's Advocates, began in St. Paul, Minnesota, in the early 1970s. The projects were courageous and profound in their simplicity. Abused women, and often their children, found safe harbor in other homes set up for that purpose. The initial programs were defiantly non-institutional and run on a shoestring. Over time, an impressive network of women's shelters was established and funded with both private and public funds. Advocates created powerful coalitions and managed to change laws, public attitudes, and societal understandings of the dynamics of abuse.

In 2008, movement leaders in Minnesota recognized that still deeper institutional changes were necessary. Uneven implementation of laws left too many women vulnerable to continued abuse. Police responders often missed critical indicators of danger. Women and children, deprived of financial support by their spouses, faced impoverishment. The justice system treated battering as a criminal issue, without coordinating with their counterparts in the social welfare system. Working closely with the St. Paul Police (a group that was itself once seen as an obstacle to reform), an experienced group of advocates created the Praxis Project and developed a blueprint for a system-wide approach to confronting domestic abuse. The approach has already transformed the way abuse is treated in St. Paul and has become a model for other communities across the state and nation.

Children and Family Services: Connecting Public Policy to Grassroots Organizing

Children and Family Services in Minneapolis had a long and distinguished history as a service organization devoted to serving the needs of largely low-income families. By the 1990s the group had incorporated a community organizing approach into its work. While continuing its clinical services, the agency implemented a strong focus on developing leaders from within the newly-emerging communities of color and immigrants it served. CFS also had a public policy wing, staffed by sophisticated "experts" on policy issue affecting the urban poor. Unfortunately, the community organizing wing of the agency and the public policy wing didn't communicate. The public policy advocates saw the organizers as "bomb throwers" who would alienate the decision makers they were trying to influence. And the organizers saw the policy people as part of the problem. It became a classic case of "street vs. suits."

In 2009, this all changed. The agency was reorganized and the director combined the public policy unit with the grass roots organizing. The change had almost immediate impact. The new structure created space for a more powerful relationship between the agency and its constituency. Low-income constituents became effective participants in issues that were important to their lives. Rather than simply providing input for professional staff to act on, they themselves determined priorities and, working with effective organizers, acted collectively to achieve their goals.

In 2009, in the grip of the Great Recession that began a year earlier, community residents identified jobs as a key need. Soon after, CFS joined other organizations in a broad coalition called HIRED and successfully lobbied the legislature to open up state construction contracts to communities of color. In the process, CFS participants learned some lessons about power. For example, in one important legislative committee hearing, coalition members arrived early and filled up the seats usually occupied by well-heeled representatives of the more privileged classes. In another, they literally surrounded an unsympathetic legislator who had been avoiding them and convinced him to change his vote. It was the power of their stories, combined with their obvious resolve, that convinced the legislator to think anew about the impact of abstract legislation on real people's lives.

This process, of directly engaging the people affected by a problem in shaping a solution, also had an impact on a very different social issue: human trafficking. Organizers from CFS, now renamed the Family Partnership, became constituents in a powerful coalition that led to a fundamental change in the way state and local agencies respond to the sexual trafficking of minors. Called the Safe Harbor Program, the Minnesota Legislature redefined trafficked adolescents from criminals to victims; and funded safe houses and supportive services to help victims start new lives. Just as advocates from the domestic abuse movement engaged a broad coalition to create the blueprint, The Safe Harbor Program engaged the legislature, courts, social service organizations, and victims themselves in a comprehensive program that redefined laws and institutional practices.

The St. Paul Federation of Teachers: Engaging Parents and Community on a Shared Educational Agenda

In Minnesota, and in states and communities across the nation, the challenge of educating low-income children—especially those from communities of color—is a major concern. In Minneapolis and St. Paul, the achievement gap between whites and students of color is stark. Some people place the responsibility squarely on teachers and, in particular, teachers unions. Teacher unions, (so the story goes), fight hard to protect their members' seniority and job security, even when those protected may not be reaching those students who need them the most. "Why" critics ask, "should the needs of adults take priority over the needs of our children?" With education comes freedom and, for many, overcoming the racial disparity in our schools is the civil rights issue of our time. It's time, these critics assert, that teachers unions become part of the solution instead of part of the problem.

In St. Paul, leaders of the St. Paul Federation of Teachers have responded by working hard to change this public narrative. Most teachers are dedicated educators. They went into the field because they wanted to make a difference. They love their profession and support their union because they understand that collective power is necessary to protect it. They increasingly understand that a public perception of teachers as simply in it for themselves, will undermine their union and their profession. Over the past several years, they have worked hard to tell their story and back it up with action. In doing so, they have created powerful coalitions with community members and broadened their collective bargaining agenda to include demands that directly impact the quality of education in low-income urban communities. Rather than simply defending their turf, they are building their union into a powerful engine of educational reform.

At the heart of their strategy is the realization that the union simply can't afford to go it alone. Genuine relationships with parents and community members are critical, not only for the preservation of the union but also for the educational success of their students. Working closely with parents, the union created a series of reform proposals called *The Schools St. Paul's Children Deserve* and presented them to the school board. The plan called for smaller class sizes, reduced testing, access to pre-K education, and more. Perhaps the most powerful component of this forward-looking strategy is the Parent Teacher Home Visit Program. Developed with the participation of parents of color, the home visits have had a dramatic impact in opening up communications between teachers and families. The parents, some of whom have been reluctant or simply unable to participate in the conventional avenues for parent involvement, appreciated the connection with their teacher. The kids love having their teacher visit home. Relationships—not public relations spinning—are forming the basis for a stronger teacher community connection.

> Relationships—not public relations spinning—are forming the basis for a stronger teacher community connection.

Hope Community: From Power Places to Power Spaces

Affordable housing is an issue facing many low-income and working class families. But too often, the physical structure called a "house" is not the same thing as the social environment called a "home," and by extension, a "community." Hope Community is an organization built on "community" principles. Founded in 1977 by Catholic nuns as temporary shelter for homeless women and their children, Hope Community has evolved into a critical housing resource with 300 units of low- and moderate-income housing, and a catalyst for civic renewal in its inner city, South Minneapolis, neighborhood.

Hope's visionary director, Mary Keefe, explained the group's approach this way: "From the beginning, we approached neighborhood revitalization as more than creating affordable housing. We are not social workers or service providers…. We are building power spaces and power places… where people can create the future of their neighborhood."

The staff members and leaders of Hope create these power spaces through direct engagement with project residents. Putting civic engagement and leadership development at the core of their work, they created "multiple entry points" for residents of all ages to engage. Projects like the Girls Empowerment Movement and Power of Vision Mural Project, use art to support youth expression and creativity. Educational support programs, career development initiatives, and a youth garden and nutrition program, are just a few other "entry points" that Hope staff and leaders have created over time.

Perhaps Hope's most ambitious civic engagement program is SPEAC—an intense leadership training program that provides youth and young adults the skills necessary to be a catalyst for change in their communities. In 2008, SPEAC became the engine in a community effort to pressure the city park board to fulfill its promise to upgrade the long-neglected Peavey Park. Through a series of listening sessions it conducted throughout the neighborhood, SPEAC members discovered that the top priority of youth was to have more public gathering places like parks. Based on what they heard, they developed a sophisticated set of proposals to make racial and economic equity a central principle of park development, and to make community participation a feature of ongoing park programming.

This deep listening is at the heart of all the Hope Community programs. Since its founding, Hope Community has brought together over 2000 community residents of all ages and cultural backgrounds to build relationships through deep listening. The principle is elegant in its simplicity, but fundamental to community building. It is through genuine encounter that the seeds of community are nurtured. It is through listening and genuine communication that houses become homes, residents become neighbors, and neighbors create a *neighborhood*.

Making Peace Possible: The Nonviolent Peaceforce

In the late 1990s, a community organizer, named Mel Duncan, was profoundly moved by a vision that flowed from his life-long commitment to peacemaking and social justice. Mel was a pioneer and strategic leader with a genius for bringing people together around critical social issues. He organized ACT, one of the nation's first organizations of people with developmental disabilities. He was the catalyst for Jobs for Peace, a coalition of labor, community, and peace organizations that passed pioneering legislation for the conversion of weapons industries to production for non-military uses. As the millennium approached, he continued his commitment to building organizational relationships beyond the usual boundaries. The Minnesota Alliance for Progressive Action (MAPA) brought community, peace, labor, GLBT, and anti-poverty organizations (among others), to work together on issues of common concern: campaign finance reform, human rights protections for gays and lesbians, creative approaches to urban and rural development, and more. There were wins and losses, but the most important thing about MAPA was the relationships formed between people and groups who had previously not worked together—relationships that would continue to grow over time.

All of this was indeed impressive, but the organization he co-founded in 2002 was the most audacious of all. In creating the Nonviolent Peaceforce, Mel and the small band of international peace activists who joined him, directly confronted one of humanity's most vexing challenges: how to bring peaceful resolution to deep and often violent conflicts around the world. In the years since, the NVPF has trained and deployed civilian peacekeeping forces in conflict zones in Sri Lanka, South Sudan, the Philippines, the South Caucuses, and Myanmar. Through slow, respectful listening and engagement with local actors, Peaceforce members have been able to defuse conflicts and facilitate positive relationships across previously hostile boundaries. Project-by-careful project, the Nonviolent Peaceforce is developing the practical knowledge necessary to create an alternative

to violence, and a body of experience to counter those whose first—
and often only—impulse is to go for the gun.

The preceding five stories are examples of strategic leadership with
a capital "S." Don't get hung up on the word. In one sense, we all do
strategic leadership in our daily lives. We use the term "strategy" as a
synonym for plan. What is your strategy (plan) for helping your child
afford college, paying the mortgage, having enough to live on when
you retire, or finding a job or that special person to share your life
with? What's your strategy (plan) for increasing the membership in
the social outreach committee in your church, or the local chapter
of your veterans' organization? Anyone who thinks about how to get
from here to there is, in the most basic sense, engaged in strategy.
Elevated to the organizational level, strategic leaders are the people
in the organization who think about how to move the organization
forward, and connect mission and
purpose to action. As the examples
above illustrate, elevated to a broader
social level, strategic leadership is
about addressing critical community
issues as they evolve over time.

> ...strategic leadership is about addressing critical community issues as they evolve over time.

Seven Characteristics of Strategic Practice

When an organization, or a coalition of organizations, embrace a
forward-looking, disciplined, and value-based approach to change,
they are engaging in **strategic practice for social transformation.**
Phillip Cryan, in his study of ISAIAH (a congregation-based social
change organization), identified the seven characteristics of strategic
practice described below. Rarely, if ever, are they fully present in any
one group or collective effort. Nor do they spring full-blown from the
vision of a single leader. As a list of principles, they are aspirational.
The realization of these aspirations requires leaders who embrace
strategic practice over time.

1. A bold, long-term vision for transformation is at the heart of the organization's work.

Long-term vision is at the heart of each effort recounted above. For example, the organizers of Praxis understood that the next stage of progress in combating violence against women, required a long-term vision for the transformation of the criminal justice system. And what could be more long term and transformational than the Nonviolent Peaceforce's work to replace aggression and force with dialogue and mutual problem solving.

2. The organization has a clearly defined, systematic and disciplined, organizing methodology.

The decision at Children and Family Services, to break down the wall between policy making and grass roots advocacy, flowed from a conscious, organizing methodology that opened up new possibilities for change. Hope Community's focus on civic engagement and deep listening across the age spectrum, has been a consistent and systematic approach to its community building work.

3. For everyone involved, the work is about personal and social transformation.

At the heart of each of these efforts, is the insight that people are transformed through genuine relationships across socially-created boundaries. From the teachers and parents who get to know each other at a deeper level, to the police officer who develops a new understanding of the dynamics of abuse, to the resident members of the Hope Community who discover a new sense of possibility in themselves and each other—personal and social transformation are joined. The energy released in this process not only changes individual lives, but when strategically directed, can change institutions as well.

4. Leadership development is central to all organizing practice.

There is that term again—leadership development! It is a conscious and systematic feature of each of these efforts. One of the most impressive examples is the youth development work at the Hope Community. The training that supports the members of the St. Paul Federation Parent Teacher Home Visit teams is a form of leadership development as well. The complex and challenging work of the Nonviolent Peaceforce teams would be impossible without effective development of conflict resolution, mediation, and community-building skills.

5. Strategies are rooted in a deliberate power analysis that understands both organization and ideas as forms of power.

All of these efforts are examples of social power: the ability of groups to act effectively to promote shared values and goals. Each group understands that power is multi-dimensional. It doesn't reside simply in numbers, money, expertise, laws, values, or ideas; but in various combinations of each. For example, leaders of the Safe Harbors Coalition understood that, in order for human trafficking to be addressed, the awareness of key decision makers and the broader public had to be raised. Putting a personal face on that awareness was an essential element of their strategy. They also understood that creating a network that spanned the boundaries between advocacy groups, agencies, and policy makers (see next page), was an essential element of organizational power. Combined with the development of effective policy ideas, the coalition was able to harness multiple elements of power to achieve their shared goal.

6. Investments are made in alliance-building to achieve results that no single organization can accomplish on its own.

One of the most impressive characteristics of all of these efforts is the understanding that lasting change requires alliances across organizations and institutions. These leaders understand that it is not enough to pressure legislators to pass laws. For one thing, those laws are administered and enforced by public departments and agencies. This was a key insight in the formation of HIRED. Coalition members understood that passing legislation requiring the Department of Transportation to insure that a percentage of jobs went to racial minorities, would have little chance of actual implementation unless staff were engaged as allies. Leaders of the Nonviolent Peaceforce have engaged in years of patient alliance building at the United Nations, non-governmental organizations, and other international governments, in order to expand support for their work.

7. To achieve major changes, you have to be willing to take risks.

Risk is a property of change. So is resistance. Major change involves risk and generates resistance at both the individual and group level. Leadership itself is a risky business. It requires reaching out and developing relationships. Sometimes the offer of relationship is rejected. It requires sharing power and embracing the seemingly contradictory idea that power actually expands the more you share it (at least much of the time). In the kind of transformational leadership we are discussing here, it also requires developing relationships with individuals and groups with whom you may not have worked before.

There is risk when advocates really start listening to the people for whom they have been advocating. Or, even more, when community members start engaging with the very institutions they have been challenging over the years. My guess is that some middle class teachers have felt risk when participating in the Parent Teacher Home Visit program. It is one thing to encounter a low-income parent at school, grade sheet in hand; and another thing to enter the parent's turf.

It is also risky to pursue long-term change when immediate tangible accomplishments may be minimal; or to engage in complex strategies that require both a trust in the member's ability to grasp complexity and the ability to effectively educate members along the way. Not every risk will be rewarded with success, but leaders can take heart in the experience of the Nonviolent Peaceforce. In the ten years since they have deployed peace teams in conflict zones around the world, they have resolved multiple conflicts without the loss of a single peacekeeper. Effective planning, genuine relationship building across deep social divisions, and excellent training, have rewarded risk taking with genuine social transformation.

Chapter 6
Reflective Leadership

It is appropriate to end our investigation of community **leadership at the place where it really starts: with each of us as unique individuals.** Leadership takes place where individual personality intersects with a group. Not everyone is a leader in every situation, but in the fluidity of social interactions most of us often act as leaders—if not every day, over the longer arc of our lives.

Perhaps the most discussed question in leadership studies is this: *are leaders born or made?* If we think leaders are born, we are more likely to see leadership as something selective and fixed. Either you have what it takes to be a leader, or not. Why, you might ask, should I step forward? I'm not cut out to be a leader. I don't have what it takes. And besides, leadership really can't be taught or developed in me—or most other members of the group. Let George do it, he's a natural-born leader.

I suspect most readers would reject this rather absolute embrace of the *leaders are born* perspective. Yet, intuitively, most also understand that there are limits to how much a person can develop as a leader. We all can't be leaders, the pragmatic voice inside us cautions. Some have more talent for it than others.

The most accurate answer to the question is that leaders are *both born and made*. All of us come into the world with our own bundle of personal traits and aptitudes. We refine them through education, both formal (schools) and informal (the playground). Through interaction with others we develop a personality. And, if our social environment permits (not a guarantee), we develop a positive and, at least partially, accurate picture of who we are.

If we have had supportive family members, teachers, and community leaders who have recognized abilities in us, we are more likely to recognize those abilities in ourselves. Not everyone is born to wield a gavel or lead a revolution. But most of us have personal traits and aptitudes that enable us to be leaders in specific situations and organizational contexts.

In Chapter 5, I suggested that effective leaders develop the ability to understand the groups they work with. In this, the penultimate chapter, I circle back to suggest that leaders must also know themselves. Not *first* know yourself and *then* get to know your group. But rather, get to know yourself through relationships with others through social learning. That requires the courage to be open to feedback and the discipline of reflection. Leadership and followership, in contexts large and small, offer each of us a looking glass and an opportunity to identify our values, skills, and commitments.

Reflective Leadership

The fact that leadership is about action—that leaders engage with others to do things—is a given. What is less obvious, but equally important, is that leadership is also about reflection. Put another way, effective leaders develop the capacity over time to understand themselves, the people with whom they work, and the social context in which leadership takes place. Effective leaders are *reflective* leaders.

> ...effective leaders develop the capacity over time to understand themselves, the people with whom they work, and the social context in which leadership takes place.

Reflection is a particularly powerful form of learning based on the relationship between thinking, feeling, and action. It happens when a leader takes action, then pauses to assess the dynamics of her action and her own contribution to it. Ideally, it also happens when leaders create a culture of reflection and make evaluation a feature of organizational life. In the leadership/followership relationship, what may start as a leadership initiative becomes the responsibility of the entire group.

Being a reflective leader requires a willingness to confront mistakes and be open to criticism from others. That in itself is a special kind of courage. After thirty years as a college teacher, I still have to wait at least two weeks before looking at my students' evaluation of my teaching. I know that teaching, like leadership, is a relationship. I am only as effective as the relationship itself. I also know that becoming a better teacher requires feedback from those I am trying to teach. But I would rather be punched in the stomach than read a critical comment about my teaching. Actually, since I register the emotion in my stomach, there is not that much difference between the two!

Leadership Traits: In Praise of Difference

Many students of leadership today, stress the importance of recognizing and harnessing the different personal traits people bring to their work in organizations of all kinds. Rather than look for a specific set of traits that define who a leader is, they recognize that all of us have gifts to offer and that really healthy organizations (and human relationships) thrive when these differences are recognized and put to good use.

For example, many of you have heard of the Myers-Briggs model of personality types. Based on the personality theory of Karl Jung, Isabel Briggs Myers and her mother, Katharine Briggs, developed a model of four basic personality preferences and a questionnaire that allows individuals to identify their personality type. I have found their work to be an effective tool for engaging students in reflecting on their own "leadership personality."

The first Myers-Briggs category helps us develop where we get our energy. **Extroverts** get their energy from the world outside the self. They enjoy spending time with others, are apt to start conversations, and tend to have many friends. **Introverts,** on the other hand, get energy from their inner world. They mostly listen and wait for others to speak first, and are more likely to have a few deep friendships.

An extrovert is the last to leave the party and the first to raise her hand when the teacher asks a question. An introvert prefers a

quiet evening with one or two friends and is more likely to ponder
the teacher's question than blurt out the first thing that comes
to mind. We often think of introverts as anti-social or not very
friendly. Sometimes extroverts
get cast as superficial—all talk,
little thought. Both are inaccurate
stereotypes. Introverts can be (and
often are) personable and outgoing;
and extroverts are capable of
contemplation.

> Introverts can be (and
> often are) personable
> and outgoing; and
> extroverts are capable of
> contemplation.

It is important to note with this, and all four of the Myers-Briggs
categories, that: (a) most of us are some mix of both types; and (b)
no type is better than another. The goal is to understand ourselves
and each other, not create hierarchies. In the questionnaire itself,
some people may register high on either the extrovert or introvert
scale while others may be balanced evenly between the two. Nor
are these categories fixed. Although trait theorists assert that these
personal preferences are innate, they also leave room for change and
adaptation. As we experience changes in our social or organizational
contexts, we may be encouraged or even forced to develop our "other
side." The introvert learns how to contribute actively to the small
group discussion. The extrovert learns to listen first before jumping in
with a comment.

Imagine you are right-handed. You can learn to use your left hand,
though probably not as effectively or "naturally" as your right. In
baseball (I promise this is the only time I will use a sports analogy),
some hitters learn to use both. While coaches like to have switch
hitters, they work to create a balanced team—one that includes both
left- and right-handed pitchers and batters. As we review each of the
Myers-Briggs personality types, think of your own natural style, how
much you can develop your "left hand," and how to be intentional
about creating a balanced and effective leadership team.

Extroversion is often associated with leadership, in part because
we imagine leaders as gregarious people who aren't afraid of the front
of the room and as people who *speak up*. But beware of ignoring the

wisdom of the introvert. When chairing a meeting, remember to ask the person in the back of the room for her opinion or perspective. Better still, structure approaches to discussion that allow time and space for all views to be heard.

The second Myers-Briggs category relates to how we see the world and gather information. **Sensors** are detail oriented. They think in concrete terms, are accurate, observant, and practical minded. A sensor is likely to know how much money is in the organization's budget, how many people can fit into the meeting hall, and the most direct route to the meeting. **Intuitives** like to use their "sixth sense," focus on the future, think theoretically, and try out new ideas. The intuitive might get lost getting to the meeting hall, but will happily lead a discussion on the organization's mission, propose a ten-point plan for ending homelessness, or engage in a lively debate on theories of social change.

I would not appoint an intuitive to keep the organization's financial records, keep the membership roster up-to-date, or record the minutes of the meeting. I (an off-the-charts intuitive) often volunteer to do the minutes, but get so wrapped up in the discussion that I forget to take down the precise wording of any motions that are made. However, I might suggest an intuitive to chair the financial planning committee, because that involves imagining scenarios that don't yet exist.

The third Myers-Briggs category addresses how we make decisions. **Thinkers** make decisions based on logic, treat everyone by the same rules, and aren't afraid to make decisions they believe are fair or "by the book" even if some might be offended. **Feelers** are aware of how decisions will impact the feelings of others. They are sensitive to the needs of members and strive to create harmony in the group. The Thinking/Feeling category is the only one consistently linked to gender, with women most often registering higher on the feeling side of the spectrum then men.

I am one of those men who scores high on the Myers-Briggs Feeling scale. As a teacher, I work hard to present the evaluation criteria for my courses clearly. I try to be fair and make sure that each student knows on what they will be evaluated. I don't play favorites and make exceptions for some but not others. In practice, this almost always breaks down. I agonize over how a given student might react to the comments I write on her paper or the letter grade I assign. Does this student deserve a B or a B plus? How is he going to feel if I give the lower grade? Will it upset the harmony I am trying to build between him and myself?

The result is stress for me and sometimes less-than-honest (and therefore less helpful) feedback for the student. On the other hand, my sensitivity to both individual and group dynamics does often create a positive learning environment. Students feel seen and heard rather than simply evaluated and judged.

In community organization contexts, issues related to the Thinking/Feeling continuum are pervasive. Does your organization have an attendance policy for board meetings? What happens if a member violates the policy? Do you enforce the policy (follow the rules) or cut the member some slack because he is dealing with family issues? An organization can't accomplish its mission if board members don't meet their obligations, but a little bit of empathy might go a long way toward keeping the relationship alive for another day.

The final Myers-Briggs category, Judging/Perceiving, is about how we organize our work. **Judgers** are task-focused, plan their work carefully, and meet their deadlines often before the last minute. Judgers like to end their workday (or volunteer assignment) with tasks completed and checked off. **Perceivers,** on the other hand, are comfortable working close to deadline, value flexibility, and are open to new insights—even when they come at the last minute.

Imagine an organization without at least one member with strong judging characteristics. Very little would get done—especially activities that are deadline sensitive. Fund raising is a common example. Many community organizations depend, at least in part, on foundation grants. Most foundations have strict deadlines. If your proposal comes in one minute after midnight on the due date, you are out of luck.

Community organizations also depend on fund-raising events: the proverbial pancake breakfasts, barbecues, variety shows, or fashion bazaars. Details, details! Want to advertise your event in the community newspaper? There's a deadline. Interested in getting a quality space to hold it in? Better ask in advance. Need volunteers to bring the food? How many and what should they bring?

The importance of leaders who can organize and execute tasks effectively, is so obvious that one wonders what value members who rank high on the perceiver side of the continuum could possibly bring to the organization. But think about that foundation grant. Where do the ideas come from that make it compelling? Or consider the fund-raiser. It's one thing to have an event that is well organized, but is the event itself exciting? Sometimes perceivers are the ones who come up with the new idea or insight that moves a task, an event, or a campaign in a creative direction.

> Sometimes perceivers are the ones who come up with the new idea or insight that moves a task, an event, or a campaign in a creative direction.

Emotional Intelligence

When we think of someone as intelligent, we are most often referring to that person's mental or intellectual capabilities. Thinking back to elementary or high school, how many of you remember the kids who seemed to always get the highest test scores, were great at math, or won the outstanding student award? Of course, many of my friends studied hard and made the most of the natural intelligence that they had. But there was no mistaking that some kids just had more academic "smarts" than others.

More recently, students of leadership have come to appreciate the importance of another kind of intelligence: emotional intelligence. According to Daniel Goleman (the leadership consultant who popularized the concept), emotional intelligence is the ability to effectively manage ourselves and our relationships. If Goleman is correct—and I believe he is—our emotional "smarts" are at least as important for effective leadership as those measured by the traditional IQ test. In fact, in a study comparing those who excelled in senior leadership roles to those who were just average, Goleman found that close to 90 percent of the difference was due to emotional intelligence rather than cognitive ability.

According to Goleman, emotional intelligence consists of four fundamental capabilities: self-awareness, self-management, social awareness, and social skill. Each capability has its own set of competencies. Self-awareness includes the ability to understand your own emotions as well as their impact on others in the group. Self-management includes the ability to keep disruptive emotions and impulses under control. Social awareness begins with *empathy*— the ability to understand other people's emotions and concerns. Social skills represent social intelligence in action: the ability to communicate clearly and persuasively, manage conflicts, foster collaboration, and articulate a compelling vision.

> ...emotional intelligence consists of four fundamental capabilities: self-awareness, self-management, social awareness, and social skill. Each capability has its own set of competencies.

Both the Myers-Briggs and Emotional Intelligence indicators can provide clues to self-knowledge. Underlying both, is the liberating idea that people can and do change. Reflecting on my own life, I can think of many moments when a friend, teacher, or colleague has cared enough to help me get a more accurate picture of myself. Some of the feedback wasn't flattering. There was the philosophy professor who was frustrated with my unwillingness to grapple seriously with the ideas of Rousseau, Locke, and Hume. He called me into his office and let me know that I was acting like a superficial windbag. I don't recommend ridicule as an especially useful form of feedback, but given this professor's personality and my behavior at the time, I think he had a point.

I also recall a photograph in our college newspaper, of an empty podium with an editorial asking why there weren't more concerts and lectures on campus. The writer was kind enough not to criticize me by name, though I was student chair of the convocations committee. This was one of the first times I was forced to recognize my tendency to seek leadership positions and then fail to follow through. Coming up with ideas for speakers and entertainers was no problem, but implementation was. All these years later, my ability to organize and follow through on tasks remains a weakness. I am aware of it now, and better at it than I was all those years ago. But I still remember the picture of that empty podium.

Years later, I was challenged by a community organizer I admired. "You are not serious about building power," she said. She meant that I was not willing to do the demanding work of organizing citizen groups strong enough to make genuine change happen. I appreciated the challenge for two reasons. First, I knew she respected me enough to offer, what she intended as, constructive criticism. Second, it prompted me to seriously reflect on the nature of social power and my own approaches to it.

Self-understanding requires both socially-acquired information and the willingness to receive that information. But what do we do with the information? Personal change takes practice. Goleman uses contemporary developments in brain science to explain why. Compared to the thinking part of our brain, the neocortex, the emotional brain operates more slowly. In order to master new behaviors, the emotional centers need repetition and practice. Scan the list of emotional intelligence competencies shown below. Choose one you would like to develop further. There is a cottage industry of coaches, consultants, and workshops that can help you learn and practice the competencies you are interested in improving. Better still, encourage your community organization to offer development opportunities and create a culture of personal and social growth.

How Emotionally Intelligent Are You?

❑ Are you curious about people you don't know?

❑ Do you know your strengths and weaknesses?

❑ Do you know how to pay attention to your own feelings and those of others?

❑ When you are upset, do you know exactly why?

❑ Can you get along with most people?

❑ After you fall, do you get right back up?

❑ Are you a good judge of character?

❑ Do you trust your gut?

❑ Are you always self motivated?

Adapted from *How Emotionally Intelligent Are You? Here's how to tell,* by Carolyn Gregiore, Updated, 01/23/2014, www.huffingtonpost.com

Transformational Leadership and the Power of Moral Purpose

Throughout this chapter, I have been emphasizing the importance of the individual personality in shaping leadership. I want to conclude by returning to the centrality of moral purpose in effective community leadership. When Socrates gave his immortal injunction, *know thyself,* he wasn't referring to the Myers-Briggs profile or an emotional intelligence score. I don't think he was much interested in personality at all. What he meant was, know yourself as a citizen, a member of the Greek *polis.* To Socrates, the search for truth was both an individual and communal quest. What is the good society? What are my responsibilities as a member of that society?

The political historian James MacGregor Burns, created the term "transformational leadership" to mark the connection between visionary, morally-based leaders, and empowered followers. When leaders both articulate and embody a morally inspired social vision, leaders and followers are transformed in the process. Many of Burns' examples are drawn from world-changing movements. His transformational leaders changed history. It's a long stretch from president of the neighborhood association to Franklin Delano Roosevelt or Martin Luther King. Yet transformational leadership can operate at the community level and be practiced by people whose power comes not from charisma, eloquence, or tactical brilliance; but from the ability to communicate a mission and a set of values that gives meaning and motivation to followers—creating new leaders in the process.

...transformational leadership can operate at the community level and be practiced by people whose power comes not from charisma, eloquence, or tactical brilliance; but from the ability to communicate a mission and a set of values that gives meaning and motivation to followers—creating new leaders in the process.

Transformational leaders don't look or act alike. Martin Luther
King inspired millions with his soaring rhetoric and put words
into action in mass protests based on the principles of nonviolent
struggle. It is easy to imagine that it was Martin Luther King's words
that inspired tens of thousands of followers to face down fire hoses
and police batons for freedom. But it was King's willingness to take
those risks himself—to literally *walk his talk*—that made him a
transformational leader. The proof of his leadership was manifest
in the thousands of member/leaders who inspired each other as the
movement expanded.

Now consider another transformational leader from the civil
rights movement: Ella Baker. She was not as famous as King, but,
within certain movement circles, even more influential. Baker wasn't
known for her speeches. She didn't lead from the podium and wasn't
always at the head of the march. As the acknowledged mother of
the Southern Nonviolent
Coordinating Committee
(SNCC), she advocated
a style of participatory
leadership focused on
developing the voice,
knowledge, and spirit of

> Give light and the people will follow.
> The major job was getting people to
> understand that they had something
> within themselves that they could
> use.   – Ella Baker

a new generation of courageous leaders. She insisted that members
learn how to make their own decisions and put the development of
the people they were organizing first. Her power as leader flowed
from her ability to teach the young people of SNCC to find power in
themselves and each other.

Different in style, personality, and approach, both King and Baker
inspired others to become leaders because they communicated and
lived a powerful moral vision. If we look at the arc of their lives,
we can see that their leadership transformed not only those who
were inspired by their vision, but the larger society as well. This is
Transformative Leadership with a capital T. Perhaps you are thinking,
"I could never have that kind of impact," or "I would never be willing

to give my entire life to a cause that great. Leave that to the heroes and saints!" I often think that way myself. In fact, I find it *comfortable* to think that way. A Martin Luther King or Ella Baker, I'm not.

Fortunately, there are transformative leaders all around us—people who strengthen society at its roots and inspire others to join in. Considered in isolation, these leaders may not merit a "capital T," but, considered collectively, a healthy society depends on them and us along with them. Concern for each other, our children, and our planet cannot rest alone on the inspirational power of the few. It is nurtured by citizens in local communities and civic organizations. In thousands of interactions across our nation and world, people are called to act for a higher purpose and, in the process, transformed—at least a little. And it is these little transformations that weave together the fabric of a fairer and more just society.

> Concern for each other, our children and our planet cannot rest alone on the inspirational power of the few. It is nurtured by citizens in local communities and civic organizations. In thousands of interactions across our nation and world, people are called to act for a higher purpose and, in the process, transformed, at least a little. And it is these little transformations that weave together the fabric of a fairer and more just society.

Who are these transformative leaders? Do you know any? Have you been one yourself? I have a simple test. If you have ever answered a call to act for the greater good, you have experienced the first pulse of transformative leadership. Whether that pulse leads to something deeper depends on how deeply you engage. One volunteer session at the homeless shelter or attendance at a rally for affordable housing is not in itself transformative. A longer-term commitment may well be. And with that deeper commitment, you will likely inspire others to get involved and help create a virtuous circle.

Throughout this book, I have suggested that community leadership has a moral dimension. Reflective leaders are willing to ask themselves tough moral questions, such as:

- What is the purpose of my life?
- What do I owe others?
- How best can I contribute to the common good?
- What heroes do I want to emulate?
- Am I living my values?
- Can I do more?
- When is enough... enough?

Reflective leaders have a conscience and are willing to wrestle with it. If this sounds grim, remember that there are deep rewards for a life of community engagement. In the words of Madge Hawkins, a pioneer for working women's rights in the 1930s and '40s, "If you want to be happy, join a radical group." Whether the group is radical or not, Madge's advice is as wise today as it was when she delivered it on her 90th birthday, many years ago.

Sources

Chapter 1

Coles, Robert. 2001. *Lives of Moral Leadership: Men and Women Who Have Made a Difference.* New York City: Random House Trade Paperbacks.

Wills, Garry. 1996. *Certain Trumpets: The Nature of Leadership.* New York City: Simon & Schuster.

Chapter 2

Block, Peter. 2008. *Community: The Structure of Belonging.* San Francisco: Berrett-Koehler Publishers.

Boyte, Harry and Don Shelby. 2008. *The Citizen Solution: How You Can Make a Difference.* St. Paul: Minnesota Historical Society Press.

Kretzman, John P. and John L. McKnight. 1993. *Building Community from the Inside Out: a Path Toward Finding and Mobilizing Community Assets.* Chicago: ACTA Publications.

Putman, Robert. 2001. *Bowling Alone: The Collapse and Revival of American Community.* New York City: Touchstone Books by Simon & Schuster.

Wellstone Action. 2005. *Politics the Wellstone Way: How to Elect Progressive Candidates and Win on the Issues.* Minneapolis: University Of Minnesota Press.

Chapter 3

Dubois, Paul Martin and Francis Moore Lappe. 1994. *The Quickening of America: Rebuilding Our Nation, Remaking Our Lives.* San Francisco: Jossey-Bass.

Janeway, Elizabeth. 1980. *Powers of the Weak.* New York City: Alfred A. Knopf.

May, Rollo. 1990. *Power and Innocence: A Search for the Sources of Violence.* New York City: Norton.

Chapter 4

Heifetz, Ronald. 1998. *Leadership Without Easy Answers*. Cambridge, MA: Harvard University Press.

Miller, Kay. "Not In My Neighborhood," *Minneapolis Tribune,* Sunday Magazine, February 11, 1990.

Preskill, Steven and Stephen D. Brookfield. 2009. *Learning as a Way of Leading: Lessons from the Struggle for Social Justice*. San Francisco: Jossey-Bass.

Wallis, Jim. 2013. *On God's Side: What Religion Forgot and Politics Hasn't Learned about Serving the Common Good*. Ada, MI: Baker Publishing Group.

Chapter 5

Cryan, Phillip. "Strategic Practice for Social Transformation," Grass Roots Policy Project.

Ganz, Herbert. 2002. "Organizing and Developing New Leaders," The New School.

Terry, Robert. 1993. *Authentic Leadership: Courage in Action*. San Francisco: Jossey-Bass.

Chapter 6

Burns, James MacGregor. 1978. *Leadership*. New York City: Open Road Media.

Goleman, Daniel. "Leadership that Gets Results," *Harvard Business Review* (March–April, 2000)

Myers, Isabel Briggs with Peter B. Myers. 1999. *Gifts Differing: Understanding Personality Type*. Sunnyvale, CA: CPP.

Payne, Charles. "Ella Baker and Models of Social Change," *Signs* (Summer, 1989).

Biographies

Author – Tom O'Connell

Tom O'Connell, has a PhD in Political Sociology from the Union Institute (Cincinnati, Ohio) and is a Professor Emeritus in Political Studies at Metropolitan State University (St. Paul, Minnesota) where he taught courses in politics, urban studies, community organizing, and leadership. O'Connell brings a lifetime of experience in community leadership as an active participant in citizen organizations working on issues from affordable housing to workers' rights; climate change to racial equality.

Contributor – Colleen Callahan

Colleen Callahan has served in a variety of roles with both community organizations and local government. She has a Masters in Public and Non Profit Administration from Metropolitan State University (St. Paul, Minnesota) and collaborated on the production of this book.